Apple's Angst

Apple's Angst

Rebecca Eckler

Doubleday Canada

Doubleday Canada and colophon are trademarks

Library and Archives Canada Cataloguing in Publication

Eckler, Rebecca
Apple's angst / Rebecca Eckler.

ISBN 978-0-385-66320-5

I. Title.

PS8609.C55A66 2010   C813'.6   C2010-902498-2

This book is a work of fiction. Names, characters, places and incidents are products of the author's imagination or are used fictitiously. Any resemblance to actual events or locales or persons, living or dead, is entirely coincidental.

Book design: Leah Springate

Printed and bound in the USA

Published in Canada by Doubleday Canada
a division of Random House of Canada

Visit Random House of Canada Limited's website: www.randomhouse.ca

10 9 8 7 6 5 4 3 2 1

For Rowan, with all my love

one

"*a*pple! Are you *insane*?" Happy demanded, viciously tearing Apple's fourth-favorite pair of jeans from her.

"Please tell me you're not *thinking* of wearing those," Happy continued, dismay dripping from her tongue. "I know you're obsessed with jeans. But please, not today! Today, you *can't be yourself*!"

Happy tossed the jeans into a corner, a revolted look on her face, as if she were tossing out a baby's dirty diaper. Her perfect ski-slope nose crinkled as if there was also a foul stench in the air. She ran her fingers through her shiny, long black hair and shot Apple a glance. Happy's green eyes said it all: "What am I going to *do* with you?"

"Hey, be *nice* to the jeans!" Apple huffed, picking up the pants, folding them, and placing them gingerly on her bed. "What did they ever do to you?"

There were already dozens upon dozens of items of clothing in the Absolutely Not pile in the corner of

1

Apple's bedroom, including jeans in every wash, shade, and style imaginable.

The heap was getting higher by the second. Apple hadn't known how much she owned until most of her clothes had been ripped from hangers and emptied from dresser drawers and she could see them in the one mammoth heap. Some of the clothes, much to Apple's shock and shame, still had price tags. This made her feel supremely guilty. Apple loved to shop, especially with Happy. Happy always managed to convince Apple she "should" buy something when they shopped together. But most of the time, no matter what was in her closet, no matter the occasion, Apple ended up in jeans and a tank top.

All that money gone to waste, thought Apple, looking at all the unused clothes, wondering if she could return any of the items, or if—genius idea!—she should actually start to wear them.

Happy hadn't approved of any of the outfits Apple had so far held up as possibilities to wear today. Every outfit Apple suggested had ended up in Happy's Absolutely Not pile, mostly because Apple kept holding up variations on jeans and a tank top.

"Didn't you hear what I said?" asked Happy. "You *can't* be yourself today."

Apple *had* heard her—she had simply pretended not to the first time.

"Oh, I heard you. So what exactly do you *mean* by that?" she asked, watching Happy pick up another pair of jeans, looking unimpressed. "Hey!" Apple cried. "I love those jeans. What's wrong with them? They're such a dark wash they could pass for a really funky pair of pants. *And* you said you loved them on me! *And* you said my butt looks fabulous in them. *And* you're the one who gave them to me, in case you forgot," she said, hoping to convince Happy before the jeans ended up in the Absolutely Not pile.

Apple suddenly wished Lyon was there, though she knew he would probably rather cover himself naked in honey and lie on an ant pile. But at least he would tell her that no matter what she wore, she looked fantastic. Thinking about her boyfriend, Apple couldn't help but smile. He had come by first thing in the morning only to drop off her favorite strawberry-banana smoothie.

"I just wanted your day to get off to the perfect start," he had told her. And though she was dressed in one of her dad's T-shirts and an old pair of sweatpants, he had also told her she looked adorable. Thanks to Lyon and his surprise visit, it *had* been the perfect start to a day.

As Happy sighed, with exaggerated tolerance, Apple was brought back to the present. Happy was speaking to Apple as if she were a very patient teacher explaining to a six-year-old how to add single-digit numbers.

"How many ways am I going to have to explain the situation to you so you'll actually understand, Apple? I *do* love the jeans. And they *do* make your butt look great. I'm sorry if I hurt your feelings. I'm sorry if I hurt the *jeans'* feelings," she said, rolling her eyes. "I do love *all* your jeans. But you just can't wear jeans today! Today is too important, even for designer hand-me-down jeans from yours truly. Even if they make your butt look delicious." Apple tried to interrupt, but it was impossible.

"And I know how you always say that Lyon loves you in jeans, but today is not about impressing your boyfriend, who would find you attractive in a garbage bag. Deal with it," Happy said, finishing her rant.

"But that's *me*," Apple argued. "Jeans are me! That's who I am! I'm a jeans-and-T-shirt type of gal. I'm at my most comfortable casual."

"I know that. We *all* know that," Happy said, glancing to the far end of Apple's bedroom, where their other best friend, Brooklyn, was sitting silently, eyes closed, hands resting on her knees, palms facing up.

Brooklyn was meditating, something she had recently taken up as an add-on to her regular yoga practice. Brooklyn was as obsessed with yoga as Happy was with fashion and Apple was with jeans.

If Happy had been looking to Brooklyn, whom they called "the Noodle" because she was so lean and flexible, for backup it wasn't happening. Not only did Brooklyn live in yoga pants, but ever since she took up meditation, she had also acquired the amazing capacity to tune out everything that was going on around her. You could dance in front of Brooklyn, making ridiculous faces and gestures, while she meditated and she still wouldn't budge.

"So what you're really saying is that they won't like ME if I wear jeans, even though that's who I am?" asked Apple. It bothered her that there could be people out there who thought like that, who would judge her based on what she was wearing. Apple liked to believe that people weren't that superficial or judgmental, even though she knew that was kind of naive.

Apple never judged people by the way they looked or dressed. Though she would admit she sometimes laughed along with Happy's biting criticisms of someone else's outfit, Apple was not the type to actively start those conversations, or even have those thoughts.

"No, what I'm trying to say is that, today, you just have to be a *better version* of yourself. At least you have to *dress* like a better version of yourself," Happy said gently, taking Apple's hand as if she were breaking bad news. "Listen, how are people supposed to take you seriously if they aren't a little envious of what you're wearing? They want people to look up to you, don't they? And people won't look up to you if you don't *look* like you're a person to aspire to! If you were going to be interviewed to be a counselor at a day camp or a salesperson at a clothing store, I'd tell you to wear jeans. But this is so, so different. This is so much bigger and more *important*. You have to impress these people. Please, please, *please* just let me pick out what you should wear. You're going to be working at *Angst* magazine! This is, like, the most important day of your life! It's *Angst* magazine!"

two

appy was probably right. If there was one thing she was an expert on, it was fashion and celebrities. Happy knew every trend that hit mainstream stores six months before everyone else. She had been into the boho fashion before the Olsen twins and Nicole Richie. Happy also knew which celebrities hooked up and broke up, practically the second it happened. Apple wouldn't even venture to guess how many times Happy, an aspiring actress, had looked at a photo of celebrities holding hands and predicted, "I give them three months." Happy was always bang-on. Likewise, Apple couldn't even estimate how many times Happy saw a celebrity photo on Perez Hilton's website, which she logged on to many times a day from her iPhone, and announced, "Perez Hilton is totally going to make fun of her for wearing that out in public."

Apple wasn't convinced. "They called this meeting because they told me they think I'm 'real.' That's the world they used. 'REAL.' They want me at *Angst* magazine because they think other teenagers can 'relate to me,'" she explained, using finger quotes as she said "relate to me." "Other teenagers wear jeans," she continued. "Hell, everyone wears jeans! Well, except you."

Today, Happy was wearing an off-the-shoulder T-shirt dress with high black boots. Happy was dressed as if *she* were the one going to an interview at *Angst* magazine. This was how Happy was always dressed, like she was about to walk a red carpet.

Apple looked at her watch. They had been in her bedroom for nearly two hours. She threw herself facedown on her bed and sighed loudly into her pillow, like she was fed up with the whole finding-the-perfect-outfit ordeal.

But Apple was only acting disillusioned. Apple was content. No, she was more than that. She felt her heart swell with joy and smiled into her pillow. Only a month ago, she would never have believed that Happy would be back in her bedroom, let alone her life.

After a month of Happy, her best friend forever, acting like Apple was a great-aunt she rarely saw, speaking to her with an over-the-top tone of politeness—"Hi, Apple, how *are* you?" and, "Hello, Apple, it's *so* nice to hear your voice"—Apple and Happy had finally got back to being on the Best Friend Track, and back to their thrice-daily phone chats and constant text messaging.

It still pained Apple to think of how she had treated Happy, all because of their classmate Zen, whom Apple had had a crush on forever. There was a point, just a couple months ago, when Apple had somehow believed that her and Happy's over-a-decade-long friendship was worth losing over him.

Oh, Zen.

Zen. Zen. Zen.

Apple had been silently in love, or at least in deep like, with Zen for years, since way before he came back to school after six months off traveling and then fell in love with Happy. Zen, with his beautiful blue eyes and the dimple in his cheek that melted Apple's heart every time he smiled, looked like a model in a surfing magazine.

When she had realized that Zen was interested in Happy, and that Happy, who had never even *noticed* Zen prior to his arrival back at school, was also suddenly very interested in him, Apple had gone down a path that could only be described as pure evilness.

Apple hated to think about how she had tried to sabotage her best friend's blossoming relationship by doling out awful advice to both Zen and Happy, in an attempt to keep them away from each other. Eeesh. What had she been thinking?

Even worse, Apple had pretended to be her *mother*, the famous Dr. Bee Bee Berg. (Yes, *that* Dr. Bee Bee Berg, the talk-show host, celebrity to millions! Yes, the one who was just named one of America's 100 most influential people. Yuck!)

Apple had broken into her mother's computer to send Happy that bad advice. Double-eeesh! No, make that triple-eeesh!

Apple and Happy's friendship had diminished to the point of hatred after Happy found out what Apple had done. Oh, the sound of that dial tone! Happy had hung up on Apple, but not before announcing stonily, "This friendship is over!"

And as if losing her best friend wasn't bad enough, it had got even worse for Apple.

Happy, in revenge mode, had then been a guest on Apple's mother's daily afternoon talk show, *Queen of Hearts with Dr. Bee Bee Berg*, telling millions of viewers how Apple had stabbed her in the back.

Watching Happy, her best friend, tell the world on live television, *on her mother's daily talk show*, about how Apple had tried to sabotage her relationship with Zen had been the most mortifying moment of Apple's entire life.

Her mother was out of town on a romantic getaway with her father when Guy, Dr. Berg's long-time assistant, had booked the guests for that day's show, so she had had no idea that Happy was going to be a guest—or what she was going to say—until moments before the show was to air. Guy and her mother hadn't even had any idea that Apple and Happy were in a fight, and certainly not over a guy!

There was nothing left for Apple to do but spontaneously walk onto the set of her mother's television show that day and apologize to Happy—in person. The studio audience booed and hissed when Apple admitted what she had done to her best friend. It hadn't even mattered that she was Dr. Bee Bee Berg's daughter. And people worshipped the ground Dr. Berg walked on!

Apple still couldn't believe she had done it.

However, at that point, she would have walked on burning hot coals to get her best friend back, which probably would have been less painful.

It was actually Apple's crazy aunt Hazel's suggestion that Apple apologize to Happy on her mother's show, and for once, out of pure desperation to get Happy's friendship back and let her know how sorry she was for being the type of girl who would choose a guy over her very best friend, Apple had listened to her aunt.

Apple usually never listened to her aunt, who, at that point, had never been in a relationship lasting longer than a vase of fresh flowers. Her aunt was known for what Apple described as her "Girl Crazy Moments," like when she would sneak into boyfriends' e-mail accounts or tell them on first dates she wanted to have babies and marry them. Crazy Aunt Hazel was the complete opposite of her well-spoken, famous sister, who saw everything in black and white, as right or wrong. Sneaking into boyfriends' e-mail accounts? Wrong. Apple's mother was as organized as Crazy Aunt Hazel was disorganized. Her mother was always optimistic, especially when it came to love, where her Crazy Aunt Hazel was a cynic, always crying out things like "I'm never going to meet anyone!" and "You can't trust any guy!"

In any case, Apple felt bad for the daughters of supermodels, the ones who didn't end up being as good-looking as their mothers. It was the same for Apple. She felt she was missing some of her mother's DNA too.

Her mother was shocked when Apple walked on stage that day, as if Madonna or Britney had appeared looking for relationship advice, not her own daughter. Apple, after all, had rarely showed any interest in her mother's talk show.

Apple's nickname had always been "the Sponge," because you'd have to wring her to get her to share any personal information. She had always kept her feelings to herself and, back then, on the diary she kept on her computer, which is why not one person had known about her Super-Sized Zen Crush.

But Apple had apologized to Happy, crying on *live* television, in front of millions. Even still, Happy would only say that Apple would have to "earn her trust back." And Apple's mother was furious to learn that Apple had sneaked into *her* computer and not only impersonated her but also given advice that was sure to ruin a relationship, not move it forward. What Apple had done to Happy was, in her mother's eyes, akin to murdering someone.

For a few awful days following Apple's teary television debut, days that felt like years to her, it seemed like everyone in the *world* hated her. Apple became *the* poster child for Bad Best Friends everywhere. Clips of her admitting what she had done went viral. There were websites dedicated to discussing Apple as a "frenemy." Bloggers called her a "toxic friend." Most everyone seemed to agree that Apple was a bad person. Even Apple couldn't help but agree. What she had done to her best friend *was* awful.

Yes, without a doubt, it had been the most awful time in Apple's life. But Apple was not *that* person. She just had a "Girl Crazy Moment" like her aunt! She had never loved anyone before. She should have told Happy how she felt, but she couldn't bring herself to talk about something so personal, even with her best friend. Yes, she was the exact opposite of her mother.

Thankfully, all of that was history now. Happy seemed to have forgiven her entirely. Zen and Happy seemed to be happy together, the most gorgeous and affectionate couple at Cactus High.

The fact that Happy was helping Apple pick out the perfect outfit for her meeting at *Angst* magazine, the must-read weekly fashion and celebrity magazine for teenagers, proved she had truly forgiven her and put her friend's evil behavior behind her. This wasn't just a favor. Happy sincerely wanted to help Apple look her best. She sincerely *wanted* Apple to have the job at *Angst*.

Happy, in fact, wanted Apple to have the job more than Apple did.

three

Happy read *Angst* magazine religiously, unlike Apple, who never understood people's obsession with celebrities and fashion, just as she never understood why people would share their relationship problems on her mother's show.

Sure, Apple flipped through *Angst* at coffee shops while waiting for friends, but Happy read it as if she were studying for an exam. Apple just didn't care about who was dating whom, or which celebrity was getting drunk and flirting with other celebrities, although she also knew that was kind of abnormal. Even Brooklyn couldn't get enough of celebrity gossip, and Brooklyn was nonstop talk about karma and how you shouldn't gossip because it would come back to bite you in the butt.

While Happy continued to busy herself in Apple's bedroom and Brooklyn remained still, Apple found her eyes resting on a framed photograph on her bedside table of Lyon and her. Lyon's arm hung lightly over Apple's shoulders in the photo, and he was glancing down at her with a look of adoration. He had given it to her a couple of weeks ago as a gift.

"You didn't have to do this," Apple had told him. "I love it—don't get me wrong—but I didn't get you anything. And you're always giving me things."

"It's no big deal," he had responded. "I was just thinking about you and I wanted to give it to you. It's my pleasure."

That was what Lyon was like.

Yes, at least *something* positive had come out of Apple's tearful, embarrassing—make that mortifying to the infinity degree—television debut. Actually, two positive things had come out of her television debut. One, she had met Lyon.

And two, the editor of *Angst* magazine was an avid viewer of *Queen of Hearts with Dr. Bee Bee Berg* and had witnessed Apple's teary admission and apology, which had led to a phone call to set up a meeting to discuss Apple's becoming the magazine's teen advice columnist.

Apparently, though Apple cringed at the thought, trying to sabotage your best friend's relationship and NOT getting the guy you've been in love with for years and LOSING your best friend over it was "real" and just what the editor was looking for in a teen advice columnist.

Apple couldn't help but think that Happy should have also received a job offer. Happy, after all, was also on the show that day and was the victim. Plus she was so much better suited for a job at *Angst*. She was so much more put together, so much more outgoing, and so much more into fashion and celebrities, which is what the glossy magazine was all about.

It was a fact that Happy was the most beautiful and well-dressed student at Cactus High, just as it was a fact that there were seven days in a week. Happy's nickname had always been "the Onion" because she was so beautiful you wanted to cry just looking at her.

"*You* should really be going to this meeting," Apple said to Happy, getting off her bed and peeling her eyes away from the photograph of Lyon. "You'd be much better giving out advice than me. And you'd know what to wear! You'd fit right in."

"I wish! I'd kill for a job at *Angst*. But you'll get me in. I know it. And you *are* good at giving out advice. Well, you were for the school newspaper. So it's not like you have no experience. Plus, they don't want just *any* teenager giving out advice to readers. You may not appreciate being the daughter of one of television's most-watched talk-show hosts, but admit it, it opens doors," Happy said, looking at a royal blue sweater briefly before tossing it dismissively into the Absolutely Not pile.

"Unfortunately," Happy continued, "my mother isn't famous. My mother is not the one and only Dr. Bee Bee Berg."

"Oh my God, Happy! I'm so glad you said that. I keep thinking they want me just because I'm the daughter of Dr. Bee Bee Berg! You think so too, right?" Apple asked. "That's the real reason they want me."

"Of course," Happy said matter-of-factly. "Do you actually think Rumer Willis gets acting jobs because she has talent? No, it's because of who her parents are. But who cares how you get in the door, as long as you do? Then you can prove yourself. And I NEED you to prove yourself so you can then get *me* in. Or at least get me some press so people know who I am and I can get an acting job somewhere!"

"I'll do my best," Apple said sincerely. "And you will get an acting job. You were destined to be famous."

"Duh!" Happy said, opening another one of Apple's drawers. "I'm a clothes whore, but my God, Apple, how many pair of jeans do you *own*?"

❧

Apple glanced at the clock on the wall. It was shaped like an apple, one of those unfortunate things that came along with being named after a fruit (Apple couldn't even count how many items shaped like apples she had received as gifts in her life). The apple-shaped clock was a gift from one of her dad's colleagues for her ninth birthday. She had been meaning to throw it out forever.

"The meeting is in less than an hour. We've got to figure something out, like, now," Apple moaned, "or I'm going to be late."

As if a director of a film had just called out "Action!" Apple's mother walked into the room. Apple breathed in deeply, counting to ten in her head, as Brooklyn had advised her to do to remain calm in stressful situations. Apple found being around her mother very stressful. She loved her mother, but her presence, even at home, was just so big and overwhelming, it exhausted Apple. She tried not to be annoyed that her mother didn't have the decency to knock, especially since it was *her* bedroom.

"Have you ever heard of *privacy*?" Apple asked her, already knowing what the answer would be.

There was no such thing as privacy in Dr. Bee Bee Berg's world—the world of talk-show television, where everyone shared every little dirty secret just to get their fifteen minutes of fame. Apple's mother's career relied on people's airing their dirty laundry. She lived and breathed it, like oxygen.

Her mother may be an expert in the etiquette of love and relationships, thought Apple sullenly, but she was clearly not an expert in any other aspects of etiquette— like knocking before entering.

"My goodness! Have we been broken into?" Dr. Berg asked, appalled, her wide eyes sweeping the room. "Your room is a disaster! What happened?"

"Hi, Dr. Berg," Happy chimed chirpily. "We're trying to find something for Apple to wear for her meeting. Help me convince her that she can't wear jeans."

"Of course she can't wear jeans," her mother huffed, heading into Apple's walk-in closet. Her mother, as always, was immaculately dressed in a white pantsuit with a string of pearls around her neck. Her hair was in its usual updo. Not a strand was out of place. Her mother had had the same hairstyle for as long as Apple could remember. And those pearls around her neck? Apple wondered if she even took them off to shower.

Happy shot Apple a "See? I told you so!" look.

Happy adored Apple's mother and had never quite understood why Dr. Berg annoyed Apple so much. Likewise, Apple had never understood why Happy got annoyed with her own parents. They were never around, spending most of their time traveling the world on exotic vacations. Apple could only dream of what it would be like to have a mother who wasn't ever around, never barged in uninvited, never asked personally questions, and especially a mother people didn't know. Happy had no idea how lucky she was!

"How is it," her mother asked, walking out of Apple's closet empty-handed, "that you own no dress pants? We should really get you some professional-looking clothes. If you want to be treated like a professional, you must dress the part. You want them to know that you're serious, that you want this job, that you'll do anything to get it! How do you think I have the number-one television show in my time slot? It's not because I dress like a slob, I can tell you that much. You have to dress for success!"

"Hear, hear!" chimed Happy, wrapping an arm around Dr. Berg's waist. "I was just telling Apple the same thing."

Dr. Berg beamed and patted Happy on the back. Apple turned away and rolled her eyes.

Happy always seemed to be way more in tune with Apple's mother than Apple ever was. It was Happy who always told Apple's mother what was going on at school or in her life. Happy treated her mother like she was a friend!

"Mom! Please!" Apple moaned. "You don't need to constantly remind us. We *know* about your popular show. We *know* about the ten self-help books you published. We know, we know, we know!"

Dr. Berg shot Apple a warning look. Apple looked away. She was *trying* to be nicer to her mother these days, but her mother made it difficult. While Apple was trying to be nicer, her mother didn't seem to be trying to be less annoying.

"Excuse me, Dr. Berg, let me in there," Happy said, pushing her way into Apple's walk-in closet for the umpteenth time. "There's got to be something in here," she yelled out. "A closet full of clothes and nothing to wear."

"Isn't that always the case for all women?" laughed Dr. Berg.

Apple tried to laugh too and get into the spirit but she couldn't quite get up for it. She thought about how unsure she felt about being the teen advice columnist at *Angst*. Or giving advice anywhere, for that matter. She had yet to admit this to anyone except Lyon.

"Just check it out and see if you like it. If you don't, then just don't do it," he had told her supportively when she mentioned her hesitation the other night.

He was so sweet, but Lyon didn't completely understand.

How could Apple complain about the opportunity to work at *Angst* magazine when everyone was so thrilled for her, even envious? It's not that she didn't see the need for a teenage advice columnist. Even Apple had needed relationship advice when she was trying to win Zen's affection, and especially when she was caught.

Everyone Apple had told about the phone call from the editor of *Angst* couldn't believe how lucky she was to land herself a gig at a magazine where people actually *worked for free* answering phones and fetching coffee, just to be able to *say* they worked at *Angst* magazine.

But Apple had fought her entire life against being her mother's daughter, and following in her mother's footsteps was like admitting she actually was proud of what her mother did for a living. She just didn't get why her mother was so interested in people's private lives. It was almost as if she was using the guests for ratings. Then again, the guests on the *Queen of Hearts* weren't forced to appear. They seemed to really want to tell the world about their straying husbands. They seemed to genuinely want everyone in the world to know that they cheated on their fiancés right before the wedding.

Apple had spent her life fighting hard to be the exact opposite of her outspoken, never-at-a-loss-for-words mother. So the fact the people at *Angst* more likely than not wanted Apple only because she was the daughter of someone famous, or worse, thought she might actually be like her mother, was off-putting to say the least.

Apple inhaled deeply again and watched her mother critically scour her clothes alongside Happy.

Did Apple really want to follow in her mother's footsteps in the advice-giving market? Wouldn't she then always be compared to her mother? Being perceived as a mini Dr. Bee Bee Berg was one of her worst nightmares. And what if she was bad at giving advice? Then people would surely make fun of her, thinking that she was *trying* to be a mini Dr. Bee Bee Berg and failing! Apple already felt the need to scream out, "They called *me*! I didn't ask for this!"

Apple had no idea what she wanted to be in the future—she just knew she didn't want to end up like her mother. Apple, as always, kind of just wanted to be unnoticed. She didn't want to bring any attention to herself, and attention was the one thing her mother couldn't seem to get enough of. Her mother loved signing autographs, accepting awards, and being asked to pose for magazines. Apple didn't understand why anyone, including Happy, would want to be *famous*.

"I'm not sure why you guys care so much," threw in Brooklyn suddenly. "I'm kind of with Apple on this. It's what's on the inside that matters." Apple, Happy, and Dr. Berg were so startled to hear Brooklyn's voice, they all stopped mid-movement. Brooklyn, apparently, was ready to rejoin the real world.

"Oh, dear God! You almost gave me a heart attack, Brooklyn," Dr. Berg fluttered, putting her hand to her heart. "I didn't even see you there. I'm not as young as I used to be. You can't just go surprising people like that! And what are you doing, my dear? How long have you been sitting like that?"

"Sorry, Dr. Berg. I didn't mean to scare you. I've been sitting like this for, I don't know, maybe an hour? You know, you should try meditation. It really calms you.

I feel so much calmer since I've started meditating," said Brooklyn, before letting out a loud yawn.

"Yeah, so much calmer that you're always falling asleep in class," Happy said.

Brooklyn shrugged. She didn't care about school or grades. She had always planned on going to India when she graduated, and she didn't see how learning calculus or science could ever help her find her inner peace or get her on a plane to India.

"Thank you, dear," Dr. Berg replied. "But I am *much* too busy to sit around and do nothing. Have you also been helping destroy my daughter's room?"

"Yeah, Brooklyn's been about as much help as that desk. I even forgot she was here," said Happy, "and I *drove* her here."

"That's the *point* of meditating. The point is to find silence within," said Brooklyn, uncrossing her legs and standing up to stretch her arms above her head. "Anyway, like I said, I think people will see the beauty in Apple no matter what she wears."

"Thank you, Brooklyn," Apple said, pointedly looking at her mother and Happy. "At least someone here understands me,"

Happy wasn't having any of Brooklyn's free-spirited nature right now.

"Brooklyn! You know I love you, but we don't have time for your mantras on life. Can you please start helping us pick out something fabulous for Apple to wear to her interview?"

"I thought you already *had* the job. Why do you care what you wear?" Brooklyn asked, rolling over on her head, gearing up to get into a handstand position.

"I don't. But *they* do," Apple said, eyeing her mother and Happy. "I guess I should look presentable. I'm meeting the editor-in-chief. I think they just want to see that I can talk without crying or something. They just want to see that I'm not a total whack job in person. I mean, the one time they saw me, I was blubbering like an idiot."

Apple waited for someone to say, "You still looked great!" but nobody did. Again she wished Lyon were around. He would tell her how great she looked. He would make her feel like she was the most important person in the room. He didn't care if she got the job or not.

four

"Try this. You look amazing in red!" Happy said, throwing a piece of clothing across the room. It hit Apple in the face.

Apple looked at the red T-shirt dress Happy had tossed over. She couldn't remember where or when she had bought it. "I found it on the floor under a pile of shoe boxes," Happy said, as if she could read Apple's mind. "It's not too wrinkled. I like it," she added, pleased. "I wish you had some knee-high black boots to go with it. Now that would look hot. Oh. My. God. You can wear mine! We're practically the same size."

"My feet are, like, two sizes bigger than yours," said Apple, looking at Happy as if she had lost her mind.

"Who cares? I can't think of one guy who wouldn't want to see you in these boots," she said, winking. "Friggin' hot hot hot! These are my come-get-me boots!"

"Happy, dear," interrupted Dr. Berg. "Is that how you girls talk today? It's foul! Remember, you should always talk like a lady. I mean, of course we all want to feel good-looking and confident, but we don't need boots to woo men, do we?"

"Sorry, Dr. Berg," Happy said, facing Apple and Brooklyn, who was still upside down, and rolling her eyes. They had to turn away from each other so as to not burst out laughing. Dr. Berg was old-fashioned, to say the least, when it came to love, language, and apparently, clothing. According to the bloggers' and critics' reviews of *Queen of Hearts* that Happy had read to Apple, her mother's old-fashioned nature was part of her appeal and charm.

"Brooklyn, please don't hurt yourself," said Dr. Bee Bee Berg, glancing at Brooklyn. "I'm worried that all the blood rushing to your brain is going to make you faint."

"Don't worry. I could stay like this for hours," said Brooklyn.

"Go! Go! Get dressed," screamed Happy, hopping on one foot as she took a boot off. "Take them!"

"Are you sure, Happy?" Apple asked.

"I'm sure! I'm so sure! My best friend is going to be the editor of *Angst* one day. The least I can do is lend her my boots!"

"Happy, I'm not going to be the editor. It's, like, an intern position," Apple muttered.

"Whatever! Just get changed already!" Happy said, shooing Apple into the bathroom.

"If you believe in yourself, it will be," called out Brooklyn.

Apple took the red dress and Happy's knee-length Prada boots into her bathroom. She slipped off her faded blue jeans and her tank top and threw the red dress over her head. Then she sat on the toilet and tried to yank the two-sizes-too-small boots over her feet.

"Oh, my God," she screamed out. "These boots will *never* fit! Help!"

Brooklyn and Happy burst into the bathroom. Happy looked like she meant business. Brooklyn was flushed from her handstand.

"Stay seated. Now stick your legs out," Happy demanded. "Brooklyn, use those strong yoga arms of yours and help me pull them on."

"These will *never* fit!" Apple moaned again. "This is ridiculous!"

"Shut up, Apple!" Happy groaned. "These boots cost $400. You should be honored that I'm letting you stretch them out. They're on! See?"

Amazingly, the boots *were* on her feet, although Apple could feel her toes curl under. The pain was instant and intense as she stood up.

"Oh, my God," Apple groaned. "My toes are killing and I haven't even taken one step."

"Here," Happy said, opening the medicine cabinet. "Take these."

She handed Apple over two Advils, turned on the tap, and filled a glass of water, which she also handed her. "It will help. Trust me. Sailor does it all the time when she goes out in heels. She takes two Advils and swears she can last four hours longer on her feet." Sailor was Happy's older sister. They definitely had a love/hate relationship, but Apple knew that they were as close as twins. Apple was often jealous that Happy had a sibling, even if they often fought like it was World War III. Sailor, next to Apple and Brooklyn, was definitely Happy's best friend. While Happy often complained about her sister, if anyone else said something even slightly negative about her, they would have to deal with the wrath of Happy. No one wanted to cross that line.

Brooklyn and Happy threaded their arms through Apple's and walked her out of the bathroom into the bedroom.

♡

Guy, her mother's flamboyant assistant and best friend, had appeared in Apple's bedroom and was checking out his hair in her full-length mirror.

"Guy should never have gotten highlights," he moaned, running his fingers through his hair. "This is why I'll never meet a man. Who would want to be seen with Guy and his awful highlights?"

Then Guy noticed Apple. "Sweetie! Oh, my God! You look amazing! You look like a model! Honestly, red is *so* your color. Guy never sees you in a dress. Guy thinks you should totally wear more red and more dresses. You have a nice little body. Who knew?" he giggled. "And those boots? Can you say fabulous? Guy thinks you look fab-u-lous!"

He was practically screeching now, getting more excited each second. He grabbed Apple's hand and started jumping up and down, like a little boy who had to use the bathroom ASAP. "Guy is so excited for you! The boots make the outfit!"

"I know!" said Happy. "Aren't they fierce?"

"Fiercely fabulous," responded Guy. "Guy wishes he had a pair."

He laughed his infectious laugh. Even Apple couldn't help but laugh.

Apple loved Guy, who was practically a part of the Berg family. He had worked for Apple's mother for more than fifteen years, since Apple's birth. Apple couldn't help but smile when he was around. He was just one of those people who was almost never in a bad mood, kind of like Lyon. Even when Guy was in a bad mood, like Lyon he managed to hide it.

Happy described Guy as a "drama king," and that's exactly what he was, and he wouldn't dispute it. Apple wished Guy, who was always so handsome and fashionable, could convince her mother to update her "look." It was about time, she thought. It was just so odd how her mother complained about Apple's sloppy clothes when she herself only wore white or cream, or if she felt wild, beige. She had been wearing the same colors *forever*.

(Although they never talked about it, Apple knew it was Guy who had convinced her mother to get a mini facelift two years ago and Botox a couple of times a year. In Dr. Berg's world, it was okay to announce all things matter of the heart, but when it came to cosmetic procedures, that was strictly personal.)

"Well, they're Happy's boots and two sizes too small for my feet. I'm going to end up in the hospital," moaned Apple. "I may never be able to walk normally again."

"Oh, sweetie. *Never* complain about designer boots.

NEVER. No price is too high, no pain too much, to look as fabulous as you do right now," Guy said.

"Exactly!" agreed Happy. "You really do look good, Apple. You look sexy yet professional. But I think you should change your bra. That one's a little lumpy. And you have to take off your underwear. You can see lines. You can't have panty lines."

"Guy agrees," said Guy. "Lines are a no-no! Even for men!"

Again he laughed his infectious laugh.

"Lines are gross, I agree," said Brooklyn, pointing to her panty-line-free butt in her tight yoga pants.

"My daughter is *not* leaving the house without wearing unmentionables," Dr. Berg said sternly.

Apple could not believe her mother had just used the word "unmentionables." What era did her mother think she lived in?

"She's not going to be like one of those entitled brats who go out and party to all hours of the night and flash their private parts at the paparazzi," Dr. Berg continued. "Those girls who are famous for being famous? Don't those girls have *mothers*? It's one thing to make a name for yourself by hard work, but to make a name for yourself for not wearing underwear?"

"Oh, come on, Dr. Berg," laughed Happy. "It's not like the paparazzi are following *Apple* around. And the dress goes down practically to her knees. She's not going to pull a Britney or Paris. That dress is just too clingy for her to wear underwear. Seriously, you have to trust me on this, Dr. Berg."

Dr. Bee Bee Berg smiled politely. "I'm so glad I didn't

know all these things when I was your age. Times have certainly changed. I'm just going to pretend I didn't hear this part of the conversation," she said. "I'm going to trust you, Happy."

"Good idea, Dr. Berg!" said Happy, shooing Apple back into the bathroom.

Happy had that effect on people. She always knew just how to get her way, whether it was getting an extension for an essay or convincing her parents to give her a credit card when she was ten.

Apple headed back into the washroom with a new T-shirt bra and took off her underwear. She was surprised how freeing it felt.

"What about my hair?" she called out, suddenly— and much to her surprise—finding herself caring about what she looked like. Everyone else was making her anxious. Even Brooklyn wanted to spray some weird scented oil on her, which, according to Brooklyn, would "calm" her. Thankfully, Happy shot that idea down.

"I think you should wear it down. I love your hair," said Happy. "Your hair is one of your best features!"

Apple had always hated her curly hair, which took hours and hours to dry naturally. There was just so *much* of it. It was the only thing about Apple, aside from her name, that made her memorable. Sometimes Apple felt like pregnant women must feel. People just couldn't stop themselves from touching Apple's boingy curls without asking. The one person she didn't mind playing with her hair was Lyon. When he pulled on her boings—while they cuddled watching a movie, for example—it felt calming and nice.

"We've really got to run if we're going to make it on time," Dr. Berg said, tapping her watch. "Whatever you do, you never want to be late on the first meeting. You have only one chance to make a first impression. That's why it's called a *first* impression."

God, thought Apple, her mother really was a piece of work, always stating the painfully obvious and somehow managing to make it sound like she was the first person to come up with the statement.

"Let me look at you one more time," Happy said, grabbing Apple and looking at her from head to toe. "Yes, you look perfect. And remember, if they're looking for another intern, don't forget to mention that you just happen to have this fantastic fashionable friend named Happy who would be more than honored to take an internship position."

"Absolutely," Apple said, giving Happy a big hug. "Thank you for your help today. I can't tell you how much I appreciate it."

"Wait!" Apple turned toward Guy, who was armed with a mascara wand, which he applied to Apple's lashes. "A little mascara and a little lip gloss. Now you are perfect!"

"Let's move!" Dr. Berg said, like a drill sergeant. Apple followed her mother down the stairs, holding on to the banister for fear she'd tumble over in Happy's high-heeled boots.

At the door, Apple called up to Brooklyn, Happy, and Guy, who stood watching her from the floor above. "Wish me luck!"

"You don't need luck," called out Brooklyn. "Your

aura is perfect. Your vibe is really good. So is your energy! I'm sending you positive vibes!"

"You don't need luck!" screamed Happy. "You have my boots. Nothing bad has ever happened to me in those boots!"

"You don't need luck," retorted Guy. "You're Dr. Bee Bee Berg's daughter! They'll want you no matter how badly you screw up."

"Thanks a lot!" Apple shot back. She could hear Happy and Brooklyn giggling at Guy's comment.

"Don't be so sensitive," Guy called out. "Guy can only *dream* that the one and only Dr. Bee Bee Berg will adopt him someday. For reals!"

Even Guy, apparently, knew that Apple was being given this opportunity to work at *Angst* magazine only because she was the *daughter of*, not because of anything she had accomplished on her own.

This was exactly what Apple didn't want to happen. As they got into the car, she saw that her mother was smiling proudly and, thought Apple, a little smugly, as if she was entirely to be thanked for Apple's internship opportunity at *Angst*.

Shoot me, thought Apple. Shoot me now.

five

"Are you nervous, honey?" Dr. Berg asked as they drove in her white Range Rover to the *Angst* magazine offices, which just happened to be on the same block as the *Queen of Hearts with Dr. Bee Bee Berg* studio. Just my luck, thought Apple.

"Wouldn't it be exciting to work so close together? You could stop by to visit and *I* could stop by to visit. It would be fun! We could do mother–daughter stuff all the time. We could meet for lunch." She glanced at Apple. "Don't worry, you'll be fine!"

Even though Apple thought she didn't care, she found herself becoming more nervous as they got closer to the *Angst* offices. Her mother seemed to know it. Her mother read faces like Apple read words.

Though Apple's relationship with her mother had been far from perfect, it had improved tenfold since Apple finally admitted how she had snuck into her e-mail and pretended to be her. Apple pressed her lips together.

It seemed like a lifetime ago that she had been so obsessed with Zen that she was willing to lose her best friend.

Apple hated to admit it, but she still thought about Zen. Often.

It wasn't as easy as Apple had thought it would be—even after everything—to suddenly stop thinking about someone she'd been secretly obsessed with for years.

And while she would never admit this to anyone, it wasn't always easy for Apple to see Happy and Zen cuddle and kiss at school. It wasn't easy to see them walk hand in hand through the hallways, or to hear about their date nights, although Apple had gotten pretty good at acting like she was totally okay with it.

Apple was still waiting for what her mother always said: "Time does heal all wounds." Did it? If so, when would Apple would thinking about Zen?

Not that she would ever admit this to anyone either—not to her mother, not even to Crazy Aunt Hazel, definitely not to Happy, and barely to herself—but her heart still skipped a beat whenever she saw Zen. Apple was certain that she didn't like him in that way anymore. Still, she knew that others gossiped about her at school, wondering if she still had a crush on Zen. But he was into Happy. Happy was perfect. Apple wanted nothing more than for her best friend to have a worthy guy as her boyfriend. Zen *was* worthy.

Even *thinking* about Zen, and the fact she *shouldn't* be thinking about Zen, made her feel guilty. Plus, Apple now had Lyon. And she really, really liked Lyon. Lyon was kind, funny, smart, handsome, generous, sweet. Apple was lucky to have him.

"Honey? I just asked you a question. Where were you? What were you thinking?" her mother asked, placing a hand on Apple's knee. "You can tell me anything. You know that, right?"

Apple cringed. Oh, how often her mother said, "You can tell me anything." The sentence made Apple's spine tingle.

Should she tell her mother how often she still thought about Zen? Apple could simply be looking out the window or sitting in class and Zen would suddenly pop into her mind. She usually didn't even know it was happening until someone interrupted her or touched her, like her mother just had.

Even when she should be focused on something important, such as this meeting at *Angst* magazine, Zen popped into her head. She wondered what he was doing now. She wondered if he thought about her at all. She wondered if he would like her in this red dress and Happy's boots. It was ridiculous, thought Apple. She shook her head, as if by doing so she could shake Zen out of her brain. What she should be wondering was if Lyon was thinking about her. There was no way she was going to admit this to her mother. Her mother would probably just say, "It's okay to think about someone else, but remember to be grateful for those you do have in your life who love you."

Suddenly, Apple had an awful thought: Did her mother *know* that Apple was thinking about Zen? Could she sense it? Oh, God. It was bad enough that people at school still gossiped that she was into Zen.

"I guess I am a little nervous," Apple said, hoping her mother had no idea.

"Well, this *is* big. Do you know how many other fifteen-year-olds would absolutely die to be in the position you're in now? To work at the highest-distribution teen magazine in the country? I never had that chance when I was fifteen. Then again, we didn't have tabloid magazines back then. No one was that interested. Or maybe they were. But with the Internet now, you can't do anything without people knowing about your life," her mother said. "Do you know that Guy did a Web search for my name the other day? It's amazing what is out there about me. I told him I didn't want to hear, because it turns out not everyone is a fan of the show. People are so critical. Making fun of my outfits, my hair! Guy just kept saying, 'The only thing worse than being talked about is *not* being talked about.' So I guess that's why everyone is so fascinated with the celebrities in *Angst* magazine. It seems people will do anything to get a mention in it. It's a very important publication, especially for up-and-coming young stars, according to Guy. The magazine can apparently make or break a career."

"Okay, I *already* told you I was nervous. Now you're just making me *more* nervous!" Apple said.

"That's good. I'd be so much more worried if you weren't nervous. I still get nervous before every *Queen of Hearts* show, and how long have I been doing it? No, don't tell me. I don't want to be reminded. It's when you're not nervous that you have to worry, because if you're not nervous, it means you don't care," her mother said, holding up her hand.

Apple didn't want to break her mother's heart and tell her that she wasn't sure she *did* care. Her mother would be mortified. In fact, Apple couldn't remember her mother ever being so proud of her as she was right now. She didn't want to disappoint her.

"Happy said I have to be a 'better version' of myself today. What if they *don't* love me, even the 'better version' of me?" Apple pressed, biting a nail.

"Don't bite your nails. They *will* love you!" her mother said confidently. "You have to believe in yourself."

"God, you sound like Brooklyn," Apple muttered.

Apple wondered how everyone around her seemed so sure of themselves and their lives, and for that matter, so sure of Apple's. How could it only be Apple who was so unsure of everything? Her big feet, which she could feel swelling in Happy's gorgeous boots. Her hair. The fact she still thought about Zen. Her ambivalence about this so-called greatest job opportunity on the entire planet. What did that mean? Was it normal?

The only thing Apple was sure of was Lyon. She thought back to the day they met, at the school Valentine's Day dance. Like the *Angst* magazine gig, Lyon was another unexpected surprise of appearing on her mother's talk show that day. He had seen a short clip of her appearance that someone had posted on YouTube, and when he told her this at the dance, Apple was mortified. But Lyon quickly explained that he thought she had been very brave to do what she did, and that not enough people say they're sorry for making mistakes. For her to have admitted she made a mistake of that kind and apologize in such a public way? Well, unlike most, Lyon thought it was extremely admirable. He thought her teary appearance was, in his words, "awesome."

Then again, Lyon thought everything Apple did was "awesome," even when he watched her do homework. He was a dream, thought Apple.

She smacked her forehead. She had forgotten to call him back. Lyon had called to check in just as Happy and Brooklyn had arrived, and Apple had rushed off the phone promising she'd call him right back. That was hours ago.

"I need to call Lyon back. Do I have enough time now?" Apple asked her mother.

"We'll be there in four minutes and fifteen seconds. You had better be fast," she answered, eyeing the clock on the dashboard. "And stop biting your nails!"

Apple reached down into her bag and found her BlackBerry. She pressed the digits of Lyon's number, turning away from her mother to look out the window. She didn't feel comfortable talking to Lyon with her mother so close. Still, Apple was *trying* to be more open with her mother about the goings-on in her life, and what could be more open than talking to your new boyfriend in front of your mother?

"Hello," Apple heard Lyon answer sleepily, as if she had woken him from a nap.

"Hey, it's me," Apple said. She could feel the tenseness in her voice, more, she thought, because her mother was so near (and for sure listening in—how could she not be?) than because of the meeting.

"Hey, baby. Where you've been? You were supposed to call me back ages ago. I've missed you," he said, in his sexy, laid-back voice. Apple felt her heart melt a little with a mixture of love and guilt for not calling him back sooner. She still wasn't used to being—what was it?— missed? adored? thought about? complimented? all of the above?

"I know. I know. I'm so sorry. It was pure mayhem trying to get ready. Then Guy showed up. This is the first chance I've had! I'm in the car with my mom now. But I promise to call you as soon as it's done. I just wanted to let you know that I didn't forget about calling you back," Apple said, even though she wasn't being entirely truthful.

"You'd better not forget about me. Does that mean I can't say anything naughty to you?" he asked with a soft laugh.

Apple giggled and blushed. "I think that would be wise."

She glanced toward her mother, who had raised her eyebrows and was looking at her curiously. Apple usually didn't giggle. She knew her mother was dying to know what Lyon was saying. She had that same intrigued look that was plastered on her face while she waited for her guests to answer questions on the *Queen of Hearts*.

"Well, I'll just think naughty thoughts, then," Lyon said charmingly.

"That's a good idea. I better go," Apple sighed. "We're almost there."

"Well, good luck. They'll love you. How could they not? They'd be idiots not to see how great you are," Lyon said confidently.

Why was Lyon so sure of her ability to make a good impression? She found herself containing annoyance with his words. Out of everyone, Lyon was the last person she should be annoyed with. He was just being supportive.

"Thanks, Lyon. I wish *you* were the editor! I promise to call you later," Apple said tensely, hoping she sounded nervous, not bitchy.

"I've heard that before," Lyon joked.

"I mean it," Apple said. "Call you soon."

She hung up and imagined Lyon in his bed. Lyon, with his perfect bed-head hair, his cool rock-band T-shirts, his Converse shoes. He was a grade ahead of Apple, a year older, and did the sweetest things for her. Yesterday he had dropped off a little teddy bear with a note attached saying, "Good luck! I know you'll kick ass."

Lyon always did things like that. He was cute and thoughtful—sometimes, Apple thought, overly so. But then she thought, What is "overly so"? Would she like it better if he did none of those things, if he never called? Apple didn't think that was a better option at all. She knew, from her Zen Crush, that being ignored by someone you were into wasn't a good way of living. She knew from Brooklyn, who had an on-again, off-again, on-again *something* with their classmate Hopper, that she was lucky Lyon treated her so well. Hopper was gorgeous, but supremely immature. Apple could see why Brooklyn was physically attracted to him—he was stunning. And he could be funny, if you were into jokes about sex and animals. But he didn't treat Brooklyn well. Even Happy occasionally complained that Zen wasn't that romantic, and that she wished he could be more like Lyon.

"Your boyfriend is perfect," Happy had told her more than once.

No, your boyfriend is perfect, Apple would always immediately think. Of course she would never say that aloud to Happy, for fear she would get the wrong impression.

"Is someone in love?" her mother asked Apple in a singsong. Apple breathed in and out deeply. While things with her mother had certainly improved, Apple still wasn't willing to shell out *all* the details of her love life. They just didn't have that kind of relationship.

Apple carefully considered what to say. She wanted to at least try to treat her mother more like a friend, like Happy did.

"Well, let's just say I'm in deep like," Apple said finally, blushing. She hoped that would satiate her mother's need to know.

"I'm happy for you, Apple," her mother said. "Your life is all coming together. You've made up with Happy, you're getting a fabulous new job, and you have a nice boy in your life who seems to be a gentleman and who seems to really adore you."

"God, now you're starting to sound like Aunt Hazel," Apple replied. "She says, 'When it rains, it pours.'"

"Well, she has a point. Just look at her! She and Jim seem very happy. This is the longest relationship your aunt has had in . . . well, ever!"

"God, Mom, please don't call him Jim. He's Mr. Kelly to me. And he'll always be Mr. Kelly. Honestly, I just want to gag whenever I think of my *math teacher* with Aunt Hazel. Gross!"

While Apple was meeting Lyon at the Valentine's Day dance, Crazy Aunt Hazel, who had driven her there, and whose relationships had previously always been disastrous, had met Apple's math teacher, who was chaperoning.

Crazy Aunt Hazel had danced that night with Mr. Kelly, and they'd been in a relationship ever since. On the one hand, it was good that they had hooked up that night, because everyone at her school started gossiping about her aunt and Mr. Kelly instead of about Apple's embarrassing appearance on her mother's show and her fight with Happy over Zen.

Apple knew her aunt and her teacher were both smitten. Hazel hadn't cried or thrown any temper tantrums *at all* since she met Mr. Kelly. And her aunt was *known* for her temper tantrums. She was famous in the Berg household for slamming doors and stealing their ice cream, after especially dates gone wrong, which had been a regular occurrence for years and years. And Mr. Kelly definitely seemed to be in a better mood since he met her aunt. There had been hardly *any* pop quizzes.

Apple wanted her aunt to be happy—she was always *so* pathetic when it came to men—but the thought of her aunt and her math teacher *together*? Yuck.

God, thought Apple, who would have ever thought her MATH teacher would end up with Crazy Aunt Hazel, who had been raised more like Apple's sister than her aunt. She was definitely immature for her age, always wanting to borrow Apple's clothes, bringing over her laundry for their housekeeper to do, eating food from their fridge, and wanting to hang out with Apple.

Apple had to admit that she had seen a lot less of Aunt Hazel since she had started dating Mr. Kelly, and sh sort of missed her and hearing about all her crazy hijinks and dating disasters.

"Let's be happy for Hazel," Dr. Berg said to Apple. "She's happy and it's our job to be supportive. We're her family."

"'For better or worse,' as Dad likes to say," responded Apple with a smirk. "And I *am* supportive. I just don't want to think about her and my math teacher, okay? I have to see him every day, remember? It's embarrassing."

Apple and her mother drove for the next few minutes in silence.

"We have arrived," her mother announced, pulling into a parking space in front of a large building.

Apple became suddenly aware that she couldn't feel her toes at all. And now she was also having a hard time swallowing because her mouth was so dry. She was nervous, no doubt about it.

Her mother stopped the car, took the key out of the ignition, and looked at Apple with a hopeful glance.

"Do you want me to come in or wait here?" Dr. Bee Bee Berg asked.

Apple was surprised. Her mother usually wouldn't have even bothered asking. Apple had assumed her mother would just walk in with her, not caring what Apple wanted. She was pleased, and impressed, that her mother was offering her a choice.

"I think I should do this on my own," Apple said, trying to sound as polite as possible. "No offense, but I think it would look really *unprofessional* to bring my *mother* in."

Apple thought she had been nice allowing her to drive her to the meeting. Lyon had wanted to take her, but she knew it would mean a lot more to her mother.

"Okay, then," her mother said. "I love you, Apple. Good luck. Stay strong. Be yourself. I'll wait for you right here."

"Love you too, Mom," Apple said.

Apple opened the car door but tripped getting out, almost falling on her face.

"Apple! Are you okay?" her mother yelped, jumping out and racing around the car to her.

"Mom?" Apple asked meekly as she straightened her dress, her heart pounding. "Can you come in with me?"

"Oh, honey! I'm so glad you asked," her mother gushed excitedly. "I'd like nothing more than to see where my daughter is going to get her first job! I want to be there for you every step of the way."

Apple tried not to roll her eyes. "Actually, Mom, I need you to come in with me because I can't walk in these boots. I need you to lean on," she said. "Literally."

"Physically, emotionally," Dr. Berg said, pulling Apple into a hug. "Whatever. I'm here for you. Now, is there anything else I can help you out with? Do you need any advice on how to—"

"Mom, please!" Apple snapped. "Just hold on to my arm and let's get this over with."

six

The offices of *Angst* magazine were beautifully styled, like a feature in an architecture magazine or a condo showroom. Everything was modern, and white and hot pink. Even the receptionist looked like she could be a model for a Victoria's Secret catalog.

Apple wondered how a model had ended up being a receptionist, and if she should call the local modeling agencies to ask if one of their clients had gone missing.

Apple held on to her mother's arm, not out of fear of her forthcoming meeting with the editor of *Angst*, Nancy—who, Apple knew from Happy, the gossip rags called "Fancy Nancy" because she was always dressed in the latest fashions from Paris and Milan—but out of fear she would topple over.

According to Happy, Fancy Nancy was as much photographed at events and galas as Apple's mother. But her mother and Fancy Nancy had never met. Apple thought this was because, although they were both famous, they traveled in different circles. Apple's mother's fans were mostly housewives and students who were home by 5 p.m., when the show aired. Fancy Nancy, Apple guessed, was the fashion guru, out at fabulously fashionable events late into the night, hanging out on the red carpet at events with younger celebrities.

Her mother walked up to the reception desk and spoke to the woman who looked like a model. "This is Apple Berg." Apple shot her mother a mortified look. "She has an appointment with Nancy," her mother continued, not noticing Apple's this-can't-be-happening-to-me expression.

Apple was fifteen—nearly sixteen—and her mother was speaking for her! It was almost as bad as having your mother in the doctor's office while the doctor asked if you were sexually active.

Apple regretted not having had Lyon drive her here.

"Yes, I am Apple Berg. I have a meeting with Nancy," Apple interrupted, trying to act composed, letting go of her mother's arm, attempting to butt in front of her. She could feel her face had turned a deep shade of red. Apple hated how easily she blushed.

"Hi, I'm Morgan. And . . . oh, my God," Morgan said, looking at Apple's mother with an intense stare. "You're the Queen of Hearts! I Tivo your show every day! My friends are going to be so, so jealous when they hear that I met you in person. I'll call Nancy and let her know you're both here. You can take a seat over there," she said, pointing at pink couches near a white coffee table. "Would you like anything to drink, Dr. Berg? A Perrier? Flat water? Coffee? Tea? Juice?"

"I'm fine, thank you, sweetie," her mother answered calmly and, Apple thought, overly politely, like she was a politician trying to charm voters.

Apple grudgingly had to give credit to her mother. She was always nice to fawning fans. Apple couldn't imagine always having to be nice to strangers who acted like they knew her.

Apple was always amazed, too, at how much *better* people on television were treated, as if celebrities were somehow more worthy than anyone else.

I'm okay, too, thought Apple. Thanks for asking me if *I* want anything!

She was more than a little annoyed. But what did she expect? Whenever she went out with her mother in public, which wasn't often, Apple was invisible. This meet-and-greet was supposed to be about her, and the receptionist seemed to care only about her mother!

If only Happy hadn't forced her to wear her boots, she'd have been able to walk in alone. She looked at her mother, who was beaming as she always did when strangers recognized her. Apple scowled as she grabbed her mother's arm and held on for dear life as they walked to the white leather couch to wait for Fancy Nancy.

"She'll be right out," announced Morgan, this time giving Apple a friendly smile. "She's just finishing up a conference call right now. There's reading material for you. If you don't mind, Dr. Berg, can I grab your autograph? I usually wouldn't do this, but my mother and friends would kill me if I didn't."

Apple wanted to gag. She wondered why people collected autographs. What was this Morgan going to do with her mother's autograph? Seriously. Sell it on eBay? She wondered how much her mother's autograph would be worth anyway.

Apple sat beside her mother on one of the couches and picked up a magazine off the table. Of course, all the reading materials were past issues of *Angst*. She picked up an issue with a photo of a huge twenty-year-old celebrity named Kenneth, whom Happy was obsessed with. Kenneth, an actor on a hit television show, had recently become so famous that his face was plastered everywhere—even on her cereal box.

"Happy is in love with this guy," Apple said to her mother, pointing to the cover. "It's too bad he's such a jerk. I can't believe he cheated on his wife of, like, four months." The gossip on America's young, hot rising star, marrying so young and then cheating on his new wife, had made headlines everywhere, even on CNN, as if it were real news.

"I can't believe he got married in the first place! What is he? Twenty? Oh, young celebrities these days," her mother said, in full-on Dr. Bee Bee Berg mode. "They grow up too fast and then, because they're acting like adults way before their time, they think that marriage is the next step. It's no wonder their marriages never last. No one should get married that young. Marriage is not just about love. It takes work, responsibility, and commitment."

To Apple, the stream of words coming from her mother's mouth sounded like a lecture, and one she had heard too many times. Apple hoped no one could over-hear her mother's rant. She didn't seem to grasp the concept of using an "indoor voice."

"I should do a show featuring young people getting married," her mother continued. "Remind me to tell Guy about the idea. Because people these days don't know how much work goes into good marriages. They get into one fight and they're out like lightning. And yet they still seem unable to stop themselves."

Yeah, you should know, Apple thought. She kept that not-so-nice thought to herself, though it was true. For months and months, around her Zen Crush time, Apple had noticed there was trouble in her own parents' marriage.

Even Crazy Aunt Hazel, who rarely noticed any-thing if it didn't have to do with her, had noticed. Her dad had slept in a different room for weeks, and he and her mother never spent any time together. Her dad spent all his spare time on the golf course and got angry with her mother for constantly talking about work. And her mother *never* stopped talking about work. To Apple, her parents seemed like strangers sharing the same house.

It was clear to Apple that her mother's work had come before her marriage. It was clear to everyone *but* Dr. Berg. It was ironic, thought Apple, that the person who told people how to have successful relationships hadn't even noticed her *own* marriage falling apart.

That was, until Apple screamed at her mother that she didn't practice what she preached, that she didn't even realize her own marriage was a sham. Thanks to

Apple's outburst, her parents were once again acting like newlyweds. Her mother made sure to spend at least one night a week going out with her dad, and they were sleeping in the same room again. In fact, it was like they had fallen in love all over again. Every Monday for weeks now, her dad had sent her mother flowers at the studio, and her mother had made more of an effort to be home earlier and talk about things other than work. And Guy now had to leave the house by 9 p.m. so her parents could spend "quality time" together.

Guy was hurt when he heard about this new rule, but he understood. Apple thought that he shouldn't be hanging around so much at their house anyway. Sure, he was amazing at his job, booking guests and keeping Dr. Berg's life organized. But Apple thought he should have more of a social life. She thought he could for sure find someone if he spent as much time on his personal life as he did on his job. If her crazy aunt could find someone, then anyone could.

"You know, he really kind of looks like Lyon," Dr. Berg said, looking at the photograph of Kenneth on the magazine cover.

"You think?" Apple asked.

"Yes. They have the same bone structure," Dr. Berg answered.

Apple looked at the photo again more closely. There was some resemblance. She couldn't believe that her boyfriend was as good-looking as this actor featured on the cover of *Angst* magazine.

Apple watched the glass doors open behind the reception desk. There was no mistaking who was coming through it. Without a doubt, it was Fancy Nancy, the editor-in-chief of *Angst* magazine, the one who had seen her on *Queen of Hearts*.

It was impossible to ignore that Fancy Nancy, along with having the face of a china doll, had presence. It was as if everyone and everything—even the fake plants in the corners—stopped breathing when she appeared. She had what Happy like to call "that It factor." Apple told herself, for the umpteenth time, to remember not to call her "Fancy Nancy" to her face.

Fancy Nancy was wearing a simple black sleeveless dress that clung to her body as if were painted on. She looked nothing short of elegant. Apple and Dr. Berg stood up immediately, in unison, and walked over to her. Apple inhaled a deep breath, finding it hard to swallow. Fancy Nancy may have had "that It factor," but Apple found her terrifying.

Fancy Nancy stuck out her hand and shook her mother's first.

"Dr. Bee Bee Berg! I am so thrilled to meet you in person. I can't believe we haven't met before. I'm pleasantly surprised that Apple brought you along. I'm sure a ton of my employees would love to meet you. In fact, we were just talking about you in our story meeting last week. We're thinking about doing a profile on you! Photos of your home, your family, your daughter. It would be a great way to introduce Apple to the *Angst* readership and learn what it's like to grow up with someone who has helped *so* many people on television," Fancy Nancy said. She wasn't exactly gushing, but she was close.

Oh. My. God. Was Fancy Nancy sucking up to her mother too? Did she really believe that her mother actually helped people by getting them to admit on television that they cheated on their husbands or were thinking about leaving their wives for younger women? Didn't she know that her mother's show, like *Angst* magazine, was pure entertainment?

Apple also couldn't believe how young Fancy Nancy seemed. She had imagined someone more like her mother, but Fancy Nancy looked just a few years older than Apple.

"That would be fantastic," said Dr. Berg, excitedly. "Why not? It would be fun. And I'm so proud of Apple and will do anything to help her and her career here at *Angst*."

"Great. I'll get my people to call your people, then, and we'll get it set up," said Fancy Nancy.

Hello? Apple thought. What about me? Why don't you ask *me* if it's all right to come into my home and do a story? What if I don't want a story about me in a magazine? And what about saying hi to me? I'm the one you called in to meet with. Me!

Finally, Fancy Nancy looked at Apple.

"And you must be the famous Apple! We are so pleased to have you join the *Angst* family. Why don't you two follow me? Morgan!" Fancy Nancy hollered, though Morgan was only two feet away.

"Yes, Nancy?" Morgan answered, rushing over to her side. Clearly, whenever Nancy said jump, you jumped. Apple was impressed. Fancy Nancy was the only woman she had ever met, aside from her mother, who even came close to having such an effect on people.

"Can you please show Dr. Bee Bee Berg around the office, introduce her to some people, especially Jan and Heather, who I know watch the show religiously, while I take Apple into my office for a little chat?"

"Sure, not a problem," said Morgan.

It took everything in Apple's power to try to forget the throbbing pain in her feet. She should have asked Brooklyn for meditating tips. It would have been good to know how to focus on something other than her feet at this moment. Apple needed NOT to focus on her feet right now, or rather the lack of feeling in her feet. She needed to be professional. Or at least fake it. That was what Guy always said—"Fake it until you make it."

Her mother reached out and gave Apple's hand a squeeze before Morgan led her in one direction while Apple followed Fancy Nancy down a long hallway in the opposite direction.

"Love the boots," Nancy said to Apple, who was trailing behind. Apple hadn't seen Fancy Nancy look below Apple's face since they were introduced. How did she notice Apple's boots when she was walking *in front* of her? It was almost as if she could smell designer shoes if they were in her presence. It somehow made wearing them—and the pain of wearing them—worth it.

Apple would have to remember to tell Happy that Fancy Nancy had complimented her boots. Happy would love that.

Apple, walking slowly and unsteadily, followed Fancy Nancy to the end of the hall. Fancy Nancy walked fast, as if she were late for an important meeting. Apple was not sure she would have been able to keep up with Fancy Nancy's energized pace even if she had been wearing flip-flops or was barefoot.

"Have a seat," Fancy Nancy said when they entered her spacious office, pointing to two black chairs. She sat behind her large oak desk. There was not one stray piece of paper. Apple had never been so relieved to sit down. She could swear she felt wetness on her pinky toe, which could only mean that her feet were blistering and bleeding. Great, thought Apple. How disgusting.

Apple looked out the window behind Fancy Nancy to the stunning view of the mountains. It was so beautiful. She found it depressing that Fancy Nancy's couldn't see the beautiful scenery as she worked. She also wondered how Fancy Nancy remained so pale—almost ghost-like—when 285 days of the year were sunny where they lived. She must pile on the level-50 sunblock every hour. There was something fascinating about seeing someone look so pale and young and yet so stylish at the same time. It was kind of like seeing a vampire. Apple was also amazed to see a treadmill and a spinning bike in her office.

"As you know, " Fancy Nancy started, "we saw you on that very touching show a while back. Ever since, everyone at *Angst* has been pretty obsessed with you. The way you admitted what you had done to your best friend, all for a guy! The way you cried! It was so *deliciously* evil. I mean, of course, we've all *been* there. But it takes a special someone to go on *television* and own up to that. It takes someone with courage. Even I wouldn't have done *that*. You're one brave girl!"

"Thanks," Apple said. "I think, " she added.

"I don't mean that in a bad way. Truth be told, we also just never knew that Dr. Bee Bee Berg had a daughter who fitted right into our target demographic. And you were so well spoken, so real, that we all think you will fit in quite nicely here. We'd been talking for ages about having a teenage advice columnist, but we had forgotten about it until we saw you on the show and thought, 'Bingo. That's her!' You have that *real* quality, and if I can be truthful, it doesn't hurt that your mother is so well known. We love celebrities around here. We live, eat, and breathe celebrities and their lifestyles."

"Thank you, I think," Apple said again, hating herself for sounding so unsure. All she had said so far was "Thank you. I think."

Fancy Nancy probably thought she was a moron and was regretting even offering her the gig, Apple thought, her confidence waning. She had the urge to tell her, "It's okay. You can change your mind. You don't have to have me here," though the thought of breaking that news to Happy and her mother was distressing.

She glanced out the glass door into the hallway. Everyone moved with purpose. Surprisingly, Apple suddenly could imagine working here. As Brooklyn would say, the place had a good vibe. It was electrifying.

"Things are getting very exciting here at *Angst*," Fancy Nancy continued. "We're branching out, too. We've just got word that we're starting a television show—once a week, but hopefully they'll pick it up at least a couple more days. It will be called *Angst TV* and will be aired on a cable network and as a podcast."

"Wow. That's great!" Apple said. "I had no idea."

"You had *no idea* that we were working on *Angst TV*," pressed Fancy Nancy, with a hint of annoyance. Apple picked up on the change in Fancy Nancy's tone immediately and realized she had misspoken.

"Oh, sure. I mean I've read that it was in the works, but I had no idea that it was actually happening. That's awesome," Apple said. She was sure her voice sounded meek.

"It *is* great. We've been working on it for a long time. We're hoping the readers who love *Angst* will also watch *Angst TV* and download the podcast from our website. We're going to be bringing the print magazine live on television, with fashion tips from famous designers and interviews with celebrities we feature that week in our magazine. We're also hoping that viewers who happen upon *Angst TV* will start reading the magazine. You must be comfortable on television, since you grew up around it, right, Apple?" Fancy Nancy asked, looking Apple directly in the eyes.

Apple didn't want to disappoint Fancy Nancy and tell her that she rarely even watched her mother's show, except when Happy and Brooklyn forced her to. But Apple was loyal to her mother. She would never admit that she didn't particularly care for the guests on her show, or for the idea of the show, to anyone except her very best friends.

"Of course. I've watched every episode," Apple found herself saying. "I'm very comfortable in front of a camera. I've grown up in the television world, as you said."

Apple couldn't believe how easily the lie slid out of her mouth. Why was she lying? She didn't have to lie to Fancy Nancy. She could have told her that she was a complete novice when it came to television, that she had no idea how her mother had done it for so many years or why viewers found the show so appealing.

"That's good. Really good. Because we want you on *Angst TV*. There's something *real* about you," Fancy Nancy said. "It will be great to get someone who looks *real* on *Angst TV*. Of course, we have a main host. She's television-ready, you know—well spoken and pretty to look at. But you're . . . well, you're human. And *real*."

Apple was beginning to hate the word "real." How many times could a person use that word in a sentence? What did "real" mean, anyway? Did that mean Apple wasn't good-looking, didn't look like she belonged on television?

"Now, let's get down to the business at hand. We need a teen advice columnist, and that will be you. And you'll also have a spot on *Angst TV* doing the advice thing for teens. But before you think this is an easy job, it's not. I think your . . . background, being the daughter of the country's most famous talk-show advice host, right off the bat gives you what people will see as experience. They'll trust you immediately. Which is good. But, Apple, I need to know how committed you are to *Angst*," Fancy Nancy asked. "Which is why I wanted to meet with you in person."

Apple suddenly felt she was guilty of something and on trial. She sat up straighter, feeling unprepared. But Apple was going to "fake it until you make it."

"I wouldn't be here if I wasn't committed. Of course I'm committed," Apple said, while thinking, My feet! My feet!

"Here at *Angst* we want people to really be part of the family," Fancy Nancy continued. "How do I say this? We don't want you just to do the advice column and share that advice on television. We want you to be here more than that. We want you to learn all the ropes of this magazine, from answering phones to organizing the fashion closet. We want you to eat, breathe, and live *Angst*."

"Okay," Apple said slowly.

"We need you here two days a week at the *very* minimum. After school, of course—we want our interns to do well at school. We need you to set a good example. And we hope you'll be here on weekends. Saturdays, Sundays. It takes a lot of work to put out this magazine. And with the new television show, the more help the better. You'll be working with a variety of editors, and basically doing whatever they ask and need you to do. If they need you to photocopy something, you do it. If they need you to take photos of clothes on racks, you do it. If they need you to go out and get them a sandwich, you do it. And, of course, you have to get your advice column in on time and practice for your television spot. Almost everyone here starts from the bottom rung and works their way up. I can't have my other employees thinking that just because you are the 'daughter of,' you can get away with receiving special treatment, even if you will have such a sought-after job from the start. Everyone around here wants to be on

Angst TV, but not everyone is going to be. You *are*. They're going to be jealous, so you're going to have to prove yourself more than anyone," Fancy Nancy said bluntly. "Can you deal with all this?"

Apple looked at Fancy Nancy, wide-eyed.

seven

"Of *course* I can deal with it. I don't want to be known just as the daughter of someone famous either. I never have," Apple said, nodding in agreement with Fancy Nancy. "I will prove myself."

"I'm glad to hear that. And your school schedule will allow you to be here every Tuesday and Thursday for a few hours? Because to launch this show and do your column and help out with other things is going to take up a lot of your time. And I mean a *lot*. You're going to have to be very organized and get your priorities straight. Your social life will suffer," said Fancy Nancy solemnly, as if she knew what she was talking about. Apple wondered if Fancy Nancy was single. Could someone as accomplished and sexy and fashionable as Fancy Nancy really be single?

"I understand. My grades are great," Apple said. "Wait . . . Tuesday? Like, you want me to start *tomorrow*?"

"Yes, tomorrow. Will that be a problem?" Fancy Nancy asked. "*Angst TV* launches in one week. We need to get you prepared. We have so much to do beforehand that everyone around here is working 24/7."

"Of course. I understand. I'll be here," Apple said. "It's no problem."

"And weekends? Is that a problem?" Fancy Nancy asked, her eyes piercing.

"No, not at all," Apple said, though she wasn't as sure about that. Weekends were usually her time to hang out with friends and spend time with Lyon and watch bad movies in her pajamas eating popcorn.

"Good," Fancy Nancy said curtly. "I can't babysit you either. So I need to know that you are 100 percent committed."

Was it just Apple, or had Fancy Nancy been a heck of a lot nicer when her mother was around?

"I am. I promise I won't let you down," Apple said. She wanted this meeting to end sooner rather than later. Apple would have promised Fancy Nancy her firstborn child if she let her out of there. Her feet were now one completely numb, her toes probably maimed for life.

"Perfect. Who knows, maybe there will be two stars in your family. At least that's what we hope! Go out and see Morgan and she'll get you a pass. When you arrive tomorrow, Michael, the head of the interns, will show you where you'll be working and explain in more detail what it is you're expected to do. You'll be sharing the office with another intern named Emme, who is fabulous and ambitious. I'm going to have to end our meeting now, because Emme is coming in. But it was such a pleasure to meet you and your mother."

"You too," Apple said, getting up. Thank God that was over. She could feel the sweat under her armpits. She should have doubled up on the deodorant. Had she even put on deodorant? She couldn't remember. She was leaning toward not.

"And, Apple?" Fancy Nancy said, looking not at her but at something that looked like an invitation.

"Yes?" Apple asked.

"You screw up at *Angst*, and it could be the end of your career in magazines and television forever," said Fancy Nancy.

"I won't," Apple gulped. "I promise."

"Good. Can you find your way out?" Fancy Nancy asked.

"Yes. Thank you. It was nice to meet you," Apple said.

Her new boss didn't look up as Apple walked herself out.

♡

"You screw up at Angst *and it could be the end of your career in magazines and television forever."*

Fancy Nancy's warning (or was it a threat?) raced through Apple's head as she worked her way through the maze of hallways to get back to the reception area. She was serious, this Fancy Nancy. Suddenly Apple couldn't help feeling in her gut that there wasn't anything she wanted to do more with her life than work in magazines and on *Angst TV*, just to prove to this

Fancy Nancy—and everyone else, including herself—that she could do it.

It would be a good challenge for Apple, to say the least. She had never even had a part-time job before. But there was something about Fancy Nancy that not only terrified her but also made Apple want to impress her.

Apple made it back to the reception area and saw Morgan, the receptionist. But her mother was nowhere to be seen. Apple was annoyed. Her feet were killing her. She wanted to leave NOW.

Just as she took a seat to wait for her mother to appear, a super-cute guy who was walking out, one Apple could swear she had seen before, momentarily distracted her. Then it hit her. Oh, my God, thought Apple.

Was that What's-his-name walking past her, leaving the *Angst* offices? No, it couldn't be. But was it? Apple could have sworn she saw—Oh God, *what's his name?* That guy on that music video channel who interviewed all those famous musicians? Happy would know his name. It was on the tip of Apple's tongue. Happy had forced Apple to watch the show—it was one of her favorites—more than once. It aired daily right after her mother's show, on a different channel. What's-his-name was cuter in person but shorter than he looked on television.

According to her mother, most television personalities were shorter in person (and also had bigger heads).

"I dig your hair," said What's-his-name, smiling at Apple. "It's very cool." Apple blushed. What's-his-name smiled at her again, this time for what seemed like a while. He looked down at her—rather, Happy's—boots and smiled appreciatively. She almost jumped back as he reached out and pulled one of her boings.

"Cute!" What's-his-name said. Apple didn't mind that someone she just met had pulled on one of her curls without asking.

Apple called out, "Thanks!" but wasn't sure if What's-his-name heard her. He had already walked out. This day certainly has been strange, thought Apple, wondering if she had dreamed What's-his-name's presence.

"Hey, Morgan," Apple said, trying to be brave. She would have to see Morgan a few days a week, so Apple knew it would be better to start off on the right foot and at least try not to be as shy as she really was.

"How did it go?" asked Morgan, seemingly sincere. Then she whispered, "I know Nancy can be harsh."

"Well, it went," Apple responded. "I think it was okay. I'm supposed to get a card from you."

"Yup. Already done. Here's your pass. Every time you come in, you swipe this card and the office doors will open for you. Nancy explained that you'd be meeting Michael tomorrow, right? You look a little wary," Morgan said, eyeing Apple. "Don't worry. Michael's a charmer. You'll love him. He's a true doll. Everyone adores him."

"I'm fine. It's just that Nancy was a little . . ." Apple didn't know exactly how to describe how she felt, and she certainly didn't want to say anything that might offend Morgan or get back to Nancy.

"I know. Like I said, she can be . . . well, harsh. But that's why *Angst* is the number-one-selling teen magazine in the country. You don't get to be the editor of something like this unless you're harsh. You can't be a success unless you really are forward-thinking and make sure people hear you. But don't worry. She's a teddy bear underneath. Or at least that's what all of us employees say. We *say* it. We're not sure if it's true, though," Morgan laughed. "With *Angst TV* launching, she's under extra pressure."

Apple didn't want to talk about Fancy Nancy anymore. She wanted to know about What's-his-name, the cute guy she'd seen on television who had complimented her, pulled her hair, and smiled at her.

"Um, that guy who was just leaving. Was that . . . ?" Apple asked. "My brain is totally fried. I can't remember his name."

"Sloan Starr? Yup, that was him," responded Morgan. "Cute, huh?"

eight

That's right, thought Apple. Sloan Starr! She wanted to slap herself on the head. How could she have forgotten his name? Happy is going to be so jealous, she thought. She'd have to play it down. It was enough that Apple was going to work here, let alone actually meet celebrities. It would put Happy over the edge.

"What was he doing here?" Apple asked Morgan, trying to not sound overly curious. She knew if she didn't get the details, though, Happy would kill her.

"Oh, celebrities come by a lot to meet with our editors. They think it will help them get good press if they meet us in person and take some photos with us," Morgan explained. "You'll get used to it. Think of it as a perk of the job," she added, with a wink.

"Does it?" wondered Apple. "Does it help them get into the pages of *Angst*?"

"What do you think? Of course it does. They're nice

to *Angst*, and *Angst* is nice to them. Plus, all the fabulous musicians love Sloan, so we love him too."

"He said he liked my hair," she admitted, realizing she was smiling.

"Oh, no. You already have a celebrity crush and you haven't even started here yet! Be careful," advised Morgan. "He's known as a womanizer. But then again, what male celebrity isn't? I have a rule to never date anyone in the entertainment industry. They're too self-obsessed."

"He only said he liked my hair!" Apple said, defending herself. "Don't worry. I have a boyfriend."

"You don't fool me," responded Morgan playfully but knowingly. "You're all flushed. I can tell you've just been bitten by the celebrity bug! It's always exciting to meet your first celebrity in person. Well, aside from your mother."

As if! thought Apple. She wouldn't admit just how out of touch she was with the world of celebrities. In fact, Apple was thinking it might be a good idea to ask Happy to give her a crash course on that world and tell her what websites she should be checking out.

"Speaking of celebrities," Apple said, "do you happen to know where my mother is?"

"Last I saw her she was regaling a group of fans in the kitchen with stories of the best and worst of the *Queen of Hearts*. I wish I could have stuck around, but if Nancy saw me away from my post, she'd kill me. I have to be at her beck and call practically 24/7. People just love your mother, don't they?"

"Yes," Apple said, trying to put on the kindest smile

she could muster. It was so like her mother to get all the attention on the day that was supposed to be about her.

"Take a seat and I'll go find her," Morgan said.

Apple noticed another girl, sitting on the couch flipping through a magazine. She looked around Apple's age, even though she was wearing a lot of makeup. The girl looked at her briefly, just long enough to give Apple a disgusted sneer before going back to her magazine. Apple knew it had to be Emme, the other intern Fancy Nancy had talked so glowingly about.

What is up with her? Apple wondered. She couldn't deny it. Even with all that makeup, the girl was pretty. She was more than pretty—Emme was in Happy's league of pretty. She was wearing something way more fabulous than Apple was. She looked as fashionable as Morgan and even Fancy Nancy. Clearly, Emme wasn't as insecure as Apple either. She seemed calm and collected, as if she did these kinds of meetings just as often as she brushed her teeth.

Apple wondered if she should introduce herself. She hated herself for even wondering. She hated that she was so shy. She always had. She had to—had to!—get over her shyness. She was now an employee—well, an intern—at *Angst* magazine. She was part of the *Angst* family, and weren't you supposed to be nice to other family members? Apple knew she would have to stop being so self-conscious if she was going to make it in this business, or at least make a good impression. Plus, the fact that Sloan Starr had just been so nice to her had given her a confidence boost that surprised even her.

And what was it Happy had said? That she had to be a "better version" of herself? What better time to actually be a "better version" of herself, even a new version of herself, than right now?

"Hi," Apple said quietly, taking a seat near the girl. The girl clearly hadn't heard her, because she didn't look up from reading. Apple's voice had sounded like a frog's croak. She cleared her throat.

"Hi, I'm Apple," she said, this time more loudly. "Are you Emme? Is that short for Emma?"

Again, the girl didn't look up from her magazine instantly, as Apple assumed she—or anyone—would when someone says hi and offers an introduction. When Emme finally did glance up at Apple—after what seemed like a minute—she looked bored.

"Yes, I'm Emme," she answered, her tone flat. "And, no, it's not short for 'Emma.' It's just Emme, like the letter."

"Oh! You're going to be interning here too, right? Nancy was just talking about you. We're going to be working together," Apple said. She knew she sounded childish and geeky and nervous.

"Exciting," Emme said, sounding anything but excited.

Luckily, Dr. Berg finally appeared. Emme went back to reading and didn't look up again.

"Ready?" Dr. Berg asked. "I think you're going to have a wonderful time here. The people are so nice. And I met a very nice young man who apparently is on television too. His name was Sloan . . . Sloan something."

"Sloan Starr," Apple finished for her, acting as if her mother should know who he was, even though

Apple hadn't remembered his name herself. "He hosts *Rock the Clock*," Apple said. "He's very famous. His show airs right after yours. Happy loves him. He interviews musicians."

"Ah, my baby gets her first job. I'm so proud of you," her mother said, pushing Apple's hair behind her shoulders. It was all Apple could do to stop from slapping her mother's hand away. "Just think of all the interesting people you're going to meet, including celebrities!" her mother continued. "It's so exciting!"

Apple glanced at Emme, who gave her a look that clearly said, "You brought your MOTHER to a job interview? What a loser!"

Emme, unlike the others, appeared not to notice just *who* her mother WAS. If she did recognize Dr. Berg, she didn't seem to care. For some reason, it bothered Apple that this Emme didn't notice or seem to care.

Apple wanted to explain to Emme about the boots and how they hurt so much and that that was the reason she brought her mother in with her. But Emme, her new co-worker, seemed far from friendly. In fact, she seemed scarier than Fancy Nancy.

"Emme?" Morgan called out as Dr. Berg and Apple were leaving. "Nancy will see you now. I'll take you there."

Apple couldn't help but look at Emme, who must have been 5 foot 10, as she got up gracefully, like an elegant safari animal. Her legs seemed to go on forever in her fishnet stockings. Her stiletto heels didn't seem to bug her at all, even though Apple was in pain just seeing her walk in them. Emme straightened the flowery silk scarf around her neck and gave Apple a quick look before picking up what looked like a very professional portfolio. She smirked at Apple as she passed by. She smirked! Emme was treating her like a pestering younger sister.

"That girl certainly has attitude," her mother whispered. So Apple was right. She wasn't being paranoid. Even her mother noticed!

This job just became even more challenging—and not in a good way, thought Apple as they made their way back to the car. She wondered if this whole working-at-*Angst* thing was one big mistake. Even though she had been excited just a few moments earlier, she couldn't help but wonder if she *did* have what it took to make it in this business. What if she had to deal with people like Emme, and their attitudes, every day? It wasn't worth it, thought Apple, even if she would get to meet celebrities in person. So not worth it.

♡

On the way home, her mother babbled. Apple barely paid attention. She couldn't get Emme's smirk and bored look out of her mind. She could tell Emme hated her already, and she had no idea why. How was she going to work beside someone with a personality like that two afternoons a week, plus weekends?

As soon as Apple got in the car, she had pulled Happy's boots off, not easy considering her feet were super swollen.

"I am in so much pain," she moaned.

"Well, it went well, didn't it?" her mother asked.

"I guess so," Apple answered.

"What do you mean, you guess so? God, Apple. Can't you ever just be happy? You have an internship that people your age would murder you for. I'm not joking. They would poison you if they could get the chance to work at *Angst*. And you get your own advice column! And you get to go on television? You just ask me if you need to know anything about being on television. You know, it's not as easy as it looks," her mother said. "You can't show any weakness on television. And people notice the tiniest details. If you change your earrings and they don't like them, they'll let you know!"

"Thanks for the added pressure, Mother!" Apple resonded, turning to look out the car window. "I can't believe I have to start tomorrow. I thought I'd have a little more time to prepare myself emotionally." Apple sighed, hoping she could stop her mother before she really started into lecture mode about the ins and outs of televisionland. Now not only would she have to deal with her mother's relationship advice, but she would have to deal with her advice on being on television.

"Well, you know what I always say . . ."

"Yes, Mom, I know. 'Why put off to tomorrow something you can do today?' 'Better to jump in feet first,'" Apple said, deadpan. She could have gone on and on with her mother's peppy phrases, but she stopped herself.

"Didn't you think Nancy was a little harsh?" Apple asked her mother, in an attempt to change the subject.

"Harsh? She seemed quite friendly. I think you're very lucky to have her as a boss. Not all first bosses are that accomplished, you know. She's worked in New York, Paris, Milan—all over the world. That woman knows her fashion. And she definitely knows how to run a magazine. At such a young age! So what if she seems harsh? Why is it that hardworking women always get a bad reputation? She's just the type of person you could learn a lot from. You don't want to let her down."

"She just acted a lot nicer to you than to me. And that girl Emme? Sitting there not looking at me? That's the person I'm supposed to work with. How am I going to deal with that?"

"Well, you're the one who always complains about being *my* daughter. Don't think I don't know that. You can't have it both ways. You can't want people *not* to give you special treatment because you're my daughter and then want people to treat you special when you think they aren't being nice to you. You're just being paranoid about the other girl. She's probably as nervous as you are. You can't judge someone in the blink of an eye. Yes, she seemed a little snooty. But maybe she's a really nice person. Be excited! It's good to get out of your comfort zone once in a while. It will be good for you to meet new people."

Apple immediately thought of Sloan Starr.

Screw Emme, thought Apple. After all, Sloan Starr had noticed *Apple*. Sloan Starr had complimented her! Though she knew she was being immature, she couldn't help but admit that the fact Sloan had noticed her made her feel special and got her heart racing.

"I'm going upstairs to soak my feet in a salt bath," Apple said when they pulled into the driveway. "If I can walk upstairs."

"Okay, but hurry down," her mother said, getting out of the car. "I've invited some people over for dinner."

"Who?" asked Apple warily.

"You'll see," her mother answered in a singsong. "Just a little celebratory dinner for my future celebrity daughter."

"Oh, God," Apple moaned, though she was actually pleased. Apple had to admit that sometimes her mother was very thoughtful.

nine

$a$pple had just gotten out of the bath when Happy and Brooklyn burst through her bedroom door. Apple wrapped a towel around her body and walked into her room.

"So how did it go?" Happy screamed. "Did the boots work? They did, right? I knew they would. Did they?"

"Yes, Happy! They worked. I start tomorrow," Apple said.

"Tomorrow?" Happy screeched.

"Yes, I know. Tomorrow! Can you believe it?"

"Well, that's kind of quick," said Happy. "We don't even have time to go shopping for new outfits. And we don't have time to go to Gossip for a manicure!"

Gossip was a spa for teenagers and a regular haunt for Happy, Apple, and Brooklyn, who loved to go there for manicures, facials, and eyebrow waxing. Apple certainly needed a manicure after today. She had bitten off all her nails.

"I know. That's what I was thinking. But you should see this Fancy Nancy. She's strict. When I said, 'Tomorrow?' she was all like, 'Is that a problem for you?' What could I say?" Apple asked her friends.

"What else did she say?" Happy demanded.

"Oh, let's see. Oh, yes, my favorite line was something along the lines of 'If you screw up at this job you'll probably never get the chance to work in magazines or television again,'" mimicked Apple.

"Harsh," Brooklyn said. "That doesn't sound very nice."

"Tell me about it," moaned Apple.

"Television?" Happy asked curiously. "Is *Angst* television really happening? It's not just a rumor?"

"Yup. They're starting a show called *Angst TV*. I'm going to be on it, apparently. I think I have to read my advice in front of the camera or something. I'm not quite sure. I'll find out more tomorrow," Apple said.

"Get out of here! Why don't I just slit my wrists now? You are so lucky!" screeched Happy, giving Apple a friendly shove, but one strong enough that Apple fell onto her bed. "I knew they were trying to get a show on air, but I didn't know it was actually happening! I didn't even know you wanted to work in television. Now you really are going to be a mini Dr. Berg."

"Don't say that! Don't ever say that again! But I know. Doing the advice column was one thing, but I also have to intern there two days a week, answering phones, making coffee. And now I have to worry about looking good on television," moaned Apple.

"Well, the making-coffee part sounds tedious," said Happy. "But getting to be on television? I'd fetch a thousand coffees to be on television regularly."

"It's not going to be fun. It's a job! And one I don't get paid for!" Apple muttered.

"Well, it's a start," said Brooklyn. "Hey, I wipe down the mats at the yoga studio for nothing, just to take free classes there. How do you think I feel wiping up other people's sweat?" Brooklyn asked.

Apple and Happy crinkled their noses.

"Oh, and the worst? There's this other intern starting with me, Emme, who is like a model by day and *Angst* intern by night. She literally gave me the dirtiest look I have ever seen. I've never been so scared of anyone in my life. She was scarier than Fancy Nancy. And I have to work with her, in the same office, four times a week," moaned Apple. She grabbed the first tank top she saw and a pair of jeans from the Absolutely Not pile and threw them on.

"Oh, you can take her," said Happy. "And if she gives you any trouble, just let me know and I'll handle it. I could definitely take her. No one messes with my best friend."

Apple smiled. Happy had always backed her up, ever since they met in first grade.

"I hope so. If not, I'm not going to last at *Angst* very long. And I don't think you can take her. She's, like, six feet tall," Apple muttered.

"Oh my God, Apple. What's with your feet? " Happy said suddenly. "They look like they've been run over by a truck!"

"Don't blame me. That's what YOUR boots did!" Apple said, looking down at her red, swollen, blistered feet.

"I just hope you didn't stretch them out too much," said Happy, picking up one of the boots and looking at it.

"Oh, by the way," Apple said, "Fancy Nancy gave you a compliment."

"Me? How does she know me? Did she mention my appearance on the *Queen of Hearts*?" Happy asked excitedly.

"Well, not exactly. She said she loved the boots," Apple said.

"She said that?" Happy asked, looking pleased, running her fingers tenderly over the boot in her hand like it was a baby.

"Yup. It was practically the first thing she said to me. Actually, I think it *was* the first thing she said to me," Apple admitted.

"See? I told you! I told you they'd be looking at what you wear. Aren't you happy you listened to me?"

"Oh, and you'll never guess who was there—" started Apple.

But before she could tell Happy about Sloan Starr (and his compliment on her hair) they heard the doorbell ring downstairs.

Apple, Happy, and Brooklyn immediately heard Crazy Aunt Hazel screech so loud that they all covered their ears in unison. And then they heard Aunt Hazel scream, "And then he got down on one knee and proposed!"

Apple looked at Brooklyn, who looked at Happy, who looked, shocked, at Apple.

There was no way, was there?

"There is no way your aunt just got engaged, is there?" Happy asked in disbelief, as if she were reading Apple's mind. "Because that's what it sounds like."

"To Mr. Kelly?" Brooklyn added. "The math teacher who practically flunked me? The one teacher I hate? No, I shouldn't say 'hate.' I don't hate anyone. Hate is bad. It's not good to put that kind of energy out there. No, I definitely don't hate him. But I do feel *sorry* for him."

"Well, in his defense, Brooklyn, you did absolutely no work," Happy said.

"Hey, you're supposed to be on my side!" said Brooklyn. "It's not my fault if I suck at math."

"I am on your side, Brooklyn. Why do you think I help you so much? Oh, my God, Apple! Mr. Kelly is going to be your uncle!" laughed Happy, giving Apple another small push.

"Don't say that! I can't hear you! I can't hear you!" Apple said, covering her ears and bending over so her hair covered her face.

"We'd better go down and congratulate her," Brooklyn said.

"I can't," Apple said. "I just can't. How am I ever going to go to math class again? This is mortifying."

"Don't be such a baby. Just think! You suck at math too. Maybe he'll take pity on you and give you a good mark!" Happy said. "After all, he's going to be part of your family!"

"And because he knows that I'm your best friend, he'll take pity on *me*," said Brooklyn. "This could be the best thing that has ever happened to me! Let's go down and find out what happened."

"I can't," moaned Apple.

"Yes, you can. She's your aunt, for God's sake. You have to congratulate her," said Happy.

"No, I mean, I can't walk. You guys have to help me walk!" Apple said.

Happy and Brooklyn each held onto one of Apple's arms and they all walked slowly downstairs to see if what they had heard could possibly be true.

Apple knew that Mr. Kelly had indeed proposed the minute she saw her aunt at the foot of the stairs. Crazy Aunt Hazel grabbed her, lifted her into the air, and swung her around like she was a toddler.

"Put me down. Are you crazy? Put me down!" screamed Apple. She had had no idea Hazel was so strong.

"He proposed! We're getting married!" she said, dancing around the living room as if she had just won a twenty-million-dollar lottery.

Apple looked at her blankly, not knowing what to say. Brooklyn and Happy started laughing.

"What is up with you guys? Why are you laughing?" Crazy Aunt Hazel demanded. "What? Did you think no man would ever propose to me? Is that it? Did you think I would never find love? Did you think I'd be alone forever and ever? Did you think no one could ever love *me*?"

"Of course not! We're just so happy for you!" said Happy, racing to give Aunt Hazel a hug. Brooklyn followed suit.

Apple noticed Mr. Kelly standing by the door, looking on proudly with his hands behind his back. He also seemed a little nervous, like he wasn't sure whether or not to walk inside. Apple felt bad for him, but not bad enough to be the one to say, "Come in!"

He was her math teacher, after all, and to see him in her home was strange, to say the least.

"Apple! Isn't this the best news ever?!" Crazy Aunt Hazel screamed.

"Yes! Yes!" Apple said, trying to sound as excited as possible. "It's very exciting!"

"I think she's just a little uncomfortable knowing that her aunt marrying her teacher," Happy whispered to Hazel, loudly enough for Mr. Kelly to hear. Happy enjoyed making people she didn't necessarily like feel uncomfortable. And making strict, geeky Mr. Kelly uncomfortable? It was too perfect an opportunity for Happy to pass up.

Apple smiled politely. "Of course not . . . well, maybe a little."

"This is definitely a night for champagne," Apple's dad, who was standing by the fridge door, announced. "If Hazel is getting married, that means she won't be hanging out here so much," he said, jokingly. "Jim, she's all yours now! Bee Bee, do we have any on hand?"

"Second shelf!" Apple's mother directed.

"Well, this certainly is a happy occasion. And it certainly is a *surprise*," Dr. Bee Bee Berg said. "You've only known each other for—what?—about ten weeks? In fact, Apple and I were talking just a couple of hours ago about people getting married so quickly these days."

"Don't ruin this for me, Bee Bee," Hazel said, her tone turning sour. "When you know, you know! And we know, right, Jim? We know we are meant to be together. We knew it from the second we met."

Hazel walked over to Mr. Kelly and brought him over to the couch, where she forced him to sit down and then, much to Apple's horror, proceeded to sit on his lap.

Apple was embarrassed. Not only was her math teacher in her house, but her aunt was sitting on his lap, in front of her parents and best friends. She would never hear the end of this.

Brooklyn and Happy again burst out in laughter. "Of course you and *Jim* are meant to be together," laughed Happy. "You and *Jim* make the perfect couple."

"Hold on there, Happy. I'm still Mr. Kelly to you!" their math teacher finally said, attempting to make a joke. But it fell flat, as his jokes usually did in class. Was there even such thing as a funny math teacher? wondered Apple.

There was so much mayhem that Apple didn't notice a pair of arms suddenly wrapping around her waist. She jumped in shock.

"It's just me!" Lyon said, handing her a bouquet of flowers and giving her a peck on the cheek.

"Ah, that's so sweet," Brooklyn said, sighing romantically. "I wish I had a boyfriend who gave me flowers."

Though Brooklyn had been hanging out recently with Hopper, she could not get him to commit to anything, not even dinner or a phone call. But Brooklyn, to her credit, or maybe thanks to her yoga and meditation, was laid back about these things. It had only recently begun to bug her that she might be more into Hopper than he was into her. Apple imagined it was especially hard on Brooklyn to be single when her two best friends were in relationships.

"Thanks. That's so nice of you," Apple said, smelling the roses then placing them on a table. She would put them in a vase later.

"So I guess it went well? All this celebration?" Lyon asked, smiling.

"It's not for me," Apple said, as Lyon gazed at her. "Really, it's not."

"It's for me!" Hazel cried out, taking a swig of champagne straight from the bottle. "Jim and I are getting married. He proposed!"

"That's great, uh, Mr. Kelly," said Lyon, walking over to shake his hand. At least Lyon didn't have Mr. Kelly as a teacher this year, thought Apple. He was lucky.

"Let's go up to my bedroom for a second," Apple whispered to Lyon. She could no longer stand to see her aunt being so, well, so much in Crazy Aunt overload. "We'll be right back," Apple called out to the rest of the room, though no one seemed to hear. Brooklyn and Happy were busy talking and sneaking sips of champagne. Guy had just walked in, joining the party, and hugging Mr. Kelly. Mr. Kelly looked extremely uncomfortable being embraced by Guy, who was screaming, "Congratulations! Guy is so happy for you! Guy has the perfect friend to make your wedding suit! Guy knows just where to find the perfect centerpieces! Guy *loves* weddings!"

ten

It was too much for Apple. She needed at least a minute or two of peace and quiet.

"So did it go well?" Lyon asked, once they were in her bedroom alone. "I want to hear everything."

"I think so," Apple said, pulling him in for a hug. She immediately relaxed in his arms.

"It must have. You didn't call me after like you promised," Lyon said lightly.

Oh, my God, thought Apple. She was the worst girlfriend ever. She had forgotten to call Lyon twice! In one day! What was wrong with her brain?

"I am so sorry. It was a crazy day and now Aunt Hazel has just announced she's getting married to Mr. Kelly after, like, three months. Doesn't that make you sick?" Apple asked.

"Well, when you know, you know," said Lyon sweetly.

"God, you sound like Aunt Hazel. That's exactly what she said," Apple laughed.

"Come give me another hug, you love cynic," Lyon said, smiling.

Apple gave Lyon another tight hug. They started to kiss. She loved how Lyon kissed so gently. She loved the feeling of his fingers tickling her back as they kissed. He had just reached under her shirt when—

"Hey, Apple," Happy said, bursting in the room. "Oops! Sorry to interrupt. Should I come back in a bit? Or perhaps you should think about getting a lock on your door."

"No, it's okay," said Apple, pulling down her shirt. She could feel her face turn red. "What's up?"

"Is it okay if Zen comes over? I told him we were all here and he wants to congratulate Aunt Hazel," Happy laughed.

"Right, Happy. You just want him to come over to laugh at Mr. Kelly," said Apple. She knew Happy too well.

"Well, duh!" She smirked.

"Fine. Whatever," Apple said.

"Great! But you two better come down soon! Your mother is asking where you went. My guess is that if she doesn't see you in the next thirty seconds, she'll be barging in like I did," sang Happy. "And I don't think you really want your mother to see you two in such a passionate embrace! Just a warning!"

"Thanks," said Apple.

Apple couldn't ignore that Lyon looked a little put out about Happy wanting Zen to come by. Of course he knew, as the whole school did, all about Apple's former Super-Sized Zen Crush. But that was over. She was with Lyon now, and Zen was with Happy. He had nothing to worry about, as Apple constantly seemed to be reminding him. And yet every time Lyon found out that she and Zen were partners on a project for school or sat beside each other in class, he seemed annoyed. Perhaps he had heard rumors at school, even though they weren't true, that Apple was still into Zen.

"Is something wrong?" she said, taking Lyon by his arm downstairs, where they went to lounge on the couch across from her aunt and her—ga!—future uncle.

"No. It's your night. Let's celebrate your new job," he said, plastering a big smile on his face.

"Internship. No pay. Real jobs, you get paid," Apple said.

"Well, I still think it's amazing," he said, planting a kiss on Apple's mouth. "God, I just wish I could get you alone. It seems like we haven't been alone in a while," he whispered in her ear.

"It's only been, like, two days," laughed Apple, smiling as she recalled their movie night.

"That's like two weeks for me," said Lyon.

"You're sweet," she said, pouting, pretending to be sad.

"How about tomorrow night I take you out for dinner? Any place you want. My treat. To celebrate your new job!"

"That sounds great," Apple said. But then she remembered. Her face fell.

"What?" asked Lyon, looking concerned.

"I can't! I start work tomorrow. It's my first day! I have no idea how late I have to stay."

Apple felt horrible. Her amazing boyfriend wanted to take her out to celebrate her new job, and now her new job was already getting in the way of her relationship.

"I'm really sorry. I just can't!" she moaned.

"Well, can I at least be your chauffeur and drop you off and pick you up after work?" Lyon asked

"There's nothing that would make me happier," Apple said, giving him another quick kiss on the mouth.

"Okay, take it to a hotel room," said Brooklyn. "There are other people here, you know! Have some consideration for us maybe-single people!"

"Oh, poor Brooklyn," said Happy. "You don't need anyone. You have your gurus and your yoga instructors and—"

"Stop trying to make me feel better, Happy. And stop making fun of me!"

"You know we love you. And Hopper *does* like you. He is just a little slow. You know that. He just doesn't understand what to do. He needs to be *told* what to do."

"Yeah," laughed Brooklyn. "It's so hard to pick up the phone."

"Don't you worry, Brooklyn," Crazy Aunt Hazel said, joining in. "If I can find my soulmate, so will you. So will you."

Then the doorbell rang.

"It's Zen! It's Zen! I'll get it," Happy said, jumping up from the couch.

"Hey, baby," she said, giving Zen a hard kiss on his lips as soon as he came through the door. "Come in. It's a party!"

"I can see that," Zen said, looking at everyone in the room.

When his eyes rested on Lyon, there was an immediate awkwardness. Or was Apple just being paranoid for the umpteenth time today? Was she just imagining that the vibe had suddenly changed in the room? Zen would barely look at Lyon, and Lyon would not meet Zen's eyes. But Lyon was always friendly, which is one of the reasons Apple adored him so much. Plus, he had to understand that Zen was dating Apple's best friend, so of course Apple would have to spend some time with him. It was inevitable.

"Hey, man," Lyon said, holding out his hand to Zen.

"Hey," said Zen, giving it a quick shake.

Zen turned to Apple.

"So, Apple, I hear you're going to be working at *Angst*!" he said. "According to Happy, it's the best magazine in the world," he added, somewhat mockingly, but with a sweet smile. Happy swatted him.

"It *is* the best magazine in the world," said Happy. "I look forward to it every week! One day I'm going to be on the cover!"

"Yup, I'm starting tomorrow," Apple said, grabbing Lyon's hand so he would be reassured—not that he needed reassuring. But Apple wanted to make him feel comfortable.

"You must be excited! I hear you're getting your own advice column," Zen said.

"I'm a little nervous, to tell you the truth," Apple said. "They're starting a television show to go along with the magazine and I have to be on television too."

"You never told me that," said Lyon, looking at her strangely, dropping her hand from his. Apple was surprised at this but pretended not to notice.

"I was going to. I just never got the chance! I don't want to admit it, but I am nervous. I want to do well there. I don't want to screw up," said Apple. "I can barely bring myself to think about it."

"Well, don't be nervous. I know you're going to do great," Lyon said supportively.

"We'll see," Apple said. "What's the worst that can happen? Well, I guess I could get fired."

Apple and her friends listened as another cork popped in the kitchen and Aunt Hazel screamed in total drunken delight. For a moment, Apple was jealous. She wished she could be as happy and carefree as her aunt, who didn't seem to have a worry in the world at this moment. Apple hadn't even started her new job and already she was imagining telling everyone she knew how she screwed up and why she got fired, ruining her future in magazines and television *forever*.

♡

Apple's body and brain felt like a deflating balloon. The celebration had died down—the celebration for Apple that had turned into a celebration for Crazy Aunt Hazel's engagement. Mr. Kelly had carried her aunt to his car after she had gotten so drunk she started doing a striptease dance for him, to the utter delight of Zen, Lyon, Happy, and Brooklyn, and to the sheer mortification of Apple and her parents.

Zen and Happy left with Brooklyn. Lyon asked Apple if she wanted to go for a walk.

Apple had always loved to walk, especially if she was anxious or needed to really think about something in silence. Walking for Apple was like meditation for Brooklyn and shopping for Happy. Walking calmed her down. It made her feel serene.

But Apple pointed down at her mangled feet, now covered with multiple Band-Aids. She couldn't imagine standing on her sore feet for one minute longer. Lyon had looked sad, like a puppy dog that needed a home.

"Okay," he said. "Call me later, then."

"It's already after eleven," Apple said. "I need sleep so I can go to school tomorrow and then become a productive member of society. I'm now a working woman, remember?"

"I'll see you at the Spiral Staircase, then," he said, and they kissed goodbye.

Apple decided to pick out what to wear tomorrow before she went to bed. She didn't want to fret about it all night. She had never cared about how she dressed before. As of this very morning, she hadn't cared! She simply was not brave enough to venture into the fashionista world like Happy. But now, even as she looked at the huge pile of Absolutely Not clothes on her bedroom floor, she decided she had nothing suitable to wear for her first official day at *Angst*, where everyone was so fashionable. She made a note to ask Happy to take her shopping with her as soon as she could find the time. Her mother wouldn't mind shelling out the cash, especially if Apple professed she needed professional clothes to make a "good impression" at her professional new job. Apple finally settled on skintight black jeans, red ankle boots, and a black short-sleeved sweater.

She could only imagine what Emme would be wearing tomorrow and how she would treat Apple. Apple consoled herself by thinking that maybe another celebrity would stop by. That would be fun.

All these years she had never really cared about celebrities, but she couldn't help but feel excited at having seen Sloan Starr in person. She was starting to understand Happy's obsession with celebrities. She could sort of see now why strangers would ask for her mother's autograph.

Somehow, Apple managed to fall asleep—amazing since her nerves felt shot with the pressure of her new job, a new advice column that all her friends would read, and the thought of appearing on television.

She woke up the next morning, though, with butterflies in her stomach. She couldn't even think about eating breakfast.

Every weekday morning, Crazy Aunt Hazel picked her up to drive her to school. Her mother and father always left the house super early to go to work, before Apple's alarm clock even went off. This had been the arrangement for years. Apple wondered if it would stay that way once her aunt got married. She doubted it. It didn't really matter. Lyon, Happy, or Happy's sister, Sailor, would pick her up. Maybe she'd have to get her license—something that, unlike most of her classmates, Apple had put off. She would never admit it to her aunt, but she liked that Hazel drove her to school. She liked hearing her Crazy Aunt Hazel's stories every morning. They had always made Apple feel sane in comparison.

"Apple, I need to ask you something very important," Hazel said as soon as Apple jumped into the passenger seat.

Apple couldn't hide her look of disbelief as she glanced at her aunt. She was in her pajamas! Flannel pink pajamas with little bunny prints on them. She looked about eight years old.

"No, I don't think that's a very good look for you," Apple said sarcastically. "But the slippers are fantastic."

"Ha ha. I'm so hungover," her aunt groaned. "I don't even remember getting home last night. There was no way I was getting dressed this morning. You're lucky I even managed to get my head out of the toilet to come get you."

"Hmm. Shocking. I wonder why you can't remember anything? Oh, right, you drank a bottle of champagne all by yourself," Apple teased.

"Stop being sarcastic. And don't mention champagne. Don't mention anything to do with alcohol. It's turning my stomach. But I was celebrating. Can you believe I'm getting married?" her aunt asked, squealing in delight, then rubbing her forehead in pain.

"No," Apple said flatly. "I can't."

"Come on. You like Jim, don't you? He's so nice and he loves me so much and I just can't get enough of him. I know he doesn't look like a god, but trust me, in bed—" Hazel started to say, before Apple interrupted.

"God, Aunt Hazel! That's my math teacher you're talking about. Can you please have some respect for me!

TMI! Too much information," groaned Apple, covering her ears and shooting her aunt a disgusted look.

"Okay, okay. But anyway, I wanted to ask you something very important, if you'd just shut up for a moment and take your hands off your ears. And it has nothing to do with what I'm wearing right now. Are you listening?" her aunt demanded.

"Yes, yes. I'm listening," Apple said.

"I want you and your mother—*both*—to be my maids of honor," she said, biting her lip in anticipation of Apple's reaction.

Although Apple wasn't exactly sure what the duties of maid of honor were, she knew it was a very important job, especially for Hazel, who just a few months ago was in constant moaning mode that she'd never find a decent man, let alone a man she actually wanted to spend the rest of her life with. Apple was touched. She could tell how much her aunt loved her at that moment, and she felt herself tearing up with love.

"Of course I'll be your maid of honor," Apple said, grabbing her aunt's hand and kissing it. "As long as you don't make me wear one of those hideous purple puffy dresses."

"Oh, you know I will! I can't have my maids of honor looking better than me," her aunt retorted.

Apple wasn't sure if Hazel was joking or not. Her aunt loved to be the center of attention, so it wouldn't be beyond her to make Apple and her mother wear something hideous just to look stunning in comparison. Apple didn't press the issue. It was *her* wedding day, after all. She would dress in whatever her aunt wanted, no matter how ridiculous or hideous—even if it was covered in bunny rabbits.

When they pulled up to the school, Apple's aunt looked out the window. Suddenly, she crouched low in her seat so she was hidden behind the steering wheel. She looked scared.

"God, you must get out of this car fast. Like right now! I can't have Jim seeing me like this!" her aunt announced breathlessly and frantically. "He's right over there! I'm sure I can see him walking into the school!"

Apple looked at her aunt like she had gone crazy.

"Are you crazy? He's eventually going to see you in those oh-so-sexy bunny pajamas. You *are* getting married. For better or worse, isn't that what they say? And didn't you spend the night together last night?"

"Oh, no, he most certainly is NOT going to see me like this! These pajamas are going to be burned before our wedding. And, no, he didn't stay over! Now that we're getting married, I refuse to sleep with him again until the actual day. I let him walk me to the door and then I locked him out! I want to at least *feel* like a virgin when I get married."

Apple shot her aunt a "You've got to be kidding me!" look. "Who are you? You're crazy!" Apple said, laughing at her aunt, who was obviously having one of her "Girl Crazy Moments."

"Oh, go to school and learn something. And good luck today at *Angst*. You need me to pick you up?" her aunt said, looking around like someone who was worried she would be caught shoplifting.

"No, Lyon is," Apple responded.

"Good, good. That's Jim for sure," Crazy Aunt Hazel said, whipping on a pair of sunglasses she had grabbed from the glove compartment. "Go! GO! Get out of here! I mean it. Now!"

"Okay! I'm going. Sheesh. You're already a bridezilla and you just got engaged yesterday! You're already a nutcase. Please promise you're not going to get any crazier than you already are." Apple opened the door.

"Get out!" her aunt hissed.

"I'm out!" said Apple, slamming the door. Please don't ever let me turn into my aunt, she thought.

eleven

$\mathcal{A}$pple walked through Cactus High, heading toward the Spiral Staircase, where her friends hung out before school, after school, and during breaks. The Spiral Staircase was located in the middle of the school. Students had to walk past it to get to any of the classrooms, the hallways, or the cafeteria.

She hadn't noticed that Zen had caught up to her and was walking beside her until he said, "Hey."

"Oh, hey, Zen. How are you?" Apple asked. She was uncomfortable being alone with him. There were so many reasons why. Not only had she tried to sabotage his relationship with Happy, but she also had admitted her feelings for him, which were unrequited. Apple admitted her ego was still bruised, but mostly she was embarrassed. Plus Apple didn't want Happy to even wonder if she was still into Zen. She worried that if Happy saw them walking together, alone, it might upset her or make her think Apple still had feelings for him.

Or what if someone else at school saw them together and passed it on to Happy, making this innocent walk seem like something more? The last thing Apple wanted to do was make Happy mad at her or not have trust in her.

And then, of course, there was Lyon, who would not like seeing her walking with Zen at all or hearing rumors about them.

"You look like you've been crying," Zen said. "Is everything okay?"

"Oh, God, yes," said Apple, amazed that her eyes were still red from her brief tear-up in the car. "My aunt just asked me to be her maid of honor and . . . oh, I don't know. It brought out the sensitivity gene in me."

"That's nice," Zen said. "Are you going to have to wear one of those horribly puffy dresses?"

"Knowing my aunt, definitely," laughed Apple.

Apple looked at the floor. She still had a hard time looking Zen in the eye. She had never had an easy time looking him straight in the eye, especially during the days of her Super-Sized Zen Crush. But she was positive she no longer liked him in that way—and she had Lyon. So why could she still not look at Zen without blushing or having her heart go pitter-patter? Though Lyon was just as handsome as Zen, in a different way, he never made it hard for Apple to breathe. The world didn't seem to stop when she was with Lyon as it had when she had been in love with Zen. Was that a good thing or a bad thing? On the one hand, she was at ease with Lyon, more so than she had ever been with Zen. On the other hand, he didn't take her breath away, and she kind of liked that swooning feeling.

"I'm heading to the Spiral Staircase," Apple said. "Are you coming?"

"No, I think I'm going to head straight to my locker. I think it's about time I cleaned the thing out. It's starting to smell," Zen said, scrunching up his nose.

"Nice!" responded Apple, shaking her head. "Okay, see you later, then."

"Apple?" Zen said.

"Yeah?"

"You look really good today. I like the boots. They're cool. And are you wearing makeup? It looks good!"

Zen's compliments made Apple blush, and she bit her lip. She had, in fact, put a bit of makeup on before leaving the house.

"Thanks, Zen. I have to look good since I'm starting work today. I figure the least I can do is try to look like I fit in there. See you later."

Apple practically skipped to the Spiral Staircase, where Lyon and Brooklyn were sitting. Happy wasn't there, which was odd. Usually Happy was the first one to arrive.

"Well, someone looks like she's in a good mood," Lyon said, getting up to give Apple a hug. Apple kissed him on the mouth.

"I guess I am. It's a big day. I'm starting at *Angst* today. I have to be on my 'A' game," Apple joked. "As my mother says, 'If you smile on the outside, you'll smile on the inside.'"

"Well, you'll definitely be the prettiest one there," Lyon said. "Are you wearing makeup? You look sexy!"

For some reason, the compliment from Lyon didn't hit Apple as hard as the one from Zen.

"Yes, I'm wearing makeup. I'm not sure about being the prettiest girl there. You should see the women who work at *Angst*. It's like their DNA was all mixed together in a bowl to make only the most perfect blue or green eyes, the thickest hair, and the fittest bodies. I swear, these women are so good-looking and so put together, it's like they're aliens."

"You're just as good-looking," Brooklyn said. "*And* you'll be the most interesting person there, no matter how you look."

"Thanks, Brooklyn. Hey, where's Happy?" Apple asked, moving aside Brooklyn's yoga mat so she could sit down.

Brooklyn looked down and started fidgeting with her hair, a surefire sign she didn't want, or didn't know how, to answer the question. Brooklyn always fidgeted with her long blond hair when teachers asked her questions, or when her overbearing mother demanded to know where she had been.

"What is it? Is she okay?" Apple asked, worried. "What's wrong?"

"She's okay," Brooklyn answered slowly. "I think. Well, I think there's just a bit of trouble in paradise right now, if you know what I mean."

"Are she and Zen fighting?" Apple asked curiously.

"A little. I'm sure it's nothing serious," Brooklyn said, eyeing Lyon as if she didn't want to say too much in front of him. "You should talk to her."

"I wonder why she didn't tell me," Apple said, more to herself than to Lyon or Brooklyn. "Okay, don't answer that. I just thought that we were good now.

I want Happy to be able to tell me if she's having problems. Even if they are about Zen."

Apple could feel Lyon's stare on her. But it wasn't her fault that her best friend was fighting with the guy Apple *used* to like. Apple had known both Zen and Happy for years, since long before she even met Lyon. He had to understand that they all had history, even if that history wasn't all good.

"Well, she might just feel uncomfortable talking about Zen to you. Especially since you have such a nice boyfriend," Brooklyn said, looking adoringly up at Lyon and then shooting Hopper, who was playing a video game on his phone, an evil look. Not that Hopper noticed.

Apple suddenly felt guilty. Brooklyn was right. Lyon was a great boyfriend. Even though they had been together for only a short time, he bought her flowers, always called when he said he would, offered to drive and pick her up all the time, and complimented her endlessly.

According to her mother, this was what every woman hoped for in a relationship. It's what, her mother said, everyone woman *deserved*.

The bell rang, signaling that the first class was to start in five minutes.

"All right, guys. I've got Philosophy on the third floor," said Lyon, jumping down three stairs. "I'll see you at lunch, Apple?"

"Absolutely!" Apple said, giving him a peck on the cheek before he took off.

"You know, Apple. You're lucky that Lyon is a year

older. That way you don't have to see him all day long. He's not in any of your classes. Poor Happy. I mean, she's fighting with Zen and she has to see him in most of her classes," said Brooklyn as they walked to math class together.

"Oh my God. I can't believe we have Mr. Kelly right now. How the hell am I going to face him, knowing that he's marrying Crazy Aunt Hazel?" Apple demanded, stopping in her tracks.

"Not only that," added Brooklyn, "but you're going to be related to him!"

"Not exactly. He's just marrying into my family. If only I hadn't shown up to that Valentine's Day dance, then Hazel never would have met him," Apple moaned as they started to walk again.

"That's called *fate*. I think that's great. If you hadn't decided to go, then Aunt Hazel wouldn't be crazy in love and getting married. Fate works in the most mysterious ways. And also, you never would have met Lyon, remember? That was fate too! The job at *Angst*? All fate," Brooklyn continued.

Apple wished she could be as positive as Brooklyn. She wished she believed in fate. Today, Brooklyn was wearing a shirt that read, "Nothing is worth more than this day." Brooklyn had a collection of T-shirts with pithy, uplifting sayings. Apple looked forward to reading them each day and often found herself repeating the phrases in her head throughout the day, trying to believe them.

When they walked into class, Apple sat down in the seat next to Happy. She was relieved to notice that

Jim—rather, Mr. Kelly—looked away as soon as she entered. He must be just as uncomfortable. Just last night, he was getting a striptease at her house. He *should* be uncomfortable, thought Apple uncharitably. Though she had to admit, it wasn't Mr. Kelly's fault she hated math so much.

"Happy," Apple whispered, "you okay?"

"Not really," Happy responded. "I had a bad night. I'm fighting with Zen."

Apple took a second to consider how to respond appropriately.

"Do you want to talk about it? I mean, not now. Later? We can meet for lunch outside and get a private area," Apple whispered back.

"That would be great. Let's meet by the big tree on the south side of the building at 11:45, okay?" Happy responded in a hushed voice.

"Okay, girls, no more talking. Let's open your textbooks to page 145 and start doing the exercises," Mr. Kelly started.

Obviously, they were not going to get any special treatment just because Mr. Kelly was going to be part of the Berg family.

"I just can't get out of my mind your aunt giving him a striptease," Happy whispered to Apple under her breath as they opened their books.

"Tell me about it," whispered Apple. "I don't think I'm ever going to get that image out of my head. EVER!"

"That was one of the funniest things your aunt has ever done! And she's done a lot of crazy things!" Happy whispered, trying not to laugh.

It was good to see Happy smile. When Happy smiled, the world smiled. When Happy was down, it was like a dark, stormy cloud covering the whole universe. And it was just so unusual for Happy to be down . . . about anything. What did Happy ever have to be down about? To the outside world, her life was pretty perfect.

"Apple," Happy whispered as Mr. Kelly turned to the blackboard. "You look great today. I couldn't have picked out a better outfit for your first day. I wish I were you."

Luckily, Apple couldn't respond. Mr. Kelly had started in on his lecture. Apple didn't know *how* to respond to Happy's comment. Everyone, after all, at Cactus High had always wanted to be *Happy*. Gorgeous, straight-A Happy, who always got what she wanted. Everyone just assumed Happy would one day be the star she was meant to be. It was her destiny. Or as Brooklyn would say, it was her "fate."

♡

At lunch, Apple raced out of her geography class and went to the planned meeting area at the back of the school grounds to find Happy. Happy was already there, delicately holding chopsticks, eating her sushi. She looked like she was deep in thought, and this made her look even more beautiful. A slight wind in the air was blowing her long, black-as-night hair, and whenever she was sad, her eyes seemed even greener.

After checking for ants, Apple plopped down beside her.

"Did anyone see you come out here?" Happy asked.

"I don't think so. Why?" Apple wondered.

"Are you sure Zen didn't see you?" she pressed.

"No, didn't see him at all," Apple answered.

Happy threw her plastic container of sushi into a bag.

"I can't even eat this. My stomach is in knots," she said.

"What's going on, Happy?" Apple said. "I'm kind of concerned."

Happy didn't answer immediately. She just stared down at the grass.

"Listen," Apple said, "I know you're probably not totally comfortable opening up to me about your relationship with Zen after everything that happened. But you are my best friend and I'm always going to support you. You can trust me."

"I know, Apple. It's just that I feel stupid about it all. I feel stupid about what I've been thinking about how I want to tell you what I'm going to tell you. I don't want you to be angry."

Apple was shocked. What could Happy have to tell her that she would worry might make Apple mad?

"What do you mean? I'm the one who tried to ruin your relationship, remember?" said Apple, pulling some grass out of the ground.

"That's history. I mean it, Apple. I totally forgive you. I feel stupid because I made such a big deal about Zen being the one for me, and then I got so mad at you for trying to ruin our relationship and now it's only been a few weeks and . . ."

"And?" Apple asked, eyeing her best friend.

"God, I'm too embarrassed to say it," she said, covering her face with her arms.

"Just say it. I went on national television and told millions of people what a bitch I was. My math teacher is about to be my uncle! And, need I remind you, he was at my house last night getting a striptease! Talk about embarrassing. My aunt drove me to school today in her pajamas! And you know you can always tell me anything and I'm not going to judge you," Apple said, placing her hand on Happy's leg. For a moment, she felt motherly.

"Yeah, but something good came out of that something bad. You got an internship at *Angst*! And Lyon!" exclaimed Happy.

"Okay, true. But I'll always be known as the girl who tried to ruin her best friend's relationship," moaned Apple.

"Like I said, I *have* forgotten about it," Happy said. "I just . . . it's just, when I think about Zen . . ." Happy started, then stopped.

"What? What about him? Spill it already," Apple pressed.

"I think I might have put the carriage before the horse," Happy said finally.

"What does that mean?" Apple asked, genuinely confused.

"Isn't that the right saying?" Happy asked, cocking her head to one side, looking perplexed.

"I have no idea. What are you trying to say? Stop talking in Dr. Bee Bee Berg clichés!"

"Okay. I just don't think I like him in that way anymore," Happy spit out.

Apple's eyes widened with disbelief. She had had no idea *this* was coming. She could barely form a sentence. But Happy was biting her lip, waiting for her to say *something*.

"Are you serious? I thought you two were joined at the hip. I thought you guys loved each other. You've even, you know . . ." Apple managed to stutter.

She thought Zen and Happy would be together for . . . well, at least a year. She had had no idea that Happy could have such a change of heart, even though Happy did change her mind often, especially about boys. Apple thought Zen had changed all of that.

"I know, I know," Happy said, burying her head in her hands. "It's just that . . . I don't know. I find myself running when I see him and hoping he won't call me, and when he does it's like he never has anything important to say and it's just become awkward between us."

"But I know he likes you. You know he likes you," Apple said, pulling pieces of grass out of the ground viciously. "Everything seemed fine with you guys just last night!"

"Well, it wasn't. We've not been getting along for a while now. We're okay if other people are around. But when we're alone? Not so much. Can I tell you something awful if you promise not to judge me?"

"Of course!" said Apple.

"Oh, God, Apple. I'm just not into him anymore," admitted Happy.

Apple tried her hardest not to continue to look as shocked as she felt, which was as shocked as if they had just been through an earthquake.

"Are you sure? I mean, maybe it's just a phase.

There's always a honeymoon phase and then the reality of the relationship sets in and it's just not as exciting. You could work on it!" Apple said. She knew she was sounding a little too much like her mother, but she was speaking the truth, or at least that's what her mother always said about relationships.

"I know myself. And *you* know me better than anyone. And you know how bored I get. And now I feel kind of stuck in this relationship because I made such a big deal about it. Looking back, I should have never gotten so angry with you. I should have never gone on your mother's show! I mean, look at me now! I don't even think I like him. And the very thought of kissing him? So not interested anymore. Maybe it is true that because I realized you liked him, that made me like him more than I really did. I'm an awful friend too," Happy said, tears welling up.

"God, Happy," Apple said, watching Happy lie back on the ground. She had no idea what to say.

"I know. I know! What am I going to do? I can't keep hiding from him. And you want to know the worst of it?" Happy asked.

"What?"

"He doesn't seem to get it. I yell at him and he doesn't even fight back. I yell at him for not buying me a bouquet of flowers that I don't even want, and it's like he doesn't hear me. I pick fights with him so he'll break up with me! And then there's this other guy . . ."

Whoa, thought Apple. Another guy? This was just getting worse, and more shocking, by the second.

Apple hadn't even started at *Angst* and she was already failing at giving relationship advice. She wasn't cut out for giving out advice. She didn't even know what to say to her best friend.

twelve

But Apple tried.

"Another guy? Who's the other guy?" Apple asked. She knew she sounded eagerly curious, so she added, "If you don't mind me asking."

She could feel her eyes darting from the ground to Happy and back to the ground.

"He's just this guy who has an appointment right before me at my shrink's. We've been talking before my weekly sessions. I'm totally attracted to him. He's so hot and disturbed."

Oh, no, thought Apple. Happy loved "hot and disturbed" guys. Happy was what her mother would call a girl who was always attracted to bad boys. Zen was anything *but* a bad boy. A "hot and disturbed" guy in the picture didn't bode well for Zen.

"Okay, Happy. One step at a time. I think you shouldn't make any rash decisions right now. This may just be a phase, like I said. And if you still feel this way in a couple weeks, we'll deal with it. Okay?" Apple announced, trying to make her words sound confident and reasonable.

"Wow, you haven't even started at *Angst* and you're already sounding so sane!" Happy said, giving a small smile.

"Well, they aren't NOT paying me for nothing," laughed Apple, trying to lighten the mood. "But I do need your help. I need you to take me shopping, like ASAP. You should see how Fancy Nancy and this bitch Emme dress. Not to change the subject or anything," Apple said, feeling bad that she had started talking about herself when clearly Happy was so distraught and had so much going on in her life.

"Ah, but they don't have your hair. Hey, how's it going with you and Lyon anyway? Tell me something good so I can take my mind off my own pathetic relationship," Happy said.

"Good. Good. He's really good to me. You know, the flowers and all. And he calls me all the time and he's driving me to *Angst* today. He's a really good guy," said Apple. She didn't want to brag, considering what her best friend was going through.

"And you look forward to seeing him, right?" Happy asked.

"Of course!" Apple answered quickly. She always did look forward to seeing him, didn't she? Apple hadn't given it much thought, though. Lyon always seemed to be around, so she barely had a chance to miss him or look forward to seeing him.

"See? That's what I want. I want a guy I look forward

to seeing all the time. And I look forward to my shrink appointments now to see this new guy."

"Maybe that's just chemistry. I mean, just because you have a boyfriend doesn't mean you can't find other people attractive," Apple said, remembering a line from one of her mother's books.

"Maybe, but I just don't feel it with Zen. I don't. I can't see a future with him, and I'm not talking about a lifelong future. But I can't even see a future with him for another week!" moaned Happy.

"Hey, have you talked to Brooklyn about this?" Apple asked.

"Sort of. But you *know* what she's like. Don't get me wrong. I love her to death. But she's all like, 'Have some wheatgrass. It'll make you feel better.' As if some disgusting liquid that looks like crap is going to somehow make me fall in love with Zen again. And she has her own issues with Hopper. So she's just not in the right frame of mind. Shit, it's time to go back to class. And go back to hiding from Zen. Thanks for listening, Apple. You're a good friend. You're my best friend. Hey, I know! Maybe *you* should start liking Zen again—would give me an easy way out," Happy said, standing up and wiping her butt to make sure she didn't have any grass on her pencil skirt.

"Ha ha," Apple said. But Happy didn't sound like she was joking. She looked and sounded serious. Could it be possible that she really was over Zen? After all that drama? Did she really want Apple to hook up with Zen?

"I know. I know. You're with Lyon. And he's perfect. But I tell you, Apple, I should have thought things through. What is wrong with me? I never think things through. I just want what I want and then when I get it, it's like, 'Hmm. Maybe I don't want this.'"

"You should talk to Dr. Coke about this," Apple suggested.

Dr. Coke was Happy's therapist. Happy had been seeing her religiously for years and had nicknamed her Dr. Coke because she always offered her a caffeinated drink at her weekly appointment. Dr. Coke probably could give Happy more objective advice. Apple knew that Happy was pretty rash when it came to decision-making, but that was part of her charm. Happy always did what she wanted to do. And she always got away with it because of her looks and charm. Besides, Apple wasn't a professional therapist.

"Trust me. I have an appointment with her today. Of course, I'm totally looking forward to it—not because I want to see her, but because I get to see the new guy I have a crush on," laughed Happy. "At least the $180 an hour my parents shell out for my appointments now seems a little more worth it."

Apple loved Happy like a sister, and of course she would be loyal to her, but she couldn't help but feel bad for Zen. Apple knew Happy too well. Though she had told her to give it a little more time, she knew that once Happy made up her mind about something, that was it. If Happy decided that she was no longer into Zen, most likely Zen would be gone by the end of the week. Poor Zen, thought Apple. He would have to deal with the fallout of being dumped by Happy.

"I'm serious, Apple. If you want to go for him, I promise I won't care," said Happy.

Apple couldn't imagine Zen being free and single again. No, she wasn't going to get excited. Because even if Happy did dump Zen, it was still wrong to go out with your best friend's ex. That was something Apple had learned on *Queen of Hearts*. It was one of the unwritten rules of female friendship. But Happy was the one who was joking that Apple should go out with him. Or was she being serious? Was it okay to take your best friend's ex when she gave you permission? Not that I should even be considering this, she thought, shaking her head. It takes two to tango, and Zen had made it painfully obvious that he wasn't into Apple. Plus, she had Lyon. She could never break Lyon's heart like that.

"Okay, one more thing I have to tell you," announced Happy. "I kissed him."

"*What*?" Apple said, stopping in her tracks.

"I know. I know! It's bad. But last week, Hot and Disturbed Guy kissed me in the restroom at the shrink's office. He waited for me after my appointment and we snuck in. It was kind of romantic, actually, considering our first kiss took place in a restroom."

"God, Happy!" Apple said, not bothering to hide her shock this time.

"I know. I'm an awful person," Happy moaned. "I cheated on my boyfriend."

"Listen, I'm on your side. Whatever you decide, I'm going to be there for you. But you sometimes are a little rash. Take some time to think things through," Apple said, hating how grown-up she sounded.

"Okay, Apple. I'll call you later," she said.

"Wait!" Apple called out. Happy turned around.

"Was it good?" she asked. For some reason, Apple needed to know.

"Was what good?"

"The kiss," said Apple.

"The kiss? It was mind-blowing," Happy said, smiling dreamily at the memory.

Apple couldn't help but smile. She knew cheating was wrong, but somehow Happy made it seem like it was no big deal. Her smile said that it had been worth it.

As Apple walked back into school, she had the feeling that she had forgotten something. It hit her. Right! She was supposed to have met Lyon for lunch! God, I'm such a bad girlfriend, thought Apple. Here I am thinking of Zen when I have the most thoughtful boyfriend in the world. Get it together, Apple, she told herself. Get your priorities straight.

She ran inside, hoping to see Lyon still at the Spiral Staircase. He wasn't there. She walked to her locker and found a note scrawled on a sticky pad stuck to it.

Sorry I missed you at lunch. Where'd you get to? Everything okay? I'll meet you out front after school. XOX L.

Could Apple have a better boyfriend? Could Lyon have a worse girlfriend than Apple, who completely forgot about their lunch plans while actually contemplating dating Zen, who she wasn't even into anymore? Apple promised herself she was going to try harder to be a better girlfriend. After her conversation with Happy, she knew she needed to put in more of an effort. But the thought of Zen, the guy she had been in love with for years, being single? Well, *that* was definitely . . . mind-blowing.

♡

Lyon pulled up to the front of the school in his black Cadillac Escalade to pick up Apple. Apple smiled every time she saw the car. It was such a tough car, with its tinted windows, and Apple couldn't help but feel like a bit of a rock star every time she got in. And knowing how sweet Lyon was . . . well, it was funny to see him drive such a monster.

"Hey!" she said, leaning over and giving Lyon a kiss and hopping in. "First, before you say anything, I just want to apologize for lunch. I know I totally bailed and it was rude. But Happy was having some major girl issues and needed to talk. I had to be there for her. Brooklyn was right. She's having issues with Zen."

"That's okay. That's one of the traits I love about you. You are very loyal. I'm just glad I have you to myself for at least ten minutes now," Lyon said. "And I'm not going to ask what the problem is. That's none of my business."

"You're too sweet," Apple said. "Seriously, you really are too nice."

"I guess I really like you. Shall we go?" Lyon asked, driving away.

"We better. It's my first day and I don't want to be late. I'm supposed to be there at 4:30," Apple said, glancing at the oversized men's watch that she had "borrowed" from her dad a month ago but never returned.

Lyon pushed the gas and they took off.

"I can't believe my girlfriend works at *Angst*, the most relevant fashion and celebrity magazine in the world," Lyon joked.

"Right. Have you ever even read it?" asked Apple, smiling at him.

"No, but I do have sisters, you know, and I occasionally flip through it. I especially love the quizzes on 'Are you too demanding?' and 'Ten ways to tell if you're really making him happy.' And those suck-up celebrity interviews with those spoiled young stars who think they're oh so important? I can't get enough." Lyon laughed.

Apple laughed too. Lyon's dry sense of humor was one of the things that had first attracted her to him.

They rode in a comfortable silence, Lyon holding one of her hands as Apple stared out the window. She thought of Happy's joke about her getting together with Zen—something that only days ago was never a possibility, but now?

"Hey, what were you thinking about just now? You looked like you were a million miles away," Lyon said, interrupting her daydream.

"Oh, sorry. I'm just thinking of my first day. I'm thinking of that girl Emme, the intern I'll be sharing an office with two days a week? I'm telling you, this girl hates me," Apple stuttered out. How can she be thinking of Zen now? With her boyfriend right beside her?

"How could anyone hate you?" Lyon asked, looking at her adoringly.

"I know. I know. I'm so lovable. But trust me, yhis girl so does not like me," Apple moaned.

"Well, see how it goes today," said Lyon.

"She also makes me want to go on a diet."

"Apple! I've never once heard you complain about weight," Lyon said, looking at her oddly.

"I know! It's her! She makes me insecure! She's so perfect! And skinny!"

"Your body is perfect just the way it is," Lyon said.

"Maybe I'll just cut out sweets," said Apple. "So don't go buying me any more chocolate. Seriously. I have to watch my weight."

"No," said Lyon, "you don't. You're perfect just the way you are."

"You don't understand. It's a girl thing," she said, smiling at him.

Lyon shrugged, clearly knowing he wasn't going to win this argument.

They arrived at the offices and Apple hesitated before getting out of the car.

"Okay, I'm nervous. What if I screw up?" Apple started. "What if I make someone's coffee wrong, or answer the phone wrong, or . . ." She hated that she sounded so insecure.

"Babe! You're freaking. I've never seen you like this before. What time do you get off?" he asked.

"I have no friggin' idea," Apple said.

"Call me when you're off and I'll come get you, okay?" Lyon said. "It will give you something to look forward to."

"Thanks, Lyon. That would be great. I'll need to see a face that's happy to see me, because I'm sure Emme will *not* be happy to see me."

Apple kissed him passionately, hopped out of the car, and walked into the offices. She felt sweaty and nervous and her heart was racing. She had to go to the bathroom, but she had no idea where it was and was too nervous to ask anyone. She would have to hold it.

"Hey, Morgan," Apple said walking up to the reception desk.

"You're late!" Morgan whispered sternly. "Hurry up and I'll try to sneak you into your office area. Let's pray that Michael hasn't shown up there yet."

"What? I was supposed to be here at 4:30. It's 4:30!" Apple said, perplexed, looking down at her watch again.

"Actually, it's 4:32. Nancy abhors lateness. She thinks it's a sign of disrespect. If anyone is even a minute late meeting her at a restaurant, she'll leave," Morgan said.

Great, thought Apple. What a way to start my first day. Who knew a lousy *120 seconds* was such big a deal? Apparently at *Angst* magazine, every second counted.

"Remember," whispered Morgan. "You're an employee of *Angst* now. That means you follow *Angst* rules and must never be late. There are other things that Michael will go over with you too. Don't look so worried. It will be fine. Just don't be late again."

"I won't. Thanks for the tip," Apple said gratefully.

She followed Morgan, who was practically running down the stairs. Apple ran after her.

"This is where you'll be working. Emme is already here. Get in quick, grab a seat. It doesn't look like Michael has shown up yet, so you're lucky. Have fun! Got to get back to my desk. God forbid I miss a phone call," Morgan said, waving goodbye after pointing Apple to a door.

Apple peaked into the room, which was smaller than her walk-in closet at home. She couldn't believe that this was where she was expected to work. It was so not like Fancy Nancy's office, with its floor-to-ceiling windows, comfy couches, and treadmill. This looked like someone's storage space or garage.

She couldn't believe that she would have to work so close to Emme, literally. If Apple exhaled, Emme would inhale her breath.

Emme didn't look up when Apple took a seat behind one of two desks facing each other. She looked very busy typing away on a computer.

"Hey," Apple said. She was not going to let this Grumpy Emme ruin her first day. Apple had to make it work with Emme. This would be her first challenge at *Angst*.

"Hey," Emme said. At least she responded. Maybe next time she'll even look up at me, thought Apple.

"So," Apple started, "do you have any idea what we're supposed to be doing?"

"I'm sure we'll find out soon enough," Emme answered, clicking away.

"What are you doing?" Apple asked, trying to sound polite. She was genuinely curious. Why did Emme seem so busy when they hadn't been told what to do yet?

"I'm just learning all about the staff here," she answered. "I'm rereading their bios. I almost have them memorized."

"Oh, that's a good idea," Apple said, thinking, Why didn't I think of that?

"You haven't *done* that?" Emme asked, as if Apple should be punished for her stupidity.

"Um, no," Apple said, feeling like an idiot.

"Of course *you* haven't," Emme said. Her tone said Apple had disappointed her but that was to be expected.

"What's that supposed to mean?" Apple asked.

Apple wasn't used to confrontation. In fact, she hated confrontation, but there was just something about this Emme that got under her skin. Emme made her feel defensive.

"I *know* who you are," Emme said unkindly. "I know that you're the *daughter* of Dr. Bee Bee Berg, the host of the *Queen of Whatever* show. I know that's how you got the job here. It's okay. I know that's how the world works and I'd better get used to it. I *am* used to it. You have the famous last name, so everything is easy for you. I'm okay with nepotism. That's how the world works. Right?"

"Um, I wouldn't say that exactly," Apple said. "In fact, I've never used my mother to get anything before in my life. *Nancy* called *me* to work here. I didn't ask my mother to get me a job here or anything."

"Well, they want you to be the advice columnist because *your mother* is already a famous advice personality. They want you on television because *your mother* is on television. It's good publicity for *Angst*," Emme said dismissively.

"Or *maybe* I'm good at giving advice," Apple shot back, trying to act like Happy would if someone treated her the way Emme was treating Apple. "Maybe I'm *good*."

Apple couldn't believe how she had stuck up for herself. Happy would be so proud of her! Apple was proud of herself! She couldn't wait to tell Happy about this conversation.

"Maybe. But did you have to go through five interviews like I did? Did they ask to see your report cards and what extracurricular activities you do? Because they did me," Emme replied. "Did you have to write a five-page essay stating why you should be allowed to work here?"

Apple didn't know how to respond. Emme was right and knew it, and she knew Apple knew it too. Apple did get this job in large part simply by being her mother's daughter. She hadn't been asked for any résumé. She hadn't been asked to show her report cards. She hadn't had to write an essay.

"Okay, you're right," Apple told Emme. "I didn't have to go through all that, but that doesn't mean I'm not going to work my ass off here, just like you."

"We'll see," said Emme in an annoying tone. "We shall see."

Apple gulped. She had no comeback. She was out of her league. And the worst of it was that Emme wasn't even wrong. She was simply stating a fact.

thirteen

T hank God, thought Apple when a tall man wearing a beautifully designed suit walked in, interrupting the uncomfortable silence between her and Emme. He rubbed his hands together and clapped them loudly twice.

"Welcome to *Angst*," he said. Emme jumped out of her seat. Apple followed suit, standing up as if she was greeting a member of the royal family. She had the urge to bend down and kiss his feet.

"I'm Michael and I'll be your boss, your guardian, and your god. Feel free to bow down to me whenever I walk into a room," he said. Apple immediately liked him. She could tell he had a good sense of humor.

"You're Michael Manchester. You started at *GQ* twelve years ago and worked at the *Times* of London before moving here to be the editorial director of *Angst*," Emme said, as if she were reciting lines from a play. "I saw your photograph and read your bio on the website."

"Very impressive," Michael responded. "You are?"

"I'm Emme," responded Emme, standing up taller, looking proud. "Nice to meet you," she added, sticking out her hand to shake Michael's.

Michael turned to Apple. "And you are?"

"I'm Apple," she answered, trying to sound professional, sticking her hand out for him to shake too.

"Well, that's certainly an *unforgettable* name, isn't it? Apple pie. Applesauce. I'm sure you've heard them all before," he said nonchalantly.

"Yes, I have," said Apple, laughing. She couldn't help it. She had met this Michael only a second ago, but she already knew that he'd be a good guy to work for. Michael reminded her of Guy, and it made her feel instantly more comfortable.

Emme shot her a sly, dirty look.

"Well, I love the name. We love unique here," Michael said. "And your name is unique. It's perfect! Now that we've all met each other and you've gotten to see your wonderful office, I'm going to take you up to see Charlotte in styling. If you work at *Angst*, you must dress the part. Follow me, my little minions."

Apple had never felt so grateful to have such an unusual name. Emme knew Michael's entire career history by memory, but all Apple had to do to be memorable was to have a unique name. Ever since she could remember, people had commented on her name. She was named Apple, because her mother had craved apples when she was pregnant and had thought it was a "delicious"-sounding name. Her mother had clearly not been thinking of Apple's future. But today, her name had paid off.

Apple and Emme raced behind Michael. Apple couldn't help but notice that nobody at *Angst* seemed to ever walk. Everyone was always running as if a fire alarm had just been set off.

"Can you feel the energy?" Michael called out ahead of them. "Can you just feel it? Feels good, doesn't it? Feels great!"

"Oh, God, yes. It's unbelievable," Emme said. "It's a dream come true."

"That's the right attitude, Emme. You're going to do well here. I can tell you're ambitious," Michael called back. Apple felt a jab of envy. Though it was clear Emme was an overly ambitious suck-up, it seemed to work. Apple wished she had more of a suck-up gene. But never before had she really had to suck up to anyone.

They were led to a room that looked like a mini Niemen Marcus department store. In fact, it was as large as a department store floor and full of just as many clothes.

Happy would be in heaven here, thought Apple. Racks of designer clothing were everywhere. Hundreds and hundreds of pairs of shoes were organized on shelves. Apple couldn't believe her eyes.

"Hey, Charlotte! The new interns are here!" Michael called out. "You want to make sure they look *Angst*-worthy?"

"One sec," a voice called out. The woman was speaking with pins in her mouth. "Fucking actresses," she muttered. "They get thinner and thinner. Even the size zeros don't fit, and we have a shoot tomorrow for our cover."

Michael explained that Charlotte was the magazine's head stylist, one of the most important and busy jobs at *Angst*.

"Okay," Charlotte finally said, standing in front of Emme and Apple. "What do we have here?"

Emme stood up straight while Apple tried her very best not to feel like she was about to be picked last for a team. Standing next to Emme made her feel short, even though Apple's height had always been average.

"Your name?" she asked, looking at Emme.

"Emme."

Apple felt relieved that she wasn't picked first.

"Perfect, Emme. You don't need to be dressed at all. In fact, I love your belt. Where did you get that little gem?" Charlotte asked.

"Paris," Emme answered. "I was on a scholarship there last year for a semester and I saw it at a vintage store."

"Gorgeous. Now you," she said, looking at Apple. "The shirt doesn't fit you exactly right. See here?" Charlotte said, tugging at her shoulders. "The material is bunching up. I'm going to give you a blazer to throw over it. Do not get it dirty. Do not take the tag off. Just tuck it in. Nancy wants everyone—even the interns—to look like they should be in the magazine. And that means fashion-forward. You work at *Angst* and people should want to dress like you. Your shoes are cute, but a little scruffy. Make sure that you clean them before coming in. Here's the blazer. Hurry! Hurry! I don't have all day! You never know who you're going to bump into in these hallways, so a little bit of advice? Always dress more up than down."

Apple silently repeated Charlotte's advice to herself three times: Always dress more up than down. Always dress more up than down. Always dress more up than down.

♡

Apple put on the cute blazer and then Michael took them back to the dungeon of the intern office.

"First things first," Michael said, sitting on a desk. "Code of conduct. When you work at *Angst* you are to act professionally. But when you are outside the offices of *Angst*, including when you are not working—and I mean from the second you walk out of this office—you are to also act professionally. You are not to be seen doing any drugs, running the streets naked, acting in any other way that would embarrass anyone one of us here. Capiche? We don't want a repeat of our last intern."

"What happened to her?" Apple asked. Because Michael reminded her so much of Guy, she forgot that she hadn't in fact known him for more than twenty minutes. She hoped she hadn't offended him by asking the question. But wasn't Emme dying to know too?

"Let's just say two words, or maybe it's one word. Whatever. Let's just say 'Rehab,'" Michael said, like he was letting them in on a big secret.

"That's not good," Apple muttered.

"Trust me, it *wasn't* good. She had a brilliant résumé, amazing design ideas, and could make someone's entire look change just by adding a brooch or a single gold bangle. She was too good at what she did. I think the stress got to her, though. Or her friends in the fashion world, if you know what I mean."

Apple didn't know what he meant until he said, "Sniff! Sniff!" Oh, right, drugs.

"She was brilliantly creative, and it was really too bad that one of the editors saw her snorting in the washroom. But that's not going to happen to you guys, right? Neither of you is going to end up in rehab. I just can't take another talented cokehead. I loved the girl. Everyone loved her, because she had the eye. Models, who are notoriously difficult, even loved her. But, alas, her time had to come to an end. We couldn't have someone like that working here. We're role models! Still, I miss her. It's just so disappointing to me when someone has that much talent and blows it."

"I understand completely," Emme said. "We're not going to end up in rehab, or at least *I'm* not." Was Apple being crazy, or was Emme trying to push her out of *Angst* already?

"Absolutely," added Apple. "I don't do drugs."

"Good. Now, as for your jobs, Apple, we need your column by Monday. And we need you to start practicing your lines for your *Angst TV* spot next week."

"*This* Monday?" Apple asked.

"Yes, this isn't a monthly high school rag, dear. We're weekly! Are you sure you're up for it?" Michael asked, not unkindly. Why did everyone here keep asking her if she was "up for it"? Apple wondered if she looked like a person who just wasn't "up for it." She'd have to get Brooklyn to read her aura later. She'd ask Brooklyn if her aura said, "I'm not up for it."

"Yes, yes. Of course. I just wanted to make sure we were on the same page," Apple answered.

"Here are the letters for you to answer. We've picked them for you. You answer three of the five. Of course, after you write your answers, they will be looked at by about three editors to make sure we're all on track. And we'll pick one for you to read on television, and you'll have to answer looking into the camera, kind of off the cuff, but I'm sure you're good at speaking from the heart. Or so we saw on that episode. And Nancy said you feel very comfortable in front of the camera," Michael continued. "Is that right?"

"Yup. I mean, yes. I do," Apple said. She felt like she should salute him. And, God, when were people going to forget her appearance on her mother's show? Her mother had told her that people had short memories, but it didn't seem that way to Apple. It seemed that everyone still remembered.

"Today, though, we need you to clean this dungeon. All these clothes in piles have to be organized by color, size, and designer. It shouldn't take more than five or six hours," Michael said.

Apple gulped. Five or six hours? When did they expect her to write the answers for her advice column? And practice for television? And, more important, would Lyon still want to pick her up in *six hours*?

"Have fun, guys. Welcome to *Angst*. We have to let you know that you have to work your way up, and what better way to work your way up than from down here?" said Michael, laughing. Obviously it wasn't the first time he had used the joke. Apple at least liked

Michael. Now she just had to work on liking Emme, if that was even possible.

"Did he just say five or six *hours*?" Apple whispered to Emme, trying for a bonding moment. She wasn't sure if Michael was still outside the door, and she certainly didn't want him to hear her complaining.

"What did you expect? This is a *job*. Did you think it would be *fun*?" Emme asked, looking at Apple like she was not the brightest penny in the till. Obviously Apple's attempt at bonding had backfired.

"Well, sometimes, yes!" Apple said. "It sounded like that girl who ended up in rehab actually did some pretty amazing and interesting things here."

Emme shook her head, looking at Apple as if she lived under a rock.

"You know how many people out there would kill to fold clothes at *Angst*?" Emme asked. "That girl may have been talented, but she royally screwed up. That's not something to be impressed about."

"I guess," Apple muttered.

"Well, it's true. So let's start folding," Emme said.

"I just don't know how I'm going to spend the next five or six hours folding clothes, do this advice column by Monday, and do my schoolwork," Apple said. She regretted it immediately.

"Oh, poor you. It's hard to work, isn't it?" Emme said. "Not that you probably have had to work a day in your life. And now you'll be a columnist here, which is what I really want to do, and you'll be on television. God knows, because my mother isn't famous, if that will ever happen for me. But I'm going to do everything in my power to prove that I'm an *Angst*-worthy employee and can do more than just fold clothes. I'm going to work my ass off."

Apple wanted to punch her. Instead, she breathed in, counted to ten, like Brooklyn always told her to do, and started folding clothes. She doubted any celebrities even knew this room existed. Nope, there was no way she was going meet anyone famous today. She was stuck folding clothes with Emme.

After two hours of Emme not saying one word, Apple actually did wonder if she would have more fun at rehab. She wondered if Emme would drive her to doing drugs. It was possible.

fourteen

"It's ten o'clock," Lyon moaned, but he didn't sound unfriendly.

"I know. I'm so sorry. That's how long it took to fold three hundred sweaters. I totally understand if you don't want to pick me up. I can call Aunt Hazel. It's not a problem," Apple said. Apple was trying not to sound annoyed. Yes, it was ten o'clock, but Lyon hadn't had to fold sweaters for the last few hours in complete and uncomfortable silence in a tiny-sized room below ground level with a new "colleague" who refused to talk. If anyone had the right to be in a bad mood, it was Apple.

"No, no. I'll be there in fifteen minutes," said Lyon. "It's no problem."

"Really?" Apple asked.

"Really."

"Okay, I should get off. I'm not sure if talking is allowed here."

Emme shot her a look as Apple hung up. She grabbed her bag and took off the blazer, hanging it neatly on a rack.

"Well, I guess I'll see you Thursday," Apple said.

"Guess so," Emme said.

"Aren't you leaving soon?" Apple asked.

"I'm just going to stick around awhile longer," Emme said.

Of course she is, thought Apple. She's such a kiss-ass. Apple could see no redeeming qualities in Emme, though she had tried for the last few hours. Aside from her being gorgeous, Apple could not think of anything else complimentary about Emme, except, clearly, that she was so ambitious.

Apple waited outside the offices for Lyon's car to pull up. Her hands were sore and her back was killing her from being hunched over a table. She raised her arms in a stretch, yawning at the same time.

"How was your first day?" a voice called out, walking past her toward the entrance of the building. It was Fancy Nancy, looking like she had just come back from a week at a spa. Apple hoped that Fancy Nancy hadn't seen her yawn. That would look bad.

"It was great," Apple said, trying to sound excited. "Just waiting to get picked up. Are you leaving now too?"

"Oh, God, no. It's only ten. I'll be lucky to get out of here by midnight. I had a dinner meeting and I'm just getting back. Is Emme still here? Did she have a good day?"

Apple couldn't lie. She wasn't cruel.

"Actually, she's still downstairs working," Apple admitted.

"Hmm, good for her," Nancy said. "I'm impressed. See you later, Apple. And say hi to your mother for me. We can't wait to do that feature. Full interview with your family and a lot of photos. It's all set up for next week. Next week is going to be busy for us, isn't it?"

"I know. I'm ready," said Apple, again trying to sound upbeat. "By the way, you look stunning."

The compliment sounded strange coming from Apple. Fancy Nancy did look stunning, but Apple wondered if she came across as sucking up. Maybe Emme had already started to rub off on her, as if sucking up were contagious.

"Ta-ta," Fancy Nancy said as she walked into the building, seeming not to hear Apple's compliment. Apple wondered if she was going up to work or to work out. She figured working out was part of Nancy's job. She had to look good when meeting celebrities, to look like one herself. Apple decided that Fancy Nancy was going to work out and then work, and probably wouldn't be home till long after Apple had fallen asleep.

One minute later, Lyon's car pulled up.

"I want to quit," Apple said as soon as she got in.

"What? No kiss first?" he asked flirtatiously.

Apple gave him a peck on the cheek.

"That's all I get?" he said, smiling. "I want a better one."

Though she didn't feel like kissing Lyon—she was too annoyed and tired—Apple leaned over and kissed him again.

"I want to quit," she repeated.

"It couldn't have been that bad," Lyon said.

"Yes, it could. And it was. I was two minutes late, and that, apparently, is akin to murdering someone. And Emme? Oh my God. She hates me. She thinks that just because Dr. Bee Bee Berg is my mother, I don't deserve to be there. And she knew everybody's background. She studied them! And the stylist thought she was dressed perfectly, but I wasn't. Then I spent hours folding and organizing clothes next to Emme, who didn't say one word except to tell me when something wasn't folded perfectly. And she's still there! She's making me look bad already. Not to mention all the homework I have to do, plus getting my advice column in by Monday. And it has to be good! This was a huge mistake. It's too much," Apple said, feeling both self-pity and self-loathing.

"Don't be so hard on yourself. You'll be fine. You'll get it all done. It takes a while to fit in somewhere new," Lyon said supportively. "It was just your first day. It's going to get easier."

"Easy for you to say," Apple huffed. She was mortified by how cruel she sounded, especially since Lyon had gone out of his way to come pick her up and was trying to give her a pep talk.

"Hey! I'm on your side, remember?" he said, eyeing her questioningly.

"I know. I'm sorry. I'm just feeling a little stressed," Apple responded tensely. "I shouldn't be taking it out on you. I'm sorry."

"Don't worry. It will get easier—it always does. You'll see."

Apple gave him a small smile. He was trying.

"Well, I guess there are a couple of cool people who work there," she said. "Like this guy Michael, who's kind of my boss, and Morgan, the receptionist. They seem really cool."

They sat in a comfortable silence until Lyon drove up into her driveway and pulled her in for a kiss. She kissed him back, even though she found her mind wondering to her unfinished homework.

"I should really go. It's late and I have three chapters of history to get through," she said, pulling back after what she thought was a passable amount of kissing time not to hurt his feelings.

"Don't go in just yet. I miss you!" Lyon said, rubbing her neck.

"I'm right here," said Apple. "But I really should go in and get started. I'm so tired."

"You know what I mean," Lyon said, pulling on one of her ringlets. "I love your hair. I think I may even be in—"

Before Lyon could finish his sentence, there was a loud, frantic knocking on the car window. Apple and Lyon both jumped.

♡

It was Crazy Aunt Hazel. Apple pressed the button by her side and the window slid down.

"Don't do that! You scared the crap out of us!" Apple stormed. "What are you thinking?"

"Sorry, but you have to look at these. There are some fabulous dresses and ideas in this magazine," she said, throwing a copy of *Heavenly Bride* onto Apple's lap. The magazine was as thick as the history book waiting for Apple to study it.

"You have to look through them with me *right now*!" her aunt demanded. "Jim and I have decided to get married in a matter of weeks, so I don't have time to mess around. We've got to get started right now! Right now! Right now!"

Apple couldn't believe it. Her aunt had *just* gotten engaged. Why did she have to rush into a wedding?

"Do you know how many times you just said, 'Right now'?" Apple asked her aunt.

"I know what you're thinking, Apple. And I already got an earful from your mother. It's just that the venue we want has an opening in a few weeks, and no more for another seven months. Jim and I don't see a need to wait that long. We don't *want* to wait. We know we want to get married. So why wait?" her aunt asked in the same crazy tone, as if she had to convince Apple as she had obviously had to convince Apple's mother.

"Right," laughed Apple. "You just want to start having sex with him again."

"Apple! I told you that in confidence," her aunt said, turning to Lyon, who looked slightly embarrassed.

"But, yes, it's true. So get out of the car, Apple! Start acting like my bridesmaid and help me!"

"Now?" Apple moaned. "But Lyon is here. And I just got home from work. And it's so late! And I have so much homework to do."

"Lyon can help," her aunt said, opening the car door and grabbing Apple's arm. "Homework can wait."

"Ah, thanks, Hazel," Lyon said. "But I think I'm going to go. Not that looking at bridal gowns doesn't sound like such a fun thing to do. See you at school tomorrow, Apple?"

"Absolutely. Thanks for picking me up. It was really sweet of you."

"My pleasure," said Lyon. He looked like he wanted to kiss her. But Apple couldn't allow that in front of her aunt, who would surely make fun of her. Plus, Hazel was eagerly pulling Apple's arm, forcing her out of the car.

The last thing Apple wanted to do was flip through wedding magazines. But she couldn't also help but feel a little bit grateful that her aunt had showed up when she did. Apple had a feeling that Lyon was about to tell her that he loved her. She definitely wasn't ready for that. She had known him for a mere few weeks! Of course, she had known him as long as Crazy Aunt Hazel had known Mr. Kelly, and now they were getting married, making that lifelong commitment to each other.

But Apple didn't really believe that people fell in love so quickly. Her crush on Zen had built up over *years*. Not that she would ever tell that to her aunt Hazel, especially now that she was in major wedding planning mode, and truthfully Apple had never seen her aunt more sure about anything. Maybe people do fall in love that fast. What did Apple know?

Did Apple love Lyon?

"Isn't life working out for everyone?" her aunt asked, singing happily as she linked arms with Apple as they walked up to the door. "I'm getting married! You have Lyon and a great gig at *Angst*!"

Apple wasn't so sure. Suddenly, she felt somewhat sad. She knew she should be happy. But she only felt anxious, pressured, and stressed, especially wondering if Lyon had been about to tell her that he loved her. Though she knew her aunt was right—she should be ecstatic about what was going on in her life—Apple wondered why couldn't she quite get there.

Thankfully, her mother rescued her from looking through bridal magazines. Apple had never been so happy that her mother was acting like a mother, as opposed to acting like Dr. Berg or a friend.

"Don't you have homework to do? Have you even eaten dinner yet?" her mother asked when they walked in. "You got home from work late! I can't believe I'm home before you are."

"I'm too tired to eat. And, yes, I was trying to tell Aunt Hazel that I have a ton of homework to do," Apple responded. She was becoming more stressed by the second, thinking of all the pages she had to get through.

"You had better go do it. But you should really eat something first. You're going to need to learn all about time management now with this new job. You'd be surprised how much one can get done in a day if one just remains focused and organized," her mother blabbered.

Apple was skilled at tuning her mother out. She didn't have that skill, however, when it came to her aunt, who practically started screaming.

"But I need Apple's opinion! She has to be here!" her aunt cried hysterically. "She knows better than either of us what is fashionable! Right, Apple? I need you! You're my bridesmaid, for God's sake!"

"Hazel, Apple has homework. This is not more important than her grades. We *can* do this. Trust me, picking out the wedding dress is the easy part. What comes after the wedding is the hard part," her mother said calmly.

Apple and her aunt exchanged glances. Her mother had scolded them both.

"You think I'm joking? Well, I'm not. Apple, go do your homework now. And, Hazel, let's start looking through the magazines. It's so ridiculous to be getting married so quickly," her mother added, clucking her tongue.

This made Hazel start to cry. Apple watched her mother wrap her arm around her aunt guiltily.

"Don't cry. Honestly, that's the last time I'll say anything about it. You know how I feel, but it's your day. It's your life. And picking out your dress is something that should be a happy occasion," her mother said, comforting her sister, who looked far from comforted.

Apple had never thought the day would arrive, but she was happier to do her homework than to deal with one of her aunt's meltdowns, no matter how funny. She felt like she was on the verge of a meltdown herself.

fifteen

It was Friday evening and Apple was almost finished getting ready to go out for dinner with Lyon when the doorbell rang. Lyon was on Apple's bed, flipping through an issue of *Angst* magazine, throwing out quips like "Did you know Sloan Starr is not in a relationship and also likes long walks on the beach? Did you know that Tommy D., that reality star, likes to make sculptures in his spare time?"

Apple didn't know why she found herself annoyed at Lyon's throwaway comments about the celebrities in *Angst* magazine, especially the one about Sloan. Sloan, after all, had complimented her on her hair! Although it wasn't much—barely anything, and Apple knew this—she still felt that Lyon was judging him without knowing him, and that was unfair. Sure, he was a celebrity, but certainly he was a person too, and he seemed nice. But Apple didn't stick up for Sloan. She hadn't even told Lyon that she had kind-of-sort-of met him. She was embarrassed that she had felt so enlivened by his compliment. It was silly. Besides, Apple now worked at *Angst*. She knew Lyon was joking, but she found it slightly disrespectful.

"Who could that be?" Apple wondered. "I'll be right back."

Apple ran downstairs. Her parents had gone to one of the many fundraising events they were invited to. Crazy Aunt Hazel and Guy both had their own keys and knew the security code, and always let themselves in, so it couldn't be either of them.

Apple opened the door. She couldn't believe who stood before her. What was *he* doing here?

"Zen! Hey!" Apple exclaimed.

He stood slouched over with a baseball cap covering his eyes.

"What's going on? Are you okay? Come in!" Apple said, opening the door wider.

"Thanks, Apple. I know this is weird, me stopping by. I was actually just playing basketball with Hopper, so I was nearby and figured I'd see if you were home. I should have called first," Zen said.

"No, it's okay. What's happening?" Apple asked, glancing worriedly upstairs, where Lyon was waiting.

"I was just wondering if I could get your advice on something," he said, smiling slightly. God, that smile, thought Apple.

"Um, sure. Of course!" Apple answered nervously. Then she added, "Are you sure you want *my* advice? Remember how well that worked out the last time, when I lied to you?"

"I know it's weird," laughed Zen.

Though they didn't ever speak about how Apple had lied to Zen and given him entirely-not-good ways to woo Happy, they both *knew* it had happened.

"Don't worry. It's forgotten about. I just don't want you to think I'm uncomfortable," said Zen. "I mean, I want you to know that I do trust you, no matter what has happened in the past with us."

"Thanks. Can I get you a drink or something to eat? I don't think we have much," Apple said, trying to make the situation of Zen showing up at her house on a Friday night—for advice, no less—seem like it was no big deal. She hadn't heard from Happy in the last couple of hours. She was probably at one of her acting classes or hanging out with Sailor or possibly even hanging out with Hot and Disturbed Guy.

"No, no. I'll be quick. It looks like you're going out. Are you?" asked Zen shyly. "I mean, you look like you're dressed to go out."

It took Apple a minute to remember that she was in fact going out, and that Lyon, her *boyfriend*, was waiting upstairs. It was as if Zen had some strange power over her, like a hypnotist.

"Oh. Yes. In fact, Lyon is upstairs. We're going out for dinner," Apple sputtered.

"Do you think he'll mind that I'm here?" Zen wondered.

"Oh, God, no. He knows we're friends. So what's happening?" Apple asked nervously, again glancing up in the direction of her bedroom. She knew Lyon would, in fact, mind that Zen was there.

"I just have to talk to someone about this. And I can't talk to Hopper because he won't get it, and you know Happy better than anyone," Zen started to say.

"Apple?" Lyon called out. They heard footsteps coming down the stairs toward them.

Apple had no reason to feel like she was about to be caught in the middle of doing something wrong, but that's how she suddenly felt. She could tell Zen did too, because he immediately walked over to the far side of the room to look at a collection of DVDs.

"Hey, baby. What's going on? Who's here?" Lyon asked, pulling her into a hug. It was only then that Lyon noticed Zen was also in the room.

"Oh, hey, Zen. What are you doing here?" he asked, looking at Apple.

"Oh, I lent Apple a DVD a while back and I was in the area, so I thought I'd pick it up. Here it is," stuttered Zen, holding up a copy of *Batman*.

"Oh, good. You found it," Apple found herself lying. She wasn't sure why. Was it really such a big deal for a male friend, one she had known for years, to come over and talk, even if she used to be madly in love with him at one point? That was over, thought Apple, so who cared? Well, Lyon, for one. And possibly Happy. Especially as Zen had come over to talk about her.

"Thanks, Apple. So we'll speak some other time, then?" Zen asked.

"Yup. Of course. See you," Apple said as Zen walked out the door.

Lyon looked at her strangely.

"Is something going on that I should know about?" he asked.

"No! Of course not! He's just a friend picking up a DVD he lent me, like, a year ago. He was playing basketball with Hopper, and Hopper lives, like, three blocks away," Apple said defensively. She had no idea why she felt so defensive. She wasn't hiding anything. All she had done was open the door. All Zen had done was take a DVD.

"So why does he suddenly want it back now?" Lyon asked suspiciously. His tone sounded accusatory. Apple didn't like it.

"I don't know. Maybe he had the urge to watch some men in tights or something. Maybe he really was just in the area and it popped into his head," Apple suggested.

"I think he likes you," Lyon said. "I think he now has a crush on you, or maybe he always did."

"Hello? You're acting crazy. He's with my best friend Happy, remember? And he didn't like me, remember?" Apple argued.

"So?" Lyon asked. "Things change. People have changes of heart all the time."

"Nothing has changed!" Apple said. She was starting to become annoyed. Since when had Lyon become so clingy and jealous?

"I'm not convinced," Lyon said. He was pouting, and it wasn't a very sexy look for him.

"Can we please just go for dinner? I need to relax. I just finished my first week at work. And Crazy Aunt Hazel left me *twenty-two* messages today about helping her find the perfect wedding dress. She's stressing me out. So please, Lyon," Apple pleaded. "Please don't stress me out too!"

"Let's go," Lyon said. "You're right. You had a hard week. I'm sorry."

Apple couldn't help but notice there was still a slight edge to his voice. Why couldn't he see that, if anyone, she was the one who should be on edge?

♡

Lyon took her to a sweet little bistro near Apple's home, one of their favorites.

Just as Apple felt herself starting to relax over tortilla chips and guacamole dip, Lyon brought up Zen again.

"I just get a weird vibe from the guy," he said.

She really didn't want to be talking about Zen, but she had to stick up for him. She had known him much longer than she had Lyon.

"Really? He's one of the sweetest people I know," Apple said. "He's always volunteering for something. He's just a nice guy."

"Listen, Apple. I'm a guy. We know what other guys are like," Lyon explained. "And I'm telling you, he wasn't there just to pick up a DVD. He wasn't happy to see us going out. He's trying to worm his way in between us. I just know it."

Apple couldn't help but laugh, accidently spitting out some of the chip she had just taken a bite of.

"I'm being serious, Apple," Lyon said.

"I didn't notice anything weird," Apple responded, putting the half-eaten chip back on her plate. She had suddenly lost her appetite, thanks to the way Lyon was acting, even though she had been starving just minutes ago.

"Well, what is he supposed to say?" demanded Lyon.

Apple didn't feel comfortable telling him the real reason Zen had come over, which was to ask her for advice about Happy. She hadn't told Lyon anything about Happy's new crush or how Happy wasn't into Zen anymore. That was their business.

"I think you're really seeing something that's not there. I really don't want to talk about this. It's so stupid," Apple said. Her usual favorite meal, steak and French fries, arrived and it suddenly didn't look so appealing on the plate. She wished she had ordered a salad instead. Her stomach was in knots. She and Lyon had never fought before, and this felt like a fight. This was their first fight.

"All right, then. Let's go on a double date with Happy and Zen next week," Lyon suggested, as if he was daring her.

Apple gulped. She couldn't think of anything she would rather not do. Who even knew if Happy and Zen would still be together next week? Apple knew that Happy had been avoiding Zen like the plague and continued to kiss Hot and Disturbed Guy before her sessions. For a minute, Apple thought of telling Lyon the truth about what was going on with Happy and Zen.

Apple knew that her aunt Hazel told her future husband—Mr. Kelly—everything about her friends. According to her aunt, there could be no secrets in a relationship and if a friend told you something in confidence and you had a husband, obviously that friend knew you were going to share it with your partner.

Still, Apple felt in her gut that if she told Lyon Happy wasn't into Zen anymore, he'd just become more jealous and would really watch out for how Zen acted toward Apple and how Apple acted toward Zen, even if there was nothing to watch out for.

"Sure. If work doesn't get in the way. And if they're available," Apple said, trying to placate Lyon.

"You'll make the time," he said. "And of course they'll be available. She's your best friend! So it's a date."

"Fine, it's a date. If that's what you need to see that Zen is NOT interested in me, then we'll do it. But you're being ridiculous," Apple said, pushing her plate back and looking away from Lyon.

Lyon didn't respond. This romantic, relaxing dinner was a bust. But suddenly Apple wanted to fix it. She didn't want to be fighting with Lyon. She knew she hadn't been the best girlfriend over the last couple of days. She had forgotten to call him back so many times. She had bailed on lunch. She had been short with him. And, in Lyon's defense, Apple *had* once been in love with Zen. Maybe it was only natural for him to act this way.

"You're forgetting one thing," Apple said.

"And what's that?" Lyon asked shortly.

"I'm interested in *you*," Apple said as Lyon handed over his credit card to the waitress.

"Sometimes, Apple, I'm not so sure," he said, much to Apple's shock. She had been trying to make up with him.

"What's that supposed to mean?" demanded Apple. She was trying to play nice, but Lyon wasn't playing nice back. She was losing her patience.

"You heard me," he said, slipping Apple's coat over her arms as she stood up. Even when Lyon wasn't in a good mood, he was always the gentleman.

Apple had a response, but not one she would voice aloud to Lyon in a public restaurant.

"Listen, I've just been overwhelmed with the stress of this new job and school. It has nothing to do with you," Apple said.

"Exactly," said Lyon. "I feel like nothing in your life has to do with me anymore."

She really didn't want to fight with Lyon. She had no idea what was happening to them. Even when she tried to be nice, they still kept on fighting. Lyon, she thought, was maybe waiting for some sort of deeper apology. What Apple wanted to say was that he was lucky she had even come out with him tonight. She had to be at *Angst* all the next day, and her aunt wanted to meet her after to go scout out some wedding dresses. Apple needed a good night's sleep.

They drove home in silence, until the silence became deafening. Apple turned on the radio. Lyon dropped her off and didn't even attempt to invite himself in. He didn't lean over to give her a goodnight kiss either—which was fine with Apple. She was in no mood to kiss him. She simply said, "Thanks for dinner," and got out of the car.

Lyon had put Apple in what her aunt called her "Bad Apple" mood. Apple didn't want to talk to anyone. She didn't even have it in her to call Happy and tell her that Zen had stopped by, or to return Brooklyn's call, or to tell anyone that she was in the middle of her first fight ever with Lyon. She knew her aunt would be pissed off that she didn't return any of her twenty-two messages. Although no one was around, Apple couldn't help but slam her bedroom door.

sixteen

It had been a strange day. Apple had arrived at *Angst* on Monday at 4:22 p.m. She had spent the entire weekend at *Angst* as well, holed up in the dungeon sorting mail, and was starting to feel more at home. She no longer felt nervous as she walked in. She had even brought her favorite water bottle, which she kept at her desk. People around the office now nodded a quick hello when Apple walked by.

"Good girl," Morgan said, winking, tapping her fashionable pink watch. It had become somewhat of a joke between them: whenever Apple arrived now, Morgan pointed out the time.

"I know. I'm a fast learner. Is Emme here yet?" Apple asked.

"Of course! She arrived about an hour ago," Morgan said. "We've never had an intern this ambitious before. Ever."

"An hour ago?" Apple winced.

"She's eager," Morgan said. "I mean, I guess that's a good thing."

Apple was tired. She had stayed up until four in the morning reworking her advice column, which was due today.

Apple was still distraught over her Friday-night dinner with Lyon but had managed to put it in the back of her mind while concentrating on her advice column. They hadn't spoken for more than three minutes the rest of the weekend, which was fine by Apple. She didn't want to have to explain one more time that Zen wasn't into her. She didn't want to have to explain just how stressed she was feeling with this new job, falling behind on her schoolwork, and not being the perfect bridesmaid for her aunt.

Apple had woken up at 5 a.m. so her mother could read her answers for *Angst*. It wasn't cheating, Apple thought, when she first wondered if she should show her mother what she had worked on. It was simply getting help. After all, she didn't want to screw up on her first assignment. Plus, Apple knew it would make her mother feel needed. Besides, this was a perk of living in the same house with someone who had doled out relationship advice for almost two decades.

"Apple, this is good," her mother had said, reading the page she had printed out. "Really good. You must have worked on this very hard. It's well written, well thought out, and very helpful."

"Okay, but you must have some advice to give me. Something could be improved!" Apple demanded. "Give me something. You must have some criticisms. I won't be offended. Tell me the truth."

"Honey, you have to be confident. And plus, this isn't exactly my demographic. These are your peers. Would the answers you wrote be answers you'd give to your friends?" her mother asked.

"I guess so. I didn't get to pick these questions, though. Michael gave them to me. I think they're made up," Apple explained.

"Well, that's sometimes how it works. You know that Guy answers all my viewers' e-mails. Viewers think they're getting a response from me, but in reality they're not. It doesn't matter, though. Guy knows me better even than your father," Dr. Berg said.

"Um, can we get back to me, please?" Apple asked.

"Honey, they're great. Really. They are. You do have a gift. I'm going to try not to take any kudos for that, but I think you may have inherited some of my talent!"

"Okay, Mom. You can go now," Apple said. "I have to find something in my closet that's *Angst*-worthy to wear to the office. Last time, my sleeves were too long or something, and then my pants weren't the right length."

Her mother had left for work and Apple had headed back to her room. The pull of her bed was too strong for her to resist.

I'll just lay here for a few minutes, she had thought to herself. After all, it was still only 6:45.

"What are you doing?" she had heard Hazel scream suddenly, right in her face. "I've been honking outside for five minutes. Why are you still in bed?"

"Oh, my God. What time is it? I just meant to go back to bed for a few minutes," Apple moaned.

"Well, you are going to be late, sweetie. Here, throw on these," her aunt said, tossing her a pair of jeans that had been lying over a chair.

"I can't wear those! Are you crazy? I'll be laughed right out of *Angst* if I wear those," Apple responded huffily. Didn't her aunt know anything?

"Since when did you become a fashion queen? Go take a shower and I'll get an outfit together for you," her aunt said. "Unlike some people who haven't yet found the time to help *me* pick out an outfit for the MOST IMPORTANT DAY OF MY LIFE."

Apple knew that the best way of dealing with her aunt when she was in a rant was simply to ignore her comments.

"Fine. But nothing slutty. They don't like slutty. They like chic and sophisticated," Apple said.

"Slutty? Me?" Crazy Aunt Hazel asked mockingly. "Make this the quickest shower you've ever had."

Apple raced into the shower and shampooed and conditioned her hair in less than five minutes. Just as she was getting out of the shower, she heard her phone ringing.

"Can you get that, Hazel?" Apple called out, trying to brush her hair. She should have done it in the shower. It was always easier that way.

Apple walked out in a towel and listened to her aunt talk animatedly on the phone. Apple mouthed the words "Who is it?"

"Here she is," Hazel said, handing the phone over. "It's Happy."

"Happy! What are you doing?" she asked. "I'm totally running behind. Crazy Aunt Hazel is about to blow up."

"I'm at home. I need an 'emotional day' off. Interested in joining me?" Happy asked.

"Yes! Oh, my God! Can we please go shopping? I have no *Angst*-worthy clothes," Apple responded, delighted.

Hazel looked at her. She shot her aunt a dirty look. Since when had her aunt become so responsible? Just months ago, her aunt was taking "emotional days" off from her job the minute a guy dumped her, which seemed to be almost every other day.

"Let's meet at Milk and Sugar and then we'll do some retail therapy," Happy suggested. "I need some retail therapy. Don't forget your credit card."

"Perfect! See you soon!" Apple said excitedly, hanging up.

Aunt Hazel looked at her disapprovingly. "So you're skipping school today?"

"I need an emotional day," Apple said. "Don't look at me like that! Just because you're getting married doesn't make you suddenly the most responsible person in the world. It's just one day! And Happy needs me."

"Fine, whatever. But I'm not going to lie to Jim about you missing math because you want to hang out with friends and go shopping," Aunt Hazel responded sternly.

"Dear God," moaned Apple. "Who are you? I want my crazy aunt back. Just don't tell Mom, okay?"

"If you don't tell her I'm borrowing her new shawl, you have a deal," her aunt said slyly. "Oh, and if you don't mind, I'll look through that pile of your clothes on the floor over there. You might be younger than me, but I know I still have the body of a teenager."

Her aunt had done a little jig in front of Apple's full-length mirror, as if to prove how youthful she was.

"Fine. Take what you want. But you can't say a word to either Mr. Kelly or my mother, okay? That's the deal," Apple warned.

"Deal. But I don't think Jim is going to be impressed with you skipping the pop quiz today," her aunt told her.

"What? First of all, I told you, do not call him Jim. And, second, how do you know there's going to be a pop quiz today?" Apple asked.

"Uh, hello? I'm sleeping with him. I know all," Aunt Hazel responded, giving her an evil grin.

"I thought you weren't sleeping with him until the wedding," Apple answered—not that she really wanted to know the intimate details of her aunt and her math teacher's sex life.

"We don't actually . . . well, you know. I'm still holding out. Aren't you impressed? But we cuddle and have sweet talk," her aunt said.

"Yeah, talking about a pop quiz sounds so romantic," Apple laughed.

"Whatever," her aunt had said, Apple's clothes falling out of her arms. "Where would you like me to drop you off?"

♡

Happy was already at Milk and Sugar, the coffee shop next to a strip of boutiques at the outdoor mall near their homes, when Apple's aunt dropped her off. She had been flipping through an obviously outdated issue of *Angst*. The pages looked like they were going to fall apart.

"Hey, babe," Apple said, leaning over and giving Happy a peck on the cheek.

"Hey. Thanks for meeting. I've texted Brooklyn to join us. She's trying to get out of class right now. Did you know that Mr. Kelly surprised the class with a pop quiz? It was already on Brooklyn's desk. But I'm not worried. Brooklyn will come up with something good to get out. You look tired," Happy said.

"I was up until 4 a.m. working on my first, and maybe last, advice column."

"Oooooh! Let me see! Let me see!" Happy demanded, grabbing Apple's bag.

"No!" Apple said, grabbing back her purse. "It's not good. It's so bad. I'm so going to be fired. They're going to realize they made a huge mistake, and my career at *Angst* magazine will be over before it really even began."

"Get over it, Apple! You're always so hard on yourself. Just hand it over," Happy demanded.

"Fine," Apple said as she handed over the sheet of paper she had worked so hard on. She cradled her face in her arms as Happy read the questions and Apple's advice aloud.

Dear Apple,

I'm in the tenth grade and have been a fan of Angst *magazine forever. I can't believe that the daughter of the Queen of Hearts is now the advice columnist at* Angst. *I'm so happy!*

Happy paused after reading that paragraph and put her finger in her mouth as if she was going to make herself gag.

"I know, right?" Apple said. "It's just the magazine trying to make them look better. They made that up. Whatever." She put her head back into her arms. Her hair, which was still wet from her hurried shower, felt cool on her flushed-with-embarrassment cheeks.

Happy continued to read.

Anyway, I really hope you can help me. I have been dating this guy for a few months. He's great. He's really sweet and gets along with my friends and family. He wants to spend all his spare time with me. My girlfriends are so jealous. They think we're perfect together. I don't want to break his heart, but I'm just not into him anymore. I'm not sure why. I would love to be, because I don't want to break his heart (let alone my friends' and family's). Should I hang in there? Or try talking to him about it? Is there any way I can get back that feeling I had for him at the very beginning? Please help. I'm in angst! (Pun intended!) XOXO Stuck.

"Oh, my God. You didn't write this for me, did you Apple?" Happy asked, squinting at Apple.

"First of all, I don't pick the questions. Michael, my boss, who is awesome, gave me five and told me to answer three of them. And who even knows what he'll do with my answers. He'll probably answer them himself if he doesn't like mine."

"It's so weird that it's *exactly* what I'm going through with Zen. It's not that I even really needed an 'emotional day' off. I just can't bear to see Zen," Happy said.

"What are you going to do?" Apple wondered.

"Let me read your answer," Happy said.

Dear Stuck,

No one knows what goes on in a relationship but the two people in it. Don't worry about what your friends will think, or your family. It's your life and your decision to make. Can you pinpoint exactly what about him is bothering you? If so, maybe you can discuss it with him. Maybe you just need to spice up your relationship. After a few months, like cheese, a relationship can go bad if you don't work on it. And relationships are about work. Try discussing it with him. And if you still feel in your heart that he's not the one, tell him sooner rather than later. You don't want to be the girl who leads a guy on if you're not feeling the love. You're young. You'll have many more loves. Good luck to you.

Happy placed the piece of paper on the table and didn't say anything at first.

"What? Do you not agree? What's wrong with it?" Apple asked desperately.

"Nothing," Happy said. "What you wrote is exactly true. I'm not sure I can pinpoint what suddenly bugs me about Zen. He's still the same Zen I fell in love with. I still love him. I'm just not . . ."

"In love with him," Apple finished for her.

"Exactly. But there's no way I can discuss it with him," Happy said.

"Why not?" Apple asked.

"I just can't! Look at me! I'm skipping school just to avoid running into him. I'm turning off my cell phone at night just in case he calls. I'm not good at dealing with these things!" Happy said.

"Happy, you're the bravest person I know!" Apple protested.

"Not when it comes to relationships. I'd rather he dump me than me have to dump him. I usually leave guys, but Zen is too, well, he's just too sweet," Happy moaned.

"Well, if you keep ignoring him, I have a feeling you're going to push him away," Apple said. She hadn't told Happy that Zen had stopped by, most likely to talk about the way Happy was acting.

"Good!" Happy said, smiling brightly for the first time since Apple had arrived.

"Really? Can you imagine life without Zen? Take a second and imagine what your life would be without him calling or taking you out. Does that thought make you feel better?" Apple pressed.

"Actually, Apple, it gives me a great sense of relief," Happy answered. "Then I can really be out with Therapy Guy."

"Poor Zen," Apple sighed.

"Poor Zen? Poor me! You're supposed to be on my side."

"I am on your side. It's just that, you know, it's Zen. He's so nice and sweet, like you said."

"And that's why this is so hard. He's too nice and sweet for me. I need a little drama. Zen is much more suited for you," Happy said. "He always was. Even now, he's always saying how in awe he is of your sensible nature."

"You are such a typical woman," Apple laughed. "At least that's what my mother would tell you. You need a bad boy. And sensible? God, that's not a compliment at all! You're making me sound like an old lady!"

"Sorry. But speaking of old, I'm not! I'm young! I should be having fun. Zen was fun. But now he's not fun. At least not for me. Like I said, you two are so much better suited for each other," Happy said, smiling slyly at Apple.

"Happy, you are not trying to fix me up with your boyfriend, are you?"

Happy lifted her eyebrows, smiling.

"You mean, my soon-to-be-ex-boyfriend? Well, you liked him. You loved him! Don't you have any feelings left for him?" Happy asked.

Apple was starting to feel very uncomfortable.

"I don't think that's how it works. You can't force people to be together. And, hello? There's Lyon, in case you forgot," Apple answered.

"Right. Lyon," Happy said, sipping her ice tea.

Just then, Happy's iPhone started to vibrate on the table. She looked at the text message and showed it to Apple. It was Zen, asking where Happy was. Happy placed the phone back on the table.

"You're not going to respond?" Apple asked.

"Nah. Don't feel like it," Happy said casually.

"You're so bad, Happy," Apple said, but she couldn't help but smile. She wished she could be as brave as Happy and just not do things she didn't feel like doing.

As if on cue, Apple's BlackBerry, also on the table, started to vibrate. She looked at it and read the text.

"Who is it?" Happy asked.

"You're not going to believe this," Apple told her. "It's Lyon. He just asked where I am and if I'm okay."

Apple placed her phone back down on the table.

"Aren't *you* going to respond?" Happy pressed, staring at Apple intensely with her green eyes.

"Nah. Don't feel like it," Apple said, imitating Happy.

Happy laughed. "See, I'm not the only one."

"No, you're right. You're not."

seventeen

Brooklyn raced in, looking like she had just finished a marathon.

"You have no idea how I had to get out of Mr. Kelly's class," she moaned. She called out to the waitress, "Can I have a large wheatgrass with some protein powder?"

"This is a coffee store, sweetie," the waitress responded sarcastically. "We serve coffee and tea."

"Okay, then I'll have a non-fat decaf soy latte with extra foam," Brooklyn ordered. "Mr. Kelly gave out a pop quiz today! What is up with that? I took one look at it and all I saw were numbers. Nothing made sense to me. I might as well have been trying to read another language."

"So how did you get out of it?" Happy asked.

"I put up my hand and said I had to go. Mr. Kelly looked at me like I was just trying to get out of the pop quiz."

"Which you were," laughed Happy.

"Well, yeah. I wanted to meet you guys! Why shouldn't I be allowed to take an 'emotional day' too?"

"So how *did* you get out?" Happy asked.

"I said, 'I'm really sorry, Mr. Kelly. I really have to go. It's an emergency.' Then he said, 'What's the emergency, Brooklyn?' So I wrapped my arms around my stomach and said it was personal. And he said if it's so important that I have to get out of a quiz, then I can tell him in front of the class what my emergency is."

"So?" Apple pressed.

"So I told him I had 'women's issues.' I told him I needed to go find a tampon immediately because I just got my period."

"Oh, my God!" laughed Apple. She tried to imagine Mr. Kelly, who somehow looked embarrassed all the time anyway, reacting to that.

"Well, it worked! I'm here. He just blushed and shooed me out of the room. Guys cannot handle the word 'period.' God, you should have seen his face when I said 'tampon.' Priceless. Anyway, what have I missed?"

Before they could answer, both Happy's and Apple's phones started to vibrate again. They looked at each other and laughed, while Brooklyn looked perplexed.

Apple looked at hers. It was from Lyon. Again. "I miss you," it read.

"Who was it from?" Happy asked Apple.

"Lyon, of course. He misses me. Yours?"

"Zen, of course. He wants to meet me tonight to talk," groaned Happy.

"What is going on with you two?" Brooklyn asked,

watching them put their gadgets back in their purses. "Aren't either of you going to respond to your boyfriends?"

"Nope!" they answered in unison. Apple looked at Brooklyn's shirt, which today read, "What is it you plan to do with your one wild and precious life?"

The T-shirt was so appropriate, thought Apple.

"Really, what is going on with you two?" Brooklyn demanded again.

"I'm hiding from Zen, plotting an exit strategy," said Happy.

"I'm hiding from Lyon, who is being annoying and overbearing."

"Enough of boy talk," Happy announced when the server brought over Brooklyn's coffee, thankfully in a takeaway cup. "Let's shop!"

So they did. Happy had the amazing ability to see something on a rack on the other side of a store and know instantly if it would fit or not. Two hours later, Apple felt fashionably satiated. Her mother was probably going to have a fit over how much money she had spent on her credit card. Apple already had planned her argument: *I needed the clothes for my job!* As her mother always said, if you look good on the outside, you'll feel better on the inside. Apple planned to throw that line back in her face too, if necessary.

She had called Hazel and asked her to pick her up and take her over to *Angst*, because Happy had made an emergency therapist appointment. Apple had a feeling it was because her new crush, Hot and Disturbed Guy, probably also had an appointment. Luckily, Apple was able to convince her aunt that she could take a break from wedding planning for twenty minutes.

"I'm coming by tonight with magazines. You're not getting out of it. You have to help me. You're my maid of honor, remember? And so far, you haven't done *nada* for me!" her aunt had griped as Apple got out of the car outside *Angst*.

"Okay, okay," Apple had mumbled. "We don't have enough time to get all the stuff you need to get done for a *wedding*."

"That's why I need your help! I want to become Mrs. Kelly, and I want to do it looking fabulous!" her aunt said dreamily.

"Okay, I can't listen to this. I'll see you later," Apple said, jumping out.

Not only had she arrived at *Angst* in a good mood, thanks to spending the day shopping with her friends, but Apple had arrived *early*.

"Hey, Emme," Apple said as she plopped her purse on the floor near her desk. She felt confident wearing one of her new outfits, a slim-fitting, simple black dress with a strap over one shoulder that had received "two thumbs up" from Happy when she tried it on. Happy's "two thumbs up" meant Apple looked really, *really* good.

"You're here early. What's up?" Emme asked.

"Just trying to show that I'm a good employee," Apple answered lightly.

"I love what you're wearing," Emme said. "Where did you get that?"

Apple couldn't believe it. It was the first nice thing Emme had ever said to her. It was the *most* Emme had ever said to her. Maybe Emme was being nice because she finally was dressed like she belonged at *Angst*.

"Thanks. I love your earrings," Apple responded. "I just bought it at one of my favorite boutiques." Apple didn't want to tell Emme the name. She didn't feel that generous.

Always compliment someone after they compliment you, Dr. Berg always advised.

"Well, here we are in the dungeon. Again. I wonder when we'll get to spend time, you know, above ground?" Emme said sarcastically.

There was no doubt about it. Emme *was* acting different. Could she possibly have a sense of humor too? Had Apple totally misjudged her?

"I thought you liked it down here. You seemed to be enjoying folding clothes for hours," Apple said carefully.

"Please! Do you think I signed up to work at the Gap? I don't think so. But I do know that I love *Angst*. I've always loved magazines. I didn't grow up with money. My family was quite poor. And I would save for weeks just to buy a *Vogue* magazine. All the other girls were buying clothes and shoes, but I was saving for *Vogue* and *Elle* and *W*. So for me to be here, even down here, is really a dream come true. I plan to work here forever. I want to be the editor someday, and if this is what I have to do to get there, I will."

"Wow," said Apple. Apple knew she lived a privileged life, as did most of her friends. She had no idea how to respond to Emme, who was suddenly being so open with her. Apple didn't need to, thankfully. Emme wasn't finished speaking.

"I'm sorry if I seemed harsh the first few days. I just really am serious about this job, and I guess I judged you, which wasn't fair." Emme sounded sincere. "I judged you because I didn't think you were going to take it seriously, or had to."

"That's okay," Apple said. "But if we're going to be stuck working beside each other in a room the size of an oven, we should probably try to get along. I'm not a bad person, I swear."

"Well, except for what you did to your best friend by trying to steal her boyfriend," laughed Emme, to Apple's horror. "Yes, I saw that episode of *Queen of Hearts*. It's still on YouTube. More than 100,000 people have viewed it, you know."

Apple was mortified. Would she ever live down what she had done?

"God, let's just say I was a different person back then. Trust me, everything has changed," Apple said.

Apple wondered what had gotten into Emme. Why was she suddenly being so nice to her? It didn't matter. Apple *didn't mind* the new Emme. Though she wasn't convinced they would be friends, this was at least better than having Emme not talk to her and shoot her dirty looks for hours. And what did she really know about meeting new people? Maybe this was how all friend-ships started. Come to think of it, Emme was the first new person Apple had met for years who had a pos-sibility of becoming a friend.

♡

Michael suddenly appeared. He looked handsome, as always, in a three-piece gray suit and a pink tie, his hair perfectly slicked back.

"Okay, you two. Today is going to be your first foray into the real world of *Angst* magazine. It's production day. No one will have time to eat. You will not have time to go to the bathroom. Whatever anyone asks you to do, you will do. Capiche?" he asked, clapping his hands twice.

"Do you mean we're—" started Emme. Apple knew she was about to ask if they were going to get out of the dungeon today.

"No time for questions. Apple, your advice column? Need it now!" Michael said sternly, but with a smile.

Apple scrambled in her bag and handed him the piece of paper. She told him she had also e-mailed him a version. Michael grabbed the piece of paper from her hands. "Great. Now, Apple, we need to get your 'head furniture' done. We need it, like, yesterday!"

"What?" Apple asked.

"Your 'head furniture.' The photo of you that goes on the top of your advice column? That's called head furniture," Michael said. Then added, "It's so cute when our new interns learn the language of the business."

"Head furniture? That's cute?" Apple said.

"No, we don't do cute here at *Angst*. Which is why I need you to go see Celia in cosmetics so she can do something with your hair and makeup."

"My hair?" Apple asked, putting a hand to her head.

"Yes, your hair. Don't get me wrong—I like your hair. But I think you need a bit of a makeover. Celia is the best. In her hands, you'll walk out feeling and looking like a model. Don't look so scared, dear. She's the best!" Michael repeated.

"Are you talking about Celia DeFenoyl? *The* Celia Defenoyl, from New York?" Emme asked eagerly.

"Good for you, Emme. That's exactly who I'm talking about," Michael said, grabbing a piece of licorice from a bowl on Emme's desk. "Keep me away from this. I'm not supposed to be eating sweets. If I have one piece, I won't be able to stop."

"Oh, my God, Apple," Emme said. "She's done everyone from J.Lo to Natalie Portman to Jessica Simpson. Damn, you are so lucky."

"Go now!" Michael demanded. "And, Emme, don't worry. I have a something just as cool for you to work on. I need you to organize all those clothes over there by shade and color."

He gave Emme a sympathetic smile.

Poor Emme, Apple thought. She felt awful that Emme was stuck folding clothes while she was going to get a makeover and "head furniture" for her own column. She felt especially guilty now she knew that working at *Angst* really was Emme's dream job, and that she was willing to do anything to work her way up to the very top. She could see why Emme had been annoyed with her from the start. Here Apple was, being treated like someone special, and Emme was folding clothes. If their positions were reversed, thought Apple, she'd be annoyed too.

Apple followed Michael into the hair-and-makeup room and stood at the door for what seemed like ten minutes before anyone noticed her. Michael had said he had a "million things to attend to" but had asked Apple if she'd like him to stick around. Apple had told him she could handle it herself. But now she wasn't sure what she was supposed to be doing.

"Yes? What is it? Why do you stand there like a statue and not say anything?" a blond pixie asked. "I see you standing there. I wait for you to say something, but you say nothing. So what is it you want?"

"I'm Apple. I'm supposed to get ready for my head furnishing or something. Michael told me to come here," Apple answered nervously.

"Oh, yes, yes. Apple. The advice columnist extraordinaire."

"Well, I'm not sure about that," Apple said modestly.

"To work in this business, you must think you are the best. You must act like you are the best, even if you know it not to be true. You must have others believe it to be true. Take a seat over there. You have a lot of hair. Gorgeous. But I have a brilliant idea for that hair," Celia said, staring at Apple like she was a science project.

Apple gulped. Her hair was the one thing that had always made her feel safe. She used it to hide her face. Everyone always complimented her on her hair. Sloan Starr had complimented her on her hair! What could Celia's brilliant idea be?

"We will straighten it!" she said.

"Oh, my friend Happy has straightened it before," Apple said, letting out a sigh of relief. "With her straightening iron. It took forever."

"Not like this. I have this new product that will straighten your hair for months. It will make it silky smooth. You will not even remember that you once had curly hair. It will be so much easier to take care of. It will bring out your cheekbones and your lips. You will be able to do so much more with it. What do you think?" Celia asked, in a tone that said she didn't really care what she thought.

Was she ready to straighten her hair for months? Did she have the choice to say no? As she was debating, Fancy Nancy walked into the room.

"Celia!" she said, with a bright smile.

"Nancy!" Celia replied, with the same warmth.

They gave each other a peck on both cheeks.

"I see you are working on Apple for her photo shoot today. I overheard you say something about straightening her hair with that new product. That's from Italy, yes?"

"Yes. Exactly. It's all the rage there," Celia said. "People fly from all over the world to buy it! They won't even ship it. You have to know exactly the right people."

"Brilliant," said Fancy Nancy.

How could she say no to Fancy Nancy—or Celia, who clearly had already made up her mind?

"Let's do it!" Apple said, trying to sound excited, like Celia and Fancy Nancy. Maybe she *should* be excited. After all, both Celia, makeup artist and hairdresser to the stars, and Fancy Nancy thought it was a "brilliant" idea.

"It will take a couple of hours," Celia said.

"Good thing you came in early today," said Nancy. "And good for you for taking risks. We like people at *Angst* who take risks."

With that, she left the room and Celia got to work, washing Apple's hair first, then massaging in awful-smelling chemical lotion, and finally, putting a plastic shower cap over her hair.

At least, Apple thought, no matter how badly this turned out, she could tell people that she got her hair done by the same person who does J.Lo and other celebrities. Apple regretted not cutting at least one of her boings off, as a memory. She felt like she imagined a six-year-old must losing her first tooth.

Happy called while Apple was sitting under a hair dryer, holding a scarf over her nose and hoping that she wasn't inhaling too much of the chemical product, the scent of which was making her nauseous.

"What are you doing?" Happy asked.

"I've been sitting under a dryer for, like, six months now. My hair is getting straightened. I think I've lost half my brain cells smelling all the chemicals," Apple whispered.

"Straightened?" Happy asked.

"Oh, yes. Apparently with this new product from *Italy* I won't have curly hair for months!"

"Months? Are you serious?" Happy asked. "But I love your hair. Are you sure about this? I love your hair exactly the way it is."

"Stop saying that. It's too late. I'm freaked out enough. I think I may cry. I couldn't say no. They weren't going to listen to me," Apple moaned. "And it happened so fast!"

"I'm sure it will turn out fine. And, hey, it's only a couple of months, right?" Happy said supportively.

"I guess," Apple responded despondently. Though she had always complained about her hair, Apple knew there was nothing worse than a bad haircut.

"I have something else you can't say no to," Happy said.

"What?" Apple asked.

"Remember how Zen texted me and wanted to meet tonight 'to talk'? I told him that I was hanging out with you at *Angst* today and couldn't meet him until later. He said that was cool. But the thing is, I don't *want* to meet him. Please, Apple, please? He'll be out front at around ten. Just get in the car with him and tell him I suddenly got sick and left early," Happy begged. "I'm hoping to hook up with Therapy Boy."

"You can't be serious, Happy! You're going to have to face him one of these days. What am I going to do with him?" Apple asked.

"Do whatever you want! I know I have to see him and have 'the talk.' Just not today. I can't. I just can't. Please do this for me."

"But what am I going to say to him?" Apple whispered. She didn't think anyone at *Angst* would appreciate her talking about anything that wasn't work-related. And she couldn't believe she was going to cover for Happy, who was meeting up with another guy!

"I don't care what you say really. Say I wasn't feeling well. Please just go for me," Happy begged.

Happy continued to plead, but Celia had finally come back to fetch Apple.

She pointed at Apple's ear. "Off! Now! We have twenty minutes to get you to the photo studio."

"Happy, I have to go," Apple said frantically.

"So you'll do it?" Happy asked.

"Yes, yes. Fine. I'll do it. Got to run!" Apple said, hanging up on Happy, who was in the middle of saying thank—

Everyone today, it seemed, was forcing Apple into doing things she wasn't entirely comfortable with. No one would let her say no. Why did Apple feel that she was letting everyone walk over her?

eighteen

N o one let Apple look in the mirror as they did her makeup and finished drying her hair. She had two people brushing out her hair and two others working on her makeup, while her back faced the mirror.

"Please let me look!" she begged over and over.

"No," was always the answer. Did she look awful? It was certainly taking a long time. Apple wondered if this was because she was "real." Perhaps people who were really meant to be in the pages of *Angst* didn't need so much time and effort put into making them look good.

"Can you please, then, just tell me what you think? You're killing me here! I can't take it!" Apple went to run her hand through her now straight and smooth-as-a-baby's-skin hair, but Celia swatted it away. "Patience, my dear. Beauty is all about patience. I say you are going to wish you were born with hair like this."

"Are you guys ready? We go to print in three hours.

We need her photo taken pronto!" Michael said walking in. "Where is she?"

"Michael? It's me!" Apple said.

"Apple?" Michael said, hopping back. "Be still my heart!"

"They made me!" Apple said.

"You look . . . you look stunning. You look . . . well, you look like a model. Celia, again, I bow to you! Will you take her to the studio in five? Apple, I feel like crying, you look so beautiful."

He reached out and held on to her hand, like he was a proud older brother. Apple suddenly felt calmer. She instinctively trusted Michael's opinion, like she trusted Guy's opinion on clothes and makeup.

"No problem," said Celia. She seemed very proud of herself.

"Can I look now?" Apple begged after Michael left.

"Yes," Celia said, spinning her chair around so Apple faced the mirror.

Apple couldn't believe what—rather, who—she was looking at. Her once shoulder-length boingy, curly hair was now so long and straight it reached halfway down her back. And Celia was right. Apple had cheekbones, and her eyes looked bigger and wider! Even Apple, who rarely thought she looked good, thought she looked . . . stunning!

Apple was so impressed with the result she jumped up and hugged Celia and the other makeup artists. "I love it. I love it!" Apple screeched.

"Celia does not make mistakes. Please, you have makeup on," she said, pulling away from Apple's embrace.

"But I'm glad you're glad. You look like a movie star now, yes? And that's what we always aspire to here at *Angst*. Follow me."

It soon became clear that although at present she may have looked like a movie star, she definitely didn't know how to act like one.

The cranky photographer apparently was not used to working with novices.

"Smile! No, not like that. You're smirking! Okay, smile! Not so much teeth! More serious!" he demanded over and over, as Apple sat.

She wanted to yell, "I'm not smirking! This is how I smile!"

"How big is this photograph going to be?" she asked Michael, who came to check in at one point.

"About the size of a postage stamp," Michael answered. "Maybe a bit larger. We'll see."

"All this for a tiny photo?" she wondered aloud.

"Oh, you'd be surprised, Apple. Our readers see the most minuscule detail. We get thousands of letters and rarely do any of them have to do with the stories—more like, 'Why are her roots showing?' and 'Where can I get that writer's glasses?' The head furniture also makes you stand out, makes readers know that you are somebody important. And we might use some of the photos for advertising purposes—we'll see," he answered casually.

"Really? Am I that important?" Apple asked.

"You are now. I read your first draft. I did a little editing. Nancy did a little editing. For your first attempt, it wasn't bad. Not bad at all. Congratulations! Next Monday the first issue featuring Apple'sAngst will be on stands and on doorsteps everywhere. Excited?" Michael asked.

"Nervous," Apple said. She felt comfortable telling Michael the truth. She realized that she had been spending more time with Michael these days than with her own family. He was starting to feel like family.

"Well, you've had a long day. You can go now. Don't forget to start practicing for your *Angst TV* spot. Basically, you're going to read a letter and you'll answer it. You're going to have to speak on your toes, but I'm sure you've learned a hell of a lot from your mother, right?" Michael asked.

Apple couldn't help but lie. "Yup."

"Is Emme still here?" Apple asked, finding herself caring about her colleague.

"I told her to go too," Michael said. "She spends so much time here! Have a good night, sweetie."

Apple smiled at Michael as she left. She ran into Emme as she was walking out of the building.

Although Emme had been nice, friendly even, to Apple earlier that day, Apple was worried she'd say something nasty about her new hair and how she looked wearing professional makeup.

"Apple?" Emme asked.

"You like?" Apple asked, jokingly shaking her now long, straight hair side to side.

"Do I like? You look gorgeous," Emme sighed.

"Come on!" Apple responded modestly.

"No, seriously. You look absolutely fantastic. Your hair is so awesome. You should straighten it more often. It looks so thick and luxurious and long. People pay tons of money to get hair extensions to look like the hair you now have," Emme said. Then she asked softly, "Can I feel it?"

"Sure," Apple said.

Emme ran her manicured hand over Apple's new hair. Apple didn't mind at all.

"Hey, you want to go out for a drink? You look old enough with all that makeup on. I don't think we'd have a problem. And I've never had a problem," Emme said with a wink.

Apple looked out the window to see Zen's white pickup truck pulling up.

"Emme, I would love to. I mean it. It's just that I've made previous plans," Apple said. She was annoyed that she had to meet Zen on Happy's behalf. She could have gone out with Emme and gotten to know her better.

"Is that your boyfriend?" Emme asked curiously.

"No! He's just a friend. His name is Zen. He's great. I do have a boyfriend. His name is Lyon. I'd love for you to meet him. Maybe we can all hang out some- time," Apple suggested. She didn't want Emme's offer to go out tonight to be a one-time occurrence.

"Sure. He looks super cute. Oh, my God, he is cute," Emme said, as Zen drove up in front of them.

"That's what everyone says at school," Apple told Emme.

"Is he single?"

"Not exactly," Apple said.

"What do you mean?" Emme pressed.

"Well, he's kind of going out with my best friend Happy," Apple answered.

"He's the one you two were fighting over?" Emme said, looking at Apple with wide eyes.

"Well, it wasn't really a fight. He chose Happy, not me," Apple said quietly. "Let me introduce you."

Emme looked at her strangely but followed her to the truck. Zen opened his window.

"Hey, Zen. This is my colleague Emme," Apple said, trying to sound chipper.

Zen looked confused. Why wouldn't he? He wasn't expecting Emme, or even Apple, for that matter. He was expecting his girlfriend, Happy.

Zen played it cool, though, even after Apple tried casually to mention that Happy wasn't going to meet him after all. Emme shot Apple a questioning glance, but there was no way Apple could explain all this to her.

Then Zen really looked at Apple. His jaw, literally, dropped.

"Jesus, you look different, Apple!" Zen said.

"Different good? Different bad?" she asked, suddenly feeling very insecure.

"Different hot," Zen said.

"See? I told you. I should go," Emme interrupted. "I don't want to ruin your evening."

"Do you need a ride?" asked the ever-thoughtful Zen.

"No, I'm good. See you, Apple. And it was nice to meet you, Zen."

"Have a good night, Emme," Apple said sincerely. "And definitely a raincheck on going out after work one day, okay?"

"Absolutely," responded Emme, before waving goodbye and walking back into the building.

Apple walked around and jumped into the passenger seat.

"So where is she?" Zen asked, obviously asking about Happy.

"She suddenly got a migraine and had to leave. She told me she'd call you later. She felt awful about it," Apple said. She hated lying to Zen, but Happy had begged her for this favor. She hated to think that Happy was out with another guy behind sweet Zen's back. And, worse, Apple was covering for her!

"Right. She is so trying to hide from me," Zen said, laughing.

"That's not true," Apple said weakly. "She really did feel sick."

"Right. Whatever. So now what? Are you hungry? Because I'm starving," Zen said.

Apple realized that she hadn't eaten anything since this morning, and even then she had only eaten a muffin.

"Actually, I'm starving too," Apple admitted.

"You want to go for a pizza?" Zen asked casually.

"I'd eat your left arm right now I'm so hungry," Apple replied.

"Okay, pizza it is," Zen said, driving off.

When they arrived at a casual, popular pizzeria, Zen pulled out Apple's chair so she could sit down. A number of students from Cactus High were there. She wondered if they would start talking about her and Zen having dinner together, alone. This could turn into a nightmare, thought Apple, if word got back to Lyon.

"Did you notice that everyone in here stared at you when you walked in?" Zen asked softly.

"No, they didn't," Apple protested, though in fact she had seen several eyes turn in her direction. For the first time in her life, she knew what it felt like to be Happy, who was always noticed wherever she went, even when she was dressed in sweats, which was rare but did happen on occasion. But were they staring at her because of her new look, or because she was with Zen?

"You look beautiful. Have I mentioned that?" Zen said.

"You're just saying that because you're weak from hunger," Apple joked.

"No, I'm not," he said. His voice sounded different. He was acting strange, Apple thought. Everyone was acting strange. First Emme had been nice to her, and now Zen was acting differently too. Apple was uncomfortable, so she launched into a description of her day at *Angst*.

She did not bring up Happy and neither did Zen. They laughed about the fact that Mr. Kelly was going to be a family member and how crazy her aunt has been over bridal magazines, and Apple confessed her mixed feelings toward Emme, who had seemed nice today but was too ambitious for Apple to be completely comfortable around.

"I can see why you would have to be careful around her," Zen said.

"What do you mean?" Apple asked.

"Well, you said that Emme didn't grow up with much, that she had to save for fashion magazines. We're very lucky. Sometimes we forget how lucky we are. I can see you just coming in, obviously from a fortunate background, and her being intimidated or jealous," Zen said, leaning back in his chair.

"Well, you saw her. She has nothing to be jealous about. She gorgeous. But you're absolutely right about the other things. Here I was thinking she was a royal bitch. She may have judged me, but I judged her too. I guess I can be a bitch too," laughed Apple.

Zen and Apple wiped their mouths at the same time.

"Also, I realized that all my friends I've known for years," said Apple. "Happy and Brooklyn have been my best friends since first grade. It's like I don't even know how to make new friends."

"Well, you should try."

"I think I'm going to," Apple said. "I'm stuffed."

"You look tired," Zen said, and signaled the waiter for the bill. When it arrived, he grabbed it before Apple could make a move. It weirded Apple out. Zen paying made it feel like a date. She furtively glanced around the room to see if anyone noticed. They didn't seem to.

"Is my face starting to fall off? I feel like I have ten pounds of makeup on," said Apple.

"Well, I prefer my women natural. You do look great, though. Let's get you home," he said.

They reached Zen's car and he went to unlock Apple's door. Suddenly, he grabbed her face and kissed her. Apple, shocked, pushed him away.

"Oh, God. I'm so sorry, Apple. I didn't mean it. It was an accident. I just got caught up in the moment," Zen said apologetically. He looked mortified. "Please forgive me. Let's pretend it didn't happen."

"No, wait," Apple said, placing a gentle hand on his arm. This time, she leaned in and kissed him. Then she tore herself away. What if someone saw them? Luckily, it didn't seem like anyone was around. She hopped into the car. Apple could not deny it. Kissing Zen was everything she imagined it would be. That is, what she *used to* imagine it would be.

Zen got in the car and pulled away. Apple was happy it was late and dark. She was sure her face was bright red. They didn't speak.

"Wait. Don't drive up to my house yet," Apple said.

"Okay," Zen said, pulling over down the street from her house.

She looked at him. He looked at her. They started kissing again.

"I don't want you to go," Zen whispered in her ear.

"I don't want to go either," she said. "But we shouldn't be doing this."

"I know," said Zen. "Let's never talk about this, okay? It will be our secret. It will never happen again."

"Good. Just as long as we're on the same page. This never happened!" repeated Apple.

"Right. But, Apple? You're a great kisser," Zen said.

"So are you, Zen. So are you," Apple said, getting out of the car, trying to find her breath. "But this *never* happened."

"Nope," said Zen, and they smiled.

Apple walked down the street to her home, grinning. She shouldn't be smiling. Still, her smile wouldn't go away.

nineteen

*a*pple blamed the chemicals it took to straighten her hair and the makeup and the fact she had barely eaten all day for her indiscretion with Zen. Before she had straight hair and a face full of makeup, she never would have cheated on her boyfriend—the boyfriend who had texted her three times and left two voicemail messages while she was making out with Zen. Not to mention that Zen was still dating Happy, even if Happy didn't want to be in the relationship any-more. Happy might be begging Apple to get together with Zen, but technically, they were still a couple. Apple's lips tingled as she walked up to her front door. What had she been thinking? The guilt started to set in, but before it could hit full force, her aunt opened the door from the inside, looking like a madwoman.

"Thanks a lot, Apple. You're, like, the worst maid of honor in history!" Crazy Aunt Hazel fumed.

"Oh, let it be," said Apple's mother, as Apple walked

past her aunt into the house. "She just got back from work and—OH, MY GOD! What did you do? What did you do?"

"What did I do?" Apple said, trying not to sound guilty.

Did her mother, who had the uncanny skill of knowing what was going on in people's minds, and who was such a great reader of people's faces, *know* that Apple had just fooled around with Zen? Was it possible the kiss was written all over Apple's face? Oh God, no, thought Apple.

"What do you mean 'What did you do'?" Apple asked, again gulping in fear.

"Your hair!" her mother said, her mouth agape.

After kissing Zen, her crush for years, she had completely forgotten about her new look.

"Oh, right! Celia, a hairdresser to the stars, did it," Apple said, relieved. "Do you like it?"

"I love it! Do you think she'll do my hair for my wedding?" Aunt Hazel asked, momentarily forgiving Apple for not being home earlier to help her pick out white wedding gowns or gloves or tiaras or whatever it was Apple was supposed to do tonight.

"No offense, but I don't think Celia does hair and makeup for brides," Apple said. She didn't mean for the words to come out snottily, but they did.

"Fine! Keep your hoity-toity hairdresser to yourself," her aunt huffed, running her fingers through Apple's hair. "Who knew your hair was so long? I want to look like you on my wedding day! It's not fair. I want good hair on my wedding day!" her aunt said, her voice starting to rise.

"I liked it better before," Dr. Berg said. "It was more you."

"That's just what I was thinking," Apple said.

Because what was not her, thought Apple, was kissing her best friend's boyfriend and cheating on her own.

"I have to go make a phone call," she announced.

"Apple! I swear to God, I'm going to kill you. You promised that you'd help me look through these magazines," Hazel moaned.

"But I really *have* to call Lyon. I haven't spoken to him all day. He's going to kill me! And I have to check in on Happy. I'll just be a few minutes, I promise," said Apple, racing upstairs to her room before her aunt could argue.

Apple shut her bedroom door and immediately dialed Lyon.

"Hey, you!" she said, trying to sound apologetic and sweet. She prayed her voice didn't give anything away.

"Hey! Where have you been?" Lyon asked.

"At work. You are going to be so shocked the next time you see me," Apple said.

"And when will I have the pleasure of that?" he asked. Apple thought he sounded snide. But who knew?

"Tomorrow night. For sure. Me and you, okay? I'm sorry I've been so busy. I'm trying to juggle this new job and my aunt's wedding and school and you, and I'm messing everything up," Apple moaned, feeling a rush of guilt. She needed to hear that he was still into her.

"No, you're not. You know I'm here for you. I just feel like I haven't seen you," Lyon said. Apple felt relieved. She was so lucky to have him.

"Tomorrow for sure, okay?" Apple said. "I miss you."

"I miss you, too, Apple," Lyon said, sounding tired.

"I miss you more," Apple said. Maybe she was going overboard, but she needed Lyon to know that she wasn't interested in Zen—or she needed to tell herself that—and that she was only interested in him. Zen and Apple's kissing had been a mistake. No one would ever find out about it. If no one knew, then it could just be forgotten about.

She hung up. She *did* miss Lyon, she realized, feeling a jolt of excitement at the thought of spending time with him tomorrow night. He was so patient with her. She looked at a photo tacked on her mirror of him and her hugging at the zoo. They had decided to go on the spur of the moment one weekend afternoon, before Apple started at *Angst*, before Zen and Apple kissed, before everything had become so confusing.

It was Lyon who made her happy. So what had made her kiss Zen? Sure, he may have kissed her first. Still, she could have stopped. But no. She had to keep it going. And let it happen again.

She was an awful person. But it would not happen again. Ever. Apple was sure that Zen wouldn't say anything to Happy. She got into bed, thinking happy thoughts about Lyon and how to make things better with him. Instead, much to her dismay, she dreamed of Zen. What was happening to Apple? She couldn't even manage to control her actions when she slept!

♥

At the Spiral Staircase Friday morning, Apple curled into Lyon's arms. Brooklyn was eating a power bar. Happy and Zen were both there too, though Happy was reading her fashion magazine and barely seemed to notice Zen giving her a shoulder massage. Apple didn't look at Zen. She couldn't, though she sometimes could feel his eyes on her.

"What's up for everyone tonight?" Brooklyn asked. "I need to have some fun."

"Lyon and I are going to try that new restaurant Eleven. *Angst* gave it a really good review," Apple said, holding on to Lyon's hand.

"They did?" Happy asked. "I didn't see that."

"It's in the next issue. I got a sneak peak at some of the pages the other day," Apple explained.

"You're so lucky to get to see *Angst* magazine before it comes out! I want to go to Eleven too. Can Zen and I come? We can have a double date," Happy said. Was Happy into Zen again? With Happy, you just never knew where her mind was from one minute to the next. Apple would be thrilled if Zen and Happy worked things out. It just seemed so much easier knowing that her best friend and Zen were into each other. It would make everything less complicated. Things could go back to normal. She had a knot in her stomach and she didn't like it, and she knew it had everything to do with having kissed Zen.

"Well," Apple answered slowly, "Lyon and I were planning on catching up. We haven't had a date night in a while." Apple knew she had to at least stick up for their night alone.

"Oh, Lyon, you don't mind, do you?" Happy said, batting her long eyelashes. "I want to go to Eleven. Don't you, Zen?"

"Sure," Zen said casually. "Why not?"

Apple had no idea what was going on. Was he suddenly into Happy again? Maybe their kiss had made Zen realize that he really did love Happy, just as the kiss had made Apple realize that she should try harder with Lyon.

"See. We all want to go, so why don't we all go together?" Happy said, making that sound like the only reasonable answer.

"Well, I only made a reservation for two," Lyon said. "It's new, so I'm not sure how easy it will be to change it to four."

"Five," Happy said. "Brooklyn has to come too!"

"I don't want to be a fifth wheel!" Brooklyn moaned. "I just wanted a fun night!"

"You're not going to be a fifth wheel. We'll all behave, I promise," Happy said. "And don't worry about changing the reservation. I think Sailor knows the manager or something. It won't be a problem. So we're all set, then," Happy said in a tone of finality.

Apple knew that Lyon wasn't going to be thrilled with the idea of this double date plus Brooklyn. She knew he was looking forward to a night alone. But there was nothing she could do. Happy was persistent, and she was Apple's best friend. There was no reason, really, that they shouldn't all go together. And after all, Lyon had wanted them to go on a double date just last week. He was getting what he asked for.

"Sure," Lyon said, knowing he had lost. "Let's do it—8 p.m. We'll meet you there."

"Great! I'm excited," said Happy, rubbing her hands together.

Apple glanced at Lyon with a look she hoped conveyed, "I'm really sorry. But what could I do?"

He rubbed her back. He understood that it wasn't her fault. If anything, Lyon was polite. He knew how important Apple's friends were to her.

Apple couldn't help but look up at Zen, who smiled down at her. Did he think this was a joke? They had just kissed the night before and now they were going out on a double date with their respective partners? It wasn't funny. It was sick.

Apple spent math class wondering what she was going to wear to Eleven. She wasn't sure who exactly she was imagining dressing for: Lyon or Zen.

Lyon, definitely. Or maybe just herself.

"Thanks, Apple, for letting us tag along tonight. I can't stand to be alone with Zen. Did he say anything to you last night?" Happy asked as they walked to their next class.

"Not really. We went for pizza because I was starving and then he just dropped me off at home," Apple said.

"Good! Thanks, Apple. And tonight will be fun! It's always easier when there are more people around. So he didn't mention me at all?" Happy wondered again.

"No, except to say that he *knows* you're hiding from him. Happy, I think you should put him out of his misery already," Apple said. "I mean, you are acting like you're still into him and really you're not. Or if you are into him, then be nice!"

"No, I know. I don't know if I'm not into him. So I should end it. I will. Soon. I promise. He's just such a nice guy. It's hard. I don't want to hurt his feelings," Happy moaned.

"Seriously, I don't even care if you hurt his feelings at this point. Well, I do, but the guy has no idea where he stands with you. And he's going to get tired and he's going to ditch you," Apple said.

"Great! Then I won't have to feel guilty!" Happy said cheerfully.

"Why do you want to go on a double date, then?" Apple asked.

"I don't know. I just really want to go to Eleven and hang with you," Happy said.

"Sometimes, I wish I could think like you," said Apple, shaking her head.

"Well, at least you're starting to dress like me! God, Apple. I think this is the very first time I've ever asked, but I may need to borrow that outfit. When did you get so fashion-conscious? I think I like the new version of Apple!"

Oh, God, if only Happy knew what Apple had done the night before. Apple was pretty sure that Happy wouldn't like the "new" Apple one little bit.

Apple certainly didn't like the new Apple at all.

twenty

$\mathcal{L}$yon and Apple drove to Eleven, arriving fifteen minutes early. The host showed them to their table for five. Sailor's best friend's father was a part owner of the restaurant and had pulled strings.

Lyon sat beside Apple and inhaled her neck. "You smell amazing, did I tell you that?"

"No, actually, you didn't," Apple said, flirtily.

"And you look amazing," Lyon continued.

Apple was wearing another of her new ensembles. Her mother and Happy were right. All those years she had spent in plain jeans? What a waste! It was so much more fun to dress up. As the stylist at *Angst* had said, "Always dress more up than down."

Tonight Apple was wearing skintight pink jeans, heels, and a low-cut, tight black tank top. Usually she would never be brave enough to show so much cleavage (not that she had much to show), but with her new hair, she really did feel like a new person.

"You look pretty hot yourself, mister," Apple said, leaning into him.

Brooklyn, Happy, and Zen arrived. Happy and Brooklyn took their seats after giving Apple and Lyon welcoming kisses on the cheek. Zen picked up his menu immediately and didn't look at Apple.

"Isn't it nice that we're all here together?" Happy sighed. As always, she looked amazing. "Apple, you look great."

"You really do look so different," Brooklyn said. "You look like you work at a fashion magazine now."

"So when does the first issue with you in it come out?" asked Zen. Apple was relieved. She didn't want to talk about her hair any longer.

"Monday," answered Apple. "I'm really nervous."

"Are you crazy?" Happy asked. "You're going to be a star! You're going to become just as famous as your mother. I have a feeling. And you know I'm always right about these things."

"Just don't forget us little people. You'll be like, 'Lyon? I used to know a Lyon, I think,'" Lyon joked, grabbing a breadstick from the wire basket in the middle of the table.

Apple laughed. "I will never turn into my mother, trust me," she said, giving Lyon a sideways hug. She couldn't help but look up and see Zen glance at her. He didn't look happy. But what did he expect? thought Apple. Sure they had kissed, but Zen knew that Lyon was her boyfriend.

"I have to go to the restroom," Happy said, suddenly getting up. "Anyone else need to go?"

Everyone shook their heads.

"Apple? Are you SURE you don't have to go?" Happy pressed.

Apple knew that was code. Happy had to tell her something in private.

"Actually, I do have to visit the ladies' room," Apple said, standing up.

Apple followed Happy to the restrooms, downstairs at the back of the restaurant. She held on to the handrails for dear life. The stairs were so skinny and she still wasn't exactly confident walking in heels.

Once inside, Happy walked over to the sink.

"Don't you have to pee?" Apple asked.

"Of course not. Do you?"

"No," Apple laughed. "So what's up?

"It worked! Zen said to me when he picked me up that he didn't think things were working out with us. He asked me if I felt the same," Happy said giddily.

"And what did you say?" Apple asked, feeling a knot grow in her stomach.

"I told him I hadn't really noticed," Happy said.

"Happy!"

"Well, I didn't want him to think that this was my idea! Am I awful?" Happy asked.

"No, you're not awful. You're just . . . you. So what did he say?" Apple asked.

"He said we should both really think if we are meant to be together. So I said that sounded like a good idea. Then we agreed to take break from each other," Happy continued.

"So you guys broke up?" Apple said, her heart beating quickly.

"Well, we're taking a break. I figure after we take this break, I'll tell him that he's right, that we're better off alone. It will ease my guilt about Therapy Guy," Happy said.

"Did he say anything else?" Apple pressed, praying that Zen didn't mention their kiss.

"Not really. We picked up Brooklyn, so we stopped talking about it," Happy said. Apple felt relieved.

"We should really get back up there," said Apple. "I guess, 'Congratulations'?"

"I know. I'm so glad we're all out tonight. This 'break' is the start of my freedom!"

They walked up the stairs slowly. "Oh, my God, Apple. I'm so rude. I never asked you how it's going with Lyon. It seems to be going well. You don't seem as annoyed with him."

"It is going well," Apple said.

"What's wrong? Something must be wrong. You don't sound very excited. Are you still fighting?" Happy asked.

"No. It's fine. He's perfect, what can I say?" said Apple.

"No guy is perfect," Happy responded. "I'm sorry, but there must be something wrong with Lyon."

Yeah, thought Apple, he's not Zen. She immediately shook her head. Even thinking that was insane and insulting.

When they got back to the table, their friends were in a heated discussion. Apple forced herself not to look at Zen.

"He's just a foolie," Brooklyn was saying as Apple and Happy sat down and placed their white linen napkins on their laps.

"A what?" asked Lyon.

"A foolie," repeated Brooklyn.

"You don't know what a foolie is?" Zen asked.

"What are you guys talking about?" Happy interrupted. "Hopper again?"

"Yes. I'm trying to explain to Zen and Lyon that Hopper and I are foolie friends. Of course they don't get it. Because Zen and Lyon are aliens. They're too nice."

"I know what a foolie is," Zen said.

"I don't," said Lyon.

"Do you live under a rock? How could you NOT know what a foolie is?" demanded Happy. "How could you have lived your whole life without a foolie friend?"

"Hey, leave him alone," said Apple, sticking up for Lyon. "Why should everyone know what a foolie is?"

"Can someone please just tell me what a foolie is already?" Lyon asked.

"Okay," Brooklyn said. "It's like having a friend with benefits. He is definitely not my boyfriend. I am definitely not his girlfriend. He can go out with whomever he likes, do whatever he likes with them, and I can do the same. And occasionally—like once a week or so—he calls me or I call him, and if neither of us has plans we'll get together and fool around."

"And you don't mind that Hopper is just a foolie friend?" Lyon asked, looking intrigued.

"No, actually. I mean I like the guy. I'm attracted to him. But I don't really feel that people are meant to mate for life. I don't believe monogamy is normal," Brooklyn said.

Brooklyn launched into her Monogamy Speech, which Apple and Happy had heard a zillion times. She said animals—and people were animals—were never meant to be monogamous, and that it's in our DNA to want to fool around with as many people as possible.

"My parents, for example, cheated on each other," Brooklyn said. "Now they're divorced. If you ask me, it makes perfect sense. Fifty percent of the population gets divorced, and I'm sure most of those divorces are a result of someone being unfaithful. So why get married in the first place? Why pretend to be something you're not? Why not have foolie friends instead?"

Apple looked down at her menu. At the words "cheated" and "unfaithful" she suddenly got a knot in her stomach. And she *knew* Brooklyn wasn't being entirely truthful. She knew Brooklyn was always waiting for Hopper and was disappointed when he didn't call. She knew Brooklyn wanted more from Hopper, no matter what she professed.

"Are you feeling okay, Apple?" Lyon asked, looking at her. "You look a little pale suddenly."

♡

"I think I just need to splash some water on my face or something," Apple said. "Just order for me. I'll be right back."

As Apple headed back to the restroom, she heard Happy say, "Oh, I'm not sure Apple really gets the concept of foolie friends either. She's never had one! Her mother is old-fashioned Dr. Bee Bee Berg, after all, who believes marriage is the be-all and end-all. Even if she did have one, I'm not sure she'd tell me. Apple never likes to talk about sex. When we were seven I used to say the word 'vagina' to her just to see her blush." Happy laughed.

Apple walked into the restroom and leaned against a stall door. She still didn't need to go. She just needed to catch her breath. She looked at her watch. A minute and a half had passed. If she didn't go up soon, someone would surely come down to get her.

She opened the restroom door—only to see Zen standing there.

"What are you doing here?" she asked. "You scared me!"

"I had to go to the restroom," he said, smiling.

"Well, I should really go back up," she said, trying to walk around him. Her arm brushed his and she couldn't help but look at him. It was always his dimples that killed her. Apple grabbed the back of his head and pulled him in for a kiss. Or was it Zen who pulled *her* in?

It felt so wrong, but so exciting, but still so, so very wrong.

Even when Apple tried to pull away, he kissed her harder. "God, Apple," he moaned. "What are we doing?"

"I don't know. I do know that we have to stop this right now," Apple said, pushing him away.

"We do?" Zen said.

"Well, if you haven't forgotten, our friends are upstairs. My boyfriend is upstairs. Happy is upstairs. This didn't happen," said Apple. "Again. this did not happen."

"I can't stop thinking about you," Zen said.

"We can't talk about this now," Apple said frantically. "I'm going to go up first. Count to sixty and then come up, okay?"

"Okay," Zen said. "But tell me one thing, Apple."

"What?"

"Do you still think about me? Like the way you did before Happy and I got together?"

Apple looked at him with newfound confidence. "Of course I do. But I have a boyfriend," Apple said. "And you and Happy just broke up. Yes, she told me."

"I made a horrible mistake not paying attention to you," said Zen. "Is it too late for us?" he asked.

"It's so complicated already," Apple moaned. "I can't think straight."

"I know. I know. But a guy can have hope, right?" asked Zen.

"Can I ask you one thing?" Apple asked.

"Sure," Zen said, showing his dimples.

"Does it look like I've just been kissed by a guy who is not my boyfriend?"

"You look perfect," Zen said.

Apple raced back up the stairs.

"What took you so long?" Lyon asked.

"My stomach hurts," Apple said. Then she added, "Where's Zen?"

"He went to the washroom. I'm surprised you didn't run into him," Lyon responded. Their food had arrived, thank God. Apple didn't know how she was going to make it through this dinner, with Lyon beside her and Zen sitting across from her.

"Anyway, as I was saying, I am fine with being his foolie friend," Brooklyn was muttering.

"God, are we still on this?" Apple asked.

"Yes. Lyon doesn't quite understand why Brooklyn wouldn't want more from Hopper," Happy explained. "Anyway, we all know you do, Brooklyn."

"Fine. I like him. But I'm not getting any more from him than a foolie. And I think I'm okay with that. There are worse guys to have as foolie friends."

"That's for sure," Happy said. "Hopper is so hot. He's a jerk, but he's yummy."

"Amen to that," Apple said.

"What do you mean by that?" Lyon asked. "I can't believe this is how you girls talk about guys!"

"Lyon, you're just as hot, if not hotter. Don't worry," Apple said just as Zen sat down at the table. He looked much happier. Even Happy noticed.

"Well, you seem like you're in a much better mood," she said, somewhat snidely.

"I am," Zen said, picking up his water glass. "Let's toast to, um, foolie friends!"

"I'll second that!" Happy said. She would never let Zen get the better of her.

"I just think you deserve better, Brooklyn," Lyon said.

"Maybe. But right now I'm happy. And that's all that matters. So thanks, Zen, for your toast. To foolie friends!" said Brooklyn.

Apple had the strange feeling Zen was toasting her.

twenty-one

They were just about to leave when Apple heard her name being called from the busy bar area at the front of the restaurant.

"Apple! Apple!"

"Who is that?" Happy asked, after taking a glance at the person whose voice was calling out for Apple. "She's disgusting pretty," Happy added.

Apple extended her neck, trying to look around her friends.

"Oh, my God. That's Emme! The girl I work with at *Angst*!" Apple said, looking over Happy's shoulder and waving at Emme.

"The bitch?" Happy asked. "That's Emme?"

"Well, she's acting a bit better lately. She was actually nice to me the other day. It's like she was a new person," Apple said.

"Be careful of her," Happy told Apple. "You're so naive sometimes, Apple. You know the saying—'Keep your friends close and your enemies closer.'" Happy asked.

"What are you saying? That's she's suddenly being nice to me because she sees me as her competition?" Apple asked.

"Yup," responded Happy.

"I don't know. Maybe she was just shy at first. You don't know her. I barely know her," said Apple.

"Just watch your back, that's all I'm saying," Happy advised.

Emme waved Apple over. Happy, Brooklyn, Zen, and Lyon followed.

Emme gave Apple a kiss on both cheeks, just as Fancy Nancy had done with Celia. This two-sided cheek kiss obviously was contagious.

"Emme," Apple began, making the introductions. "These are my best friends, Happy and Brooklyn. And you remember Zen from when he picked me up."

"Of course," Emme said, also giving Zen a two-pecked cheek kiss. Zen look awkward, as if he wasn't used to such sophistication. Happy either didn't care that a beautiful girl was being friendly, even flirty, with Zen or was too busy checking out the rest of the guys at the bar and didn't notice. She wasn't even doing a very good job of hiding the fact she was looking around.

"And this," said Apple, pulling Lyon close, "is my boyfriend, Lyon."

"It's nice to meet you," Emme said politely, giving him a peck on the cheek. When Lyon turned away momentarily, Emme gave Apple the thumbs-up sign and whispered, "He's cute!"

"Come join us," Emme said. "I have a table over there with a couple friends. We're drinking sangria. The food tastes like crap, but they make one killer sangria."

"I'm in," Happy said. Apple could tell that Happy was "in" because she wanted to check out Emme, to see what she was really like, and also because she was always ready for an adventure.

"Me too," said Brooklyn. She had been checking her phone constantly all night. They all knew she was hoping for a foolie call or text from Hopper. Hanging out would be a good distraction.

"I don't know," said Lyon. "I have to get up early tomorrow."

"Me too," said Zen.

"Oh, don't be such downers! I want to get to know you, since I'm working so closely with your girlfriend," Emme said, giving Lyon a soft punch on the arm while winking at Zen. "We just finished our first issue. We need to celebrate, right, Apple?"

"You know what? We *should* celebrate!" Apple said. It hadn't hit her that they should be celebrating. Why not?

They all scrunched around a table. The waiter didn't even pause when Emme ordered another round of sangria.

Apple and her friends glanced furtively at each other. The waiter didn't even bat an eyelash when they ordered or ask for ID. It made Apple feel very grown-up. And adventurous.

"We are so breaking *so* many rules," said Apple to the table after taking her first sip. Emme was right. The sangria tasted delicious.

"What do you mean?" asked Lyon.

"You want to explain, Emme, or do you want me to?" Apple asked.

"I'll explain," said Emme, who was clearly already a little tipsy—in a good way. "Well, at *Angst*, we are supposed to represent the magazine at all times—24/7, we are supposed to be on our best behavior. We are not supposed to drink, party, or be seen with no underpants. It's like we're in a nunnery. Except we get to dress great! We so should not be drinking underage here, that's for sure!"

Lyon grabbed Apple's hand. His expression was disapproving. Apple pretended not to notice.

The waiter arrived back at the table and filled up everyone's glasses.

"Cheers to being bad," Emme said, raising her glass.

Apple took another small sip. What were the chances that Fancy Nancy or Michael or Celia or any of the employees at *Angst* would be at Eleven tonight? They worked seemingly nonstop. And the crowd was so young.

"And here's to foolies!" Brooklyn said.

"Hear! Hear!" shouted Emme. "I have two."

"Okay, so apparently everyone knows what a foolie is," Lyon laughed. "And what do you mean you have *two*?"

"I think every girl should have a friend with benefits," Emme said. "I have one who goes to my school and another who lives down the street."

"Doesn't that get confusing?" Lyon asked.

"No, not really. It's surprisingly easy," Emme answered nonchalantly.

"Do they know about each other?" Brooklyn asked.

No. Not because I think they'd care. Why is it okay for men to fool around, but when it comes to girls, people have a problem with it? People think that you're a slut—or that the guys are just using you and you're letting yourself be used—when really you're using them," Emme said. She sounded so sure of herself, which made her seem more sophisticated.

"Yes! Exactly," said Brooklyn. "That's what I've been trying to explain!"

Apple leaned over to Happy and whispered in her ear, "See? Emme's not so bad, right?"

"I'm just looking out for you. But you're right. She seems fun," Happy agreed.

It was after midnight when Lyon finally said, "I think we should get you home. I think you've had enough to drink, Apple."

"Ah, poo you," said Happy. "I want Apple to stay. It's Friday night! We're having fun."

"I'll stay with you," Emme said.

"Brooklyn? You in?" Happy asked. Brooklyn was busy texting.

"Wait . . . Nope going to catch a ride with Lyon, if that's okay. I need him to drop me off somewhere," Brooklyn said, beaming, waving her BlackBerry. Obviously, Hopper had texted her.

"Foolie friend!" Emme, Apple, and Happy screeched in unison.

"Okay, it's *definitely* time to get you home," Lyon said to Apple, grabbing her arm. "You're drunk."

"I am not!" Apple heard herself say in an overly loud voice. She laughed. "Am I screaming?"

"You barely ate anything at dinner," said Lyon.

"Well, I am watching what I eat," she heard herself say.

"You should see the models. They're so skinny," said Emme, nodding. Lyon shot Emme a look.

"Well, I'm out of here too," said Zen. Happy didn't even look at him as he left. He didn't look at Happy or Apple.

"Are you coming, Apple?" Lyon pressed, still holding on to her.

"You know, you go. I'm going to stay," Apple said, shaking off his arm.

"Yay!" Happy squealed. "I like the new Apple! She's fun!"

"I don't," Lyon said under his breath but just loud enough for Apple to hear. Apple shot him a look.

"I'll call you tomorrow," Lyon said to Apple, kissing her on the cheek like she was his great-aunt or grandmother. "But I really think you should call it a night soon. Be safe?"

"I will, party pooper," Apple said, and went back to talking to her girlfriends. She hadn't had this much fun in a long time. She deserved it. And really, she hadn't celebrated her gig at *Angst*. The party meant for her the day she got the job had turned into a party for her aunt's engagement. Plus she would do anything to forget Zen's and Lyon's disapproving stares. Right now, drinking and laughing with her new colleague and her oldest friend in the world was exactly what Apple wanted to be doing.

♡

On Monday morning, Apple's BlackBerry vibrated at her ear. She had left it on her pillow. She looked her clock and let out a groan. It was 6:50 a.m.

"I just saw you on a bus! You're on a bus!" her aunt Hazel screamed when Apple groaned out a "Hello?"

"You're on the whole side of a bus!" her aunt screamed again.

Apple shook herself awake. "What do you mean? What are you talking about?" Was Apple dreaming?

"I'm on my way to your house now and a bus drove by and there's a huge, massive photo of you. And under it, it says, 'Read Apple's Angst. Every Monday in *Angst* magazine'!" her aunt screeched.

"Oh, my God! They must have used a photo from my photo shoot! Do I look okay? Do I look fat? Should I be embarrassed?" Apple was suddenly wide awake and self-conscious.

"Are you kidding? You look unbelievable! I can't believe you're on the side of a bus! I'll be there shortly. I have the magazine with me! See you in five!" her aunt said, hanging up.

Apple jumped out of bed and raced downstairs. Her mother, of course, was already there, dressed in an off-white cashmere sweater and beige pants, with her string of pearls around her neck, ready to be the Queen of Hearts for the day.

"Why are you up?" her mother asked. "It's so early."

"Aunt Hazel called. Apparently I'm on the side of a bus!" Apple said airily, grabbing a mug and pouring herself a cup of coffee.

"What?" her mother asked.

"*Angst* magazine is advertising my advice column on buses! And Aunt Hazel said there was a huge photo of me," Apple said, sitting down across the table from her mother.

One second later, Aunt Hazel raced in, her hair as messy as Apple had ever seen it—and Apple had seen this a *lot*—armed with a copy of *Angst*.

"I'm here! I'm here!" she said, flipping through the magazine excitedly. "I haven't even looked at your column yet, Apple. I was so distracted after seeing your massive face on a bus that I had to force myself to pay attention to my driving. Oh, look! There's a photo of you on the front page at the top. It says 'Apple's Angst: Page 62.'"

Hazel proceeded to try to find the page. It was painful to watch, like watching a five-year-old attempt to tie her own shoelaces when she doesn't know how.

"Give it to me!" Apple said, trying to grab the magazine from her aunt's hand. "I want to see it first."

"Actually, I'm the one who brought it over, so I'm the one who gets to see first," Aunt Hazel whined, starting to walk away from Apple, guarding the magazine.

"That's ridiculous," Apple yelled, chasing her aunt. Hazel was running around the table, holding the magazine away from Apple, who was yelling, "Give it to me!"

"Grow up, Apple," her aunt yelled.

"*You* grow up!" Apple shot back.

"Enough!" Dr. Berg barked, pounding her mug on the table. "Hazel, bring the magazine to the table and we'll all sit down and look at it together. Like adults!"

Apple and Hazel sat down, like scolded children, and Hazel handed the magazine to Apple's mother.

"Page 62! Page 62!" her aunt screeched.

"God, calm down," Apple muttered. "And did you brush your teeth? I can smell your breath from here!"

Her aunt took the opportunity to blow air in Apple's face.

"God, Hazel! Gross!"

Her mother flipped to page 62 while Apple and her aunt watched over her shoulder. There it was: a huge photo of Apple with her professionally made-up face and her new straight hair. The photograph was so much larger than what Michael had said it would be. It was as big as a picture frame, not a postage stamp. Her photo filled one page, and on the facing page was Apple's advice.

"That doesn't even look like me!" Apple said in awe.

"Sure it does, honey," said Aunt Hazel. "It's just a better-looking you! It's the same photo I saw on the bus."

"I'm not sure if I should take that as a compliment or an insult," Apple said.

"Can you please explain this photo on a bus?" her mother asked.

Crazy Aunt Hazel explained about seeing Apple on the side of a bus that drove past her, then said, "Shhh. Let's all be quiet and read Apple's Angst."

They sat in silence reading the questions and Apple's advice, which Apple could already recite by heart.

"Is this question about me?" Hazel screamed after a moment.

"Why do you think *everything* is always about you?" Apple asked her aunt.

"Because it's ME! And it does sound vaguely familiar. I thought you learned your lesson about making up fake questions?" her aunt clucked.

"Hazel! Stop being such a narcissist. I don't even get to pick the questions. The editors tell me which ones to answer. Happy thought the first question was about her!" Apple said.

"Swear on your life?" her aunt pressed, looking at her suspiciously.

"Yes, I swear!" Apple said, crossing her heart with her finger.

Her aunt proceeded to read the second of Apple's questions out loud.

Dear Apple,

My best friend is getting married in three months. She's twenty-five years old and she says she's in love with the guy. They've been dating for only a month. I don't know how to tell her that I think it's way too soon. Every time I try to broach the subject she shuts me down and tells me I'm just jealous because I haven't found someone who wants to marry me. I'm not jealous. I'm worried. They barely know each other.

"And, sweetie, no offense," Dr. Berg said. "You aren't twenty-five."

"Shut up!" snapped Aunt Hazel. "I may not be twenty-five, but Jim thinks I look it!"

"And look what Apple's advice is!" her mother said meaningfully.

Her mother proceeded to read what Apple had written.

I, too, think it's a little quick for them to get married. Ask her if her future husband knows her bra size. If he doesn't, then they don't really know each other. But it sounds like your friend will be going ahead with the wedding. You can say your two cents and must leave it at that. That is, if you want to remain friends. Friends, after all, are there to be supportive. Tell her your concerns, but then be there for her.

"Does Jim know your bra size?" Apple asked, eyebrows raised, looking at her aunt.

Hazel suddenly looked worried. "No, he doesn't," she said, biting the inside of her cheek.

Her aunt got up from the table, pacing back and forth, biting her nails.

"Oh, come on, Hazel. It's an advice column for *teens*. That line about the bras was meant to be funny," Apple said, laughing. "Don't take it seriously."

"Although it is kind of true," muttered Dr. Berg.

"Okay, Bee Bee. We all know you think it's too soon for me to get married," Apple's aunt said tersely.

"That's not true!" her mother protested.

"Yes, it is," Apple said under her breath.

"Okay, it is. But that doesn't mean I'm not going to support you, Hazel, just as Apple said," her mother said, placing her hands on Hazel's shoulders.

Apple tuned out the conversation between her aunt

and her mother. She kept staring at her photograph and felt proud about being in *Angst* magazine.

Apple's BlackBerry kept announcing new messages. Everyone she knew—and some she hadn't seen or heard from in years—was sending her congratulatory messages, telling her how great she looked. There was one from Guy, who wrote, "Another star is born!"

Zen had texted, "Beauty and brains. When can I see you?"

It was too early to deal with Zen, thought Apple, though she had no idea when it would be a good time to deal with Zen. She now knew how Happy had felt, needing to hide from him.

twenty-two

*A*pple knew when she walked into school that morning that everyone was talking about her and looking at her differently. She could tell people were in awe. So many students had told her they saw her column and her photo on the bus that Apple had lost count. So this was what it was like to be known for something people admired, Apple thought. She hated herself for admitting it. But . . . she liked it. She felt taller. Every strand of her new long, straight hair, which was now so easy to run a brush through, seemed to be saying, "I'm a star."

Apple was wearing a short green dress Happy had convinced her to buy, with long gold chains hanging around her neck. She had never felt so confident in her life. The more people stared, the taller she stood.

Happy and Brooklyn had grabbed her arms as soon as she arrived and couldn't stop talking about how excited they were for her. Apple hadn't had a chance to even see Lyon. She wondered where he was and couldn't wait to hear his reaction.

Apple didn't look at Jim—Mr. Kelly—as she sat down beside Happy in class.

"Can you believe this, Happy?" Apple asked. "It's like everyone knows who I am now."

"It is quite unbelievable," Happy answered. "I'm proud of you. You're just going to become a bigger star when *Angst TV* starts. When is that?"

"It airs next week, but we start taping today! I can't believe I'm saying this, but I'm kind of excited," Apple said.

"You are? I thought you loathed going on television," Happy said. "I thought you were dreading it."

"I don't know. Maybe I was just being a brat about it. Now I'm excited," Apple admitted.

"You should be excited. People would die to be in your position," Happy said, in a tone Apple couldn't read.

Apple didn't think Happy sounded very proud. She sounded, Apple thought, kind of jealous. But Apple wasn't sure if that was it. Not once in their entire friendship had Happy ever had reason to be jealous of Apple.

"Pop quiz," Mr. Kelly announced.

The class moaned.

"We just had one last week," complained Hopper loudly.

"And you all did poorly on it—that is, those of you who decided to show up," Mr. Kelly said to the class.

Apple and Happy and Brooklyn glanced at each other, suppressing a smile.

The quiz was passed back from desk to desk.

Apple took one look at the questions and knew she was going to fail. She hadn't been keeping up with her schoolwork at all, what with *Angst* and hanging out with her friends. She had spent all day Saturday at *Angst*, organizing the shoe closet, and most of Sunday she had spent in bed, trying to catch up on sleep.

She glanced at Happy, who was already hard at work. No matter what was going on in Happy's life, she always got straight A's. Brooklyn, however, was spinning her pen in her fingers, not writing anything. Apple felt better knowing she wasn't going to be the only one who failed.

The clock ticked. Apple tried to concentrate on the quiz, but her mind was stuck on the fact that her photograph was all over town and that people in school were looking at her now as if she were famous.

"Time's up!" Mr. Kelly said. "Pass the papers forward."

Apple couldn't believe how quickly the time had gone.

She scribbled across the top of her quiz, "Sorry, Mr. Kelly. I have women's issues today and couldn't concentrate. Cramps!" If it worked for Brooklyn, maybe it would work for her. Plus, Mr. Kelly was going to be family. He should be understanding.

Apple didn't even feel that bad about it. She was excited to get to *Angst* and see what the reaction was to the first issue. Working at *Angst* was so much better than this whole school thing. It was certainly more fun than math class, or any of her other classes, for that matter. For the first time, like Brooklyn, she felt she had a higher purpose than school. She was also excited to see Emme.

At the end of the day, as Apple was racing out, Happy wished her luck. "I'm sure you'll do fine. In fact, you seem like you actually are a person who should be seen on television. You already seem like a new person."

♡

"Okay, Apple's up next!" Michael yelled out to no one in particular, though there were many people scurrying around. "Is she almost ready?"

"I'm almost finished with her," Celia, the makeup artist, called out to Michael. "Dear, your skin is nearly flawless. You're lucky to be young," she said, speaking to Apple. Apple wasn't used to being so pampered. The blush brush felt nice against her skin. "Of course, television does make you see flaws," Celia added, "but we shall make you beautiful and definitely flawless!"

They were at the *Angst TV* studio, down the lot from where the *Queen of Hearts with Dr. Bee Bee Berg* filmed.

Unlike her mother's show, *Angst TV* was taped. Everyone, including Apple, was nervous, but at least it wasn't live, thought Apple. They could do reshoots until they got the interviews perfect.

Already Apple had watched the host interview the writer of a famous series of teen books on vampires, a musician who just had a song land at number one on the charts, and Vicky Barlo, a socialite turned actress who had shown up with her dog and demanded four cans of lemonade, two for her and two for the dog. Apple was too shy to introduce herself to any of the celebrities—not that she could have even if she wanted to. All of them traveled with so many people. It was fascinating to see. Even the vampire writer had six publicists come with her to the taping. It was mayhem, but everyone seemed excited. And at least Apple could tell her friends she sat in the same makeup chair as Vicky Barlo and Chris Jons, the musician, whose songs Happy knew by heart.

"Apple? Apple?!" Apple suddenly heard her name being called out. No. God. No. It couldn't be, could it? It was. Apple would recognize that voice anywhere. She couldn't believe it. What was *her mother* doing here? How had Dr. Berg even gotten in?

"What are you doing here?" Apple hissed at her mother.

"Don't blink," said Celia as she applied mascara. "Look toward the ceiling."

"It's my daughter's first time on her own television show, and you think I wasn't going to be here to witness it?" Dr. Berg said, as if Apple had just asked her what one plus one was.

"First of all, it's not MY television show. I have a whole one minute to talk about an advice letter. That's it! One minute," Apple said, trying to keep her face still as she hissed at her mother.

"Honey, one minute in televisionland is the equivalent to one year in the real world. That's a whole sixty seconds where everyone out there is focusing only on you," her mother responded.

"Thanks, Mom. Are you trying to make me more nervous?" Apple asked.

Her mother ignored her and looked at Celia.

"Don't you think that's a little too much makeup?" Dr. Berg asked Celia. "She's only fifteen. We don't want to make her look older than she is, do we? I think she's pretty beautiful the way she is."

Apple couldn't believe her mother. Not only had she shown up uninvited, but now she was giving out makeup advice to Celia? Did she ever stop giving out advice to anyone about anything?

"Mom! My God. I've seen you get ready. You *cake* the makeup on before your show," Apple muttered.

"I need to," her mother said. "I'm not your age. And is that what you're going to be wearing?"

Why was her mother always so critical? She didn't like her hair. She didn't like what she was wearing. How could her mother think she was being supportive at all?

The saleslady who helped her had told her she looked fabulous. Happy thought her outfit, a tight bodysuit with a ballet-type skirt, looked fabulous too. Even Michael had said it was perfect, and she trusted Michael even more than she did Happy when it came to clothes now.

"Yes, it is," said Apple, shooting the makeup artist a look that she could hopefully read as "Help me!"

Thank God, Celia understood.

"You know, I'm not sure you should be here," Celia said to Dr. Berg. Apple couldn't believe it. No one had ever kicked Dr. Bee Bee Berg out of anywhere before. Apple closed her eyes. She didn't want to witness her mother's reaction.

"Of course I should. I'm her *mother*. I'm *Dr. Bee Bee Berg*! The Queen of Hearts!"

Celia continued to work on Apple's face.

Yes! thought Apple. She had found the one person who hadn't heard of her mother. Was it possible? She felt the urge to hug Celia.

"Well, I don't care whose mother you are. I don't care right now if you're the Queen of England. I can't concentrate with other people crowding me. And I really need to finish Apple's face. They need her in about two minutes," Celia said. "You had better just leave."

"Fine, then," her mother huffed. "I have my own show to get back to, in case you didn't know. I guess I'll just watch you on television with everyone else next week, Apple. But remember, the photo shoot is also tonight. So try not to be late."

Right. *Angst* magazine's photo shoot featuring Apple's family. They were going to shoot the Bergs in their home, as a behind-the-scenes look at one of the country's most-watched television hosts. Apple was dreading it, but at least she'd have her makeup already professionally done.

Apple opened her eyes as she said goodbye to her mother.

She couldn't help but notice the disappointed and hurt expression on her mother's face. Her mother had had the same expression on her face when Apple had raced out the door this morning, slamming it in her face. She had accosted her over her bowl of cereal, telling her to always look straight into the camera, be calm, and talk to the camera like she was talking to a good friend.

Then she told her that she should wear red. Apple had managed to drown her out. When her mother had asked, "Are you listening to me?" Apple had looked at her sleepily and said, "What?"

But Apple didn't have time to think about her mother's hurt feelings now. She had to concentrate on the task at hand. She didn't want to screw this up. If the reaction she got after people saw her on television was anything like the reaction she had gotten after people saw her on buses and in *Angst* magazine, well, that was definitely something she didn't want to screw up.

twenty-three

efore she knew it, Apple was sitting on a stool. Bright lights shone in her face. She still couldn't help but feel a little bad about her mother being kicked out, but she didn't have time to dwell on it. She had to forget that hurt expression on her mother's face.

"Are you ready?" Michael asked.

"As ready as I'll ever be," said Apple, looking at the camera a foot away from her.

"You're going to be great. Ready? Action," called out Michael. Apple recited the lines she had practiced in front of her mirror during every spare moment she had the last two days. Michael kept reading the question again and again. "One more time," he kept saying.

"Okay, we got it," he finally announced, after Apple had repeated herself seven or eight times. To Apple's pleasant surprise, everyone clapped, including Emme, who had been allowed to watch, and Fancy Nancy, who had been on set all day, making sure everything ran smoothly for the first taping of *Angst TV*. Michael walked over to her and took her by the hand, helping her down.

"Good job, kid," he said, which made Apple laugh. Michael was only in his mid-twenties. He was almost a kid himself.

Apple sighed. But it wasn't a sigh of relief, exactly. That was amazing, she thought. She felt like she had just ran a marathon, her adrenaline was pumping so quickly. There was something about being in front of the camera this time around that didn't seem so scary. It felt natural. She had been confident, a feeling Apple so rarely had before today. Maybe she *was* her mother's daughter. It didn't seem so bad. She had never received so many acknowledgments in her life. Being on the side of a bus had already done wonders for her social status. Three girls in the fifth grade had even asked for her autograph this morning, and that was just because she was in *Angst* magazine. Now, the *staff* at *Angst* magazine were clapping for her, like she was a pop star who had just performed a sold-out concert!

Apple accepted warm hugs from Michael, Celia, Morgan, and Emme, and their glowing compliments.

"Are you leaving now?" Emme asked as Apple grabbed her purse.

"Yes, but don't worry. I'm still going to be working. I have to do a photo shoot with my mom for this magazine. They want to do a behind-the-scenes of the Queen of Hearts," Apple said, rolling her eyes.

"Well, I have to stay and help them clean up here. Do you want to go out one night this weekend? A few of my friends are getting together and it would be great for you to meet them. They're fashion girls and so much fun. There's a big VIP party for a skateboard company."

"Sure," said Apple. "That sounds like fun."

"Okay, I'll text you the details. See you Saturday at work, and then we'll party afterward," Emme said.

"See you," Apple said, kissing Emme on both cheeks. It was only after Emme double-kissed her back that Apple realized it didn't feel strange to do that anymore.

"Great job today, Apple," called out Fancy Nancy. Apple was more than pleased. She felt like skipping, but she never would. Television stars didn't skip. Still, even Fancy Nancy thought she had done well, and Fancy Nancy was not the type to give out compliments generously.

Lyon was waiting out front for her in his car. She hadn't spoken to him all day, and when he had offered to pick her up, Apple had readily agreed and texted him the address. She did need a lift, after all, from someone. It might as well be Lyon, her boyfriend, whom she felt she hadn't seen in forever.

"Hi, baby," he said as Apple hopped into the passenger seat. He seemed fidgety and nervous.

"Is something wrong?" Apple asked, picking up his vibe immediately.

"Not really," Lyon said, pulling away.

"Are you sure?" Apple asked.

"Yes, why?" Lyon said, sounding agitated.

"You just seem, I don't know, nervous or something," Apple said. "God, you wouldn't believe how awesome it was to film my television spot. I can't believe I'm saying this, but I actually think I did an okay job. People clapped when I finished. Can you believe it?"

She waited for Lyon, in his usual way, to say something supportive like, "Of course you did great!"

But it didn't come. She felt mildly hurt. What was up with him? Here she was, for the first time possibly ever, pleased about something she had done, and Lyon didn't even seem to be listening to her. He was her *boyfriend*, after all. Shouldn't he be happy that she was so happy and excited? She couldn't help but notice that he was driving extremely slowly, way below the speed limit. And Apple didn't have time for his slow pace. She needed to get home for the photo shoot.

She didn't want to be rude. She wanted to know if something was bothering Lyon, but she really was in a rush. Everyone was waiting to do this photo shoot at her house, and Apple needed to be there, like, ten minutes ago.

Looking at her watch, Apple asked again if something was wrong.

"It's just that . . ." Lyon started to say, before becoming silent again.

"What? What is it? If you have something to say, just say it," Apple said, realizing that she was snapping at Lyon. She didn't want to snap at him, but why was he acting so strange?

He started to drive faster.

"I'm really sorry, Lyon. I didn't mean to sound like that. I just have so much to do, and it was such a long day, and now I still have to do this photo shoot. I'm sorry if I snapped at you. I'm really sorry. I didn't mean it to come out that way," Apple pleaded. "I'm sorry."

"It's okay. You're busy. I understand," he said, looking at her forgivingly.

"Thanks. So was there something you wanted to talk about?" Apple asked, praying there wasn't. "Because it seems like you have something on your mind."

"No, it's okay," said Lyon.

It didn't take a teen advice columnist or any genius to know that Lyon did have something to say. Apple knew he was probably going to say something along the lines of "I miss you," or "You didn't call me back." She knew she should be reassuring, but her nerves were fraught. She had eaten only a half a sandwich at lunch because she was so nervous, and she could feel hunger pangs, which also made her grumpy. It was no wonder she was snappish. Apple *really* didn't feel like being reprimanded by Lyon for her faults as a girlfriend right now. She was already painfully aware of her faults as a girlfriend.

"Should I come in and watch?" Lyon asked as he drove into Apple's driveway.

"Um," Apple hesitated, fidgeting her hands. She knew it wouldn't be a big deal for Lyon to come in. No one would mind. Except Apple, who didn't want to have to babysit Lyon while also getting photographed. For some reason, the thought of having Lyon around watching her get her photo taken made her nervous. She liked being Confident Apple. But she didn't really want Lyon to see that side of her—she wasn't sure she would be as confident if he was around.

"That's okay. I can see you don't really want me there," Lyon jumped in before she answered.

"It's not that," Apple said, grabbing his hand. "It's just that it could take a while and I don't want you to get bored."

"It's fine," said Lyon, disappointed. She knew that he was looking, or waiting, for her to say, "Come in! Come in!"

But Apple knew it would be easier if he didn't come in. She just wanted to get the shoot over with, have something to eat, and get into bed.

"So, I'll see you, then?" Lyon said, looking in front of him.

Apple knew he was playing some sort of game. She'd heard and seen this time and time before. She knew that when Lyon said, "So I'll see you, then" and left it as a question, he wanted her to make the next move and say something like "I'll see you tomorrow, of course!" or "I'll call you after."

But Apple suddenly felt exhausted. She didn't have time for these sorts of relationship games. Why didn't Lyon get that? Why couldn't he see that she was under pressure, and that the last thing she needed right now was for him to add more stress and make her feel bad for not wanting him to watch her photo shoot? This was a big day for her—a *life-changing* day—and Lyon should be making her life easier, not more difficult.

She wasn't going to allow him to play games. After all, she was *Apple* of Apple's Angst. People had just applauded her!

"Okay, speak later. Thanks for the drive," Apple said, jumping out of the car.

But she felt awful. She was being a royal bitch and she didn't understand why. She turned around at the front door, realizing she had made a mistake. She wanted to chase after him and tell him that of course he was welcome to come in and watch. But it was too late. All Apple saw was the back of his car speeding off.

"You're here. Finally," her mother said, opening the door. "She's here! We can get things moving now!" Apple was sure her mother had been waiting by the window for her to arrive.

After two hours of posing for the photographer— shots of Apple and her mother; Apple, her mother, and Crazy Aunt Hazel; Apple and her father; and a couple of solo shots of Apple and then of Dr. Berg—they were finished.

"I can't believe I'm going to be in *Angst* magazine," her aunt kept repeating. "I can't wait for *all* my ex-boyfriends to see me! And see what they've missed out on!"

"Well, that's a lot of men," Apple joked.

Apple's father had even been game for the photos, which was odd, considering he loved his privacy. "I'll do anything for my daughter," he laughed, shaking the photographer's hand while apologizing for not knowing how to pose. Her mother, aside from occasionally bossing the photographer around, seemed to enjoy herself. She, of course, was an expert in getting her photo taken, and told the photographer her good angles and refused to pose showing her "bad side."

After, Apple went upstairs and looked at her Black-Berry. She had missed twelve calls. There were some from Happy, Zen, Brooklyn, and Emme. She couldn't stand to *smile* for one more second, let alone talk to anyone, tonight. She shut off her BlackBerry and passed out, but not before washing all the makeup off her face. If there was one thing Apple was going to make sure of, it was that she wasn't going to get pimples. Now that she had to worry about being on television, there was no way she was going to look like anything other than . . . well, a person worthy of being featured in a magazine and on television.

♡

Apple had no idea what Emme said to the doorman at the club, but they were whisked inside immediately, with the rest of the partiers, into a private room separated by a velvet rope.

Emme began to introduce her friends to Apple. Apple was trying hard to remember the names of the three new faces in front of her.

"How was the behind-the-scenes shoot?" Emme asked once they all were seated. She wasn't sure if Emme was making fun of her or not. They hadn't had time to talk today at work about anything but work. They had taken inventory all day of designer clothes that had been sent in and had to be sent back. Emme would call out the designer names, and Apple would log them into the computer.

"I think it went okay. I barely remember doing it," responded Apple.

"At least you were so great on *Angst TV* reading out your advice. You really are a natural. Like mother, like daughter, huh?" Emme said, giving her a friendly shove.

"Thanks!" Apple said, still pleased with herself.

"How is your boyfriend?" Emme asked.

Apple couldn't believe it, but she found herself wanting to open up to Emme. Maybe it was because she didn't know Emme all that well, so she figured she would be more objective and less judgmental than her best friends, who had known her forever. Or maybe she had learned what happened if you keep secrets too long. Last time, when she had kept her Zen Crush to herself, the whole world had ending up knowing. Apple felt she was going to burst with everything that had gone on her personal life in the last little while.

"I don't know. Things are a little strained. I'm not sure what's going on. He seems mad at me. But, in his defense, I haven't been spending much time with him. It's not because I don't want to. I literally don't have the time," explained Apple.

"Well, didn't Nancy tell you that your social life would suffer?" Emme asked. "She told me that."

"Yes, she did. But I had no idea to what extent!" Apple said.

"Well, why don't you ask him to come out? It's still early. He can meet us here," suggested Emme.

Why hadn't Apple thought of that? The idea of inviting Lyon out with her and Emme hadn't even crossed her mind, even though she and Lyon had spent nearly every Saturday night together since they met. But Apple knew that Lyon didn't really seem to like Emme. He had told her in passing a few days earlier that he was worried Emme would be a "bad influence" on her. Apple had laughed that notion off. How old did Lyon think she was? She didn't need to be told whom she could be friendly with.

"I don't know if this is his scene," Apple responded, looking around. She wasn't sure it was her scene either, but she was enjoying herself. The club was pulsating with loud music, people were out on the dance floor, and everyone seemed to be in a good mood. Apple wanted to be around people who were in a good mood, letting loose, enjoying life. She didn't want the strain of being around Lyon, and that's what being around him had started to become. They always seemed to be were on the verge of being in a fight these days.

"I think if you really wanted to see him, you'd make the time to see him," Emme said, with a lilt in her voice. "There is something more to this story, isn't there? Something you're not telling me."

Emme was right. If Apple did really want to see Lyon, she'd make the time for him, wouldn't she?

"Well, there is something else," Apple admitted. "I haven't told anyone, so you have to promise not to say anything!"

"I promise," said Emme, looking Apple straight in the eyes.

Apple told Emme all about kissing Zen. She couldn't believe she told her, but the secret had been haunting her. She supposed she could have told Crazy Aunt

Hazel, but Hazel was too busy in wedding mode and wasn't exactly thrilled that Apple hadn't been at her beck and call, helping her with the planning and dishing out advice on what kind of napkins should be on the tables. She already knew what her mother's reaction would be if she told her. Dr. Berg would be like, "Didn't you learn your lesson already?" or "Once a cheater, always a cheater. You don't want to be that person!"

"I'm the most horrible person," Apple moaned. "After I tried to steal him away from Happy, who is my best friend in the entire world, and she forgave me, I *still* kissed him! I'm not that person. I swear I'm not!" Apple said.

"Well, didn't you say they were having problems anyway?" Emme said. If she was shocked at hearing Apple's admission, she wasn't showing any sign of it. "Didn't you say Happy wanted you and Zen to get together?"

"Yeah, so?" asked Apple

"Well, it takes two to tango. You may have kissed him, but he kissed you too. You're not entirely to blame."

"You think?" asked Apple.

"Yes, and no offense, but between me and you, Lyon seemed a little clingy that night we met," said Emme. "He seemed a little overbearing for a boyfriend. But that's just my opinion."

"You know what? He has been!" Apple said.

"Who needs that?" groaned Emme. "Trust me, they get worse! Once a jealous guy, always a jealous guy."

Emme seemed so sure of herself that Apple found

herself believing what she said to be true. Lyon *was* being clingy! He *was* always acting jealous! Where once Lyon had simply seemed supportive, now Apple was seeing him in a new light.

"It's our little secret. Just forget about it. Let's have fun!" Emme said, looking around the club, bobbing her head to the beat of the music.

"Okay," said Apple. Was Apple being ridiculous? Emme didn't seem fazed by her cheating on her boyfriend at all. In fact, it seemed to please her, as if Apple had made her proud.

"But maybe I should text Happy and Brooklyn," Apple said. "It feels like I haven't seen them forever either. I want to make time for them."

Apple texted Happy and Brooklyn. Instantly, she got responses. They both wanted to come and meet Apple and Emme and Emme's friends. Apple texted the address.

"Put that thing down and let's dance," said Emme. "Happy doesn't even like Zen anymore, so just forget about it. He was just a foolie! I know you're still thinking about it. Come on! Let's dance!"

"Are you serious?" asked Apple, tensing up.

"Yes! Come on. You have to loosen up a bit. Live life!" said Emme.

"But I'm such a bad dancer! I have no rhythm," moaned Apple.

"Who cares? Just have a drink! Don't look, but someone is taking a photo of you with her cell phone," Emme said, trying to look nonchalant.

"What?" Apple asked. "Where?"

"Oh, my God," Emme said, grabbing Apple's arm before she could get an explanation. "You'll never guess who's here!"

"Who?" Apple asked, turning her head to where Emme was looking.

"Sloan Starr! Oh, my God, this night is going to be so good!" she screeched.

twenty-four

"Sloan Starr is here?" Apple asked. She didn't even try to pretend she wasn't excited to hear the news.

"Yup. Over there! With his entourage," Emme said.

Apple glanced to a table, where Sloan Starr sat surrounded by a gaggle of other people.

"You know, I met him. Well, very briefly. He complimented me on my hair after my first meeting with Fancy Nancy," Apple said to Emme. "Well, he complimented me on my hair when it was curly." For a moment, Apple was nostalgic for her curls. Ever since she had gotten her hair straightened and it was always neat, everything else in her life seemed to have gotten messed up.

"You should totally go over and say hi," Emme suggested.

"Are you insane? He'll never remember me," Apple responded.

"Who cares? You'll remind him. It's your job now

to interact with celebrities. You work at *Angst* magazine. Think of it as part of your duty. It's your job," Emme pressed.

Apple took another sip of her sugary drink and contemplated Emme's words.

"You know what?" Apple said, standing up. "I'm going to do it. Why not?" The liquid courage was setting in.

Emme held up her hand for a high-five and grinned.

Apple straightened her dress and asked Emme if she had lipstick on her teeth.

"You look gorgeous," Emme said. "Go forth and be brave!"

Apple walked over to where Sloan Starr was sitting, crammed into a booth with about eight others. She almost turned around when she was a couple of feet away. But Emme was right, and she couldn't turn back now. She did work at *Angst* magazine and she supposed it was part of her job to make nice to celebrities.

"Hey, remember me?" Apple asked loudly and boldly, extracting her inner Happy, bending down and looking at Sloan Starr directly. "My hair is different. I work at *Angst* magazine. We met a couple weeks ago. You were walking out and I was in the reception area."

Sloan looked at her and Apple felt her heart sink. She was mortified. He didn't seem to remember her at all.

"*Angst* magazine? I was in the waiting room?" Apple repeated. "I used to have very curly hair."

"Right! Hair Girl!" he said, slapping his hands on the table. "The one with the gorgeous curls."

"Right!" Apple said and laughed with relief. She hadn't exactly made a fool of herself. "Well, it's different now. Obviously."

"I like it," said Sloan. "I'm really digging it. It's hot! Why don't you sit down? Join us!"

Sloan patted a spot next to him, and immediately the guy sitting next to him got up and left, making room for Apple. She sat down.

"Hi," said Apple. She didn't have anything else prepared to say.

"Hi," Sloan said. "Again."

They stared at each other. Apple's confidence was beginning to wane. She needed to think of something to say other than hi.

She looked over at Emme, who was beaming at her. Apple waved her over. Emme jumped up. When she got to the table, Apple introduced her to Sloan Starr. Immediately, Emme made herself comfortable.

"So how did you end up at *Angst*? You want to be a tabloid reporter or something?" Sloan asked Apple.

"Right. Don't you know who she is?" Emme asked, laughing. Obviously, Emme had been listening in on their conversation. Apple knew what Emme was about to say, but for some reason she didn't care. Apple was thrilled to be surrounded by new people, and amazed at how confident she had been to stride up to Sloan. Now he was talking to her! Every girl in her right mind would want to be in Apple's position.

"She's the daughter of Dr. Bee Bee Berg! You know, the Queen of Hearts," Emme said, giggling. "You're in the presence of . . . well, the *Princess of Hearts*."

"No kidding," said Sloan, looking at Apple with even more appraisal. "Dr. Bee Bee Berg has, like, a huge following!"

For once, Apple was completely proud to be her mother's daughter. Who knew her mother's name would impress cute, young celebrities like Sloan Starr?

"Do you have a boyfriend, Princess of Hearts?" Sloan asked.

"Do you have a girlfriend?" Apple shot back. She couldn't believe how easy it was to flirt with him.

"She does have a boyfriend, but there's trouble in paradise," Emme said to Sloan, "so you might have a shot."

Apple wasn't sure if she should be mortified or grateful that Emme had shared this news with Sloan.

"We should hang sometime." Sloan grinned at Apple. "In fact, I'm coming by *Angst* next week as a guest on *Angst TV*. They begged me to come. You should come watch. That will make it more interesting for me, if there's a beautiful girl hanging around."

"If they'll let me hang out," Apple said. "I mean, I will be there. I have a one-minute spot on the show each week, but I'm not sure if they'll let me stick around to watch people's interviews."

"Don't worry. I'll make it happen," Sloan said. "So you're a TV star too?"

"Well, not like you. I mean, you get to meet and interview all the really cool people. And all my friends watch your show. I have no idea if anyone will even watch *Angst TV*, let alone the one minute I'm on it."

Sloan nodded. "You think I'll ever meet your mom?" he asked.

"What?" Apple said, laughing.

"She's just so . . . she's so entertaining. Well, not her so much. But her guests? Who really has that much shit going on in their lives that they're willing to share? It's like watching a train wreck. You can't turn away."

"I know exactly what you mean," said Apple.

Sometime later in the night, Emme whispered in her ear, "See? I bet you've forgotten all about Zen and Lyon! Who are they, anyway, but just guys you've grown up with and go to school with?"

Apple found herself entranced with Sloan. He was gorgeous, charming, funny, and extremely confident in himself. Being around such confident people made Apple more confident too. Maybe confidence was contagious. She couldn't remember laughing so hard in a long time. And she had forgotten all about Zen and Lyon. Emme was right.

Emme took out her camera phone and started taking pictures of her friends. Apple wasn't sure, but it seemed like Emme was also taking photos of her talking to Sloan. Apple *hoped* she was. She'd get Emme to e-mail them to her so she could forward them to her friends. This was a night worth remembering.

Two hours later, sweat pouring from her face, Apple was both exhausted and exhilarated. She hadn't realized how late it now was. Though technically she didn't have a curfew, she knew if her parents heard her walk in at this hour, they would be far from thrilled. She had danced with Sloan, talked animatedly with his friends, and drunk too much. She hailed a cab and thought about how much fun she'd had. She wanted to leave on a high note. She had offered to leave money on the table for their drinks, but Sloan had explained that it was taken care of, that he had some sort of arrangement with the club. Apple didn't question it. Emme's friends were fantastic. Sloan's friends were fantastic. It wasn't until she got home, letting herself in quietly as a mouse, and had shut her bedroom door that she realized Brooklyn and Happy hadn't shown up. What had happened to them? Apple found out soon enough, after grabbing her BlackBerry from her bag.

"We're outside! Can't get in. List!" was Happy's first text.

Happy's second: "Come get us!"

Her third: "Where are you?"

Finally, her fourth: "It's been thirty minutes. The doorman doesn't believe we're with you."

The fifth: "We've left."

Apple felt horrible, but there was no point in apologizing at this hour, especially by text or e-mail. It would be easier to explain in person. Her friends would understand. If Happy had been in the presence of Sloan Starr, surely she would have forgotten to check her texts as well.

♡

Monday morning, Apple walked into Cactus High. She had spent almost all day in bed on Sunday, recovering from her Saturday night, and she felt energized, like she had drunk ten cups of coffee. She hadn't done any homework in days and the assignments were piling up, but she brushed the thought away. She hadn't spoken with her friends the day before, as she'd spent most of her time sleeping and, when she was awake, organizing her clothes. Apple rushed to the Spiral Staircase, where Brooklyn and Happy had already gathered. Her aunt had been furious with Apple in the morning because Apple was running late. She couldn't decide what to wear and her aunt had huffed, "My God, you are driving me crazy. I want the old Apple back. The one who wore jeans and a tank top and didn't give a rat's ass about looking stylish. That Apple was so much easier. AND SHE DIDN'T KEEP PEOPLE WAITING!"

Apple had apologized to her aunt, and now she had to apologize to her friends for the mix-up on Saturday night.

"I'm so sorry," she said to Happy and Brooklyn immediately, when she reached them.

Brooklyn gave her a half-hearted smile.

"What *happened* to you?" Happy asked. "We texted you, like, a billion times."

"I know. I'm so sorry. I didn't get them until I got home. I was dancing, so I didn't get your messages," explained Apple.

"You were *dancing*?" Brooklyn asked. "I can't believe it!"

"I was," Apple said and she felt a smile creep on her face. Just thinking about how much fun she had had Saturday night made her gleeful.

"Please don't be pissed off. Honestly, it was just a mix-up. I should have checked for messages, but I totally forgot. You're not going to believe who I was hanging out with! Once you hear, you're not going to be as pissed off, I promise," Apple said, eager to spill the news about Sloan Starr.

"I'm *not* pissed because *I* didn't get to meet Sloan Starr and you were hanging out with him, even though *I'm* obsessed with how gorgeous he is and envy his job," Happy said crankily. "I'm pissed because you invited us out and then forgot about us! And you're the one who asked us to meet you there."

"I'm so sorry! I just—" Apple started to say. "Wait! How did you know that I was hanging out with Sloan Starr?"

She watched Happy and Brooklyn exchange glances.

"What?" Apple pressed her friends. "How did you guys know?"

Brooklyn handed her her iPhone. Apple grabbed it and looked at what was on it. She couldn't believe what she saw on the website Brooklyn had pulled up. It was a photograph of Apple looking very cozy with Sloan Starr. It looked like she was practically sitting on his lap. Had she really been that close to him?

"I don't believe this!" Apple cried. "What site is this?"

Happy told her it was one of the gossip websites—one that Apple had heard of but had never checked out.

"You're a celebrity now," Happy said, sounding not overly friendly. "It says so right here under your picture. 'Apple Berg, of *Angst* magazine and daughter of the Queen of Hearts, getting cozy with Sloan Starr.'"

"Obviously, you were having too good a time with Sloan Starr to remember your old friends," Happy continued.

"That's not true, Happy. I invited you!" Apple

protested. She thought Happy was acting immature. But her mind was on the photo on that website. How had it gotten there?

"How do you think Lyon is going to feel when he sees this?" Brooklyn asked. "I mean, you know what I mean. I would feel bad if I were him, seeing my girlfriend like that."

Apple hadn't even thought about that. She was still so shocked her photograph was on a gossip website. It was true that the photograph made Apple look very cozy with Sloan, and that she was spending time with another male who wasn't her boyfriend. Plus Apple knew now she couldn't tell Lyon that she had worked late at *Angst*, as she had planned to do if he asked what she had done on Saturday night.

"It wasn't like that!" Apple protested. "We just talked! I'll make it up to you guys. I promise. Please don't tell Lyon."

"Of course we're not going to tell him," said Happy, speaking for both her and Brooklyn. "But people are talking about it. All Sailor's friends are asking her for more information about it. Lyon is going to find out, unless he lives under a rock."

Apple grabbed Brooklyn's iPhone one more time to look at the photo.

"I do look good, though, right?" Apple asked. "I mean, I don't look fat or ugly, right?"

Her friends simply nodded. Apple pretended not to notice the look they exchanged—once again, it was meant to happen behind her back, but Apple saw it, right in front of her face.

It was at that point that Apple realized her life really was changing drastically. She felt like she was having an out-of-body experience. Students in the hallways were looking at her and whispering as she walked by. Obviously, many other students aside from Brooklyn and Happy had seen the photo of her and Sloan. Apple wasn't sure if she felt embarrassed or pleased. But then, Apple thought, how many people get to hang out with Sloan Starr at a cool nightclub? Of course they're talking about her. Who wouldn't?

twenty-five

"I just don't think we're working out," Lyon said a couple of weeks later. He was driving her from school to *Angst* magazine. He had waited patiently—though, Apple noted, with a gloomy look on his face—as some of the younger students talked to Apple, asking for her autograph. A couple of them even asked if she was dating Sloan Starr. Apple just smiled politely. She didn't want to let them down, since they seemed to adore her and to want her to be dating Sloan. She felt that if she admitted the truth she would let them down. Apple barely spent any time with Lyon anymore. They saw each other briefly in the mornings, but Apple had been arriving to school later and later each day as she focused more and more on her appearance. Apple could only half blame this on choosing an *Angst*-worthy outfit. She had been staying out late at night a lot as well, going out to trendy hotspots with Emme after work, making it nearly impossible to drag herself out of bed in the mornings. Lyon had never mentioned the photo on that gossip website of her with Sloan Starr. She had a feeling that he knew about it, and she was grateful that he didn't ask about it or demand an explanation. What could Apple say? She was not guilty of anything. She hadn't done anything but have some fun and meet new people. Apple hadn't brought it up either.

"Are you breaking up with me?" Apple asked. She was genuinely surprised. She wasn't expecting this, especially from Lyon, who only weeks ago had adored her.

"Well, I think we both should acknowledge that this isn't working right now," Lyon said.

"What's not working?" Apple asked, playing dumb. She wondered if this was how Happy had acted when she was trying to break up with Zen. But what else was she supposed to say?

"Us! This relationship," Lyon said, hitting the steering wheel in frustration. She had never seen Lyon so angry before. "If you can even call it that."

"You're the one breaking up!" Apple protested. "I mean, don't you want to at least work on it?"

"Oh, come on, Apple. We haven't gone out together in so long. We barely speak on the phone. The only time I see you is when I'm driving you to or from work, and now that you're getting your own driver, I won't even get the privilege of being your chauffeur," he huffed. "Obviously, you just don't have the time, or want to make time, for me."

All of what Lyon was saying was true. A few days ago, Fancy Nancy had been walking into the office when she spotted Apple waiting outside to be picked up. Michael had already told Apple that Fancy Nancy had seen the pictures of her with Sloan Starr, and he said that she had seemed amused and even proud of Apple. Fancy Nancy had told Apple that she shouldn't have to wait to be picked up. She told her to go ask Morgan to give her the number of a car service, and Morgan explained that whenever Apple need a drive, she should call the driver ten minutes ahead of time, and he'd drive her home. Permission to use a car service was one of the perks of being a VIP employee at *Angst*. Michael, Celia, and Charlotte, the head stylist, all had drivers. Emme had been so jealous at this news, but Apple assumed that Emme would be tagging along with her.

"This is not what I want in a relationship," Lyon continued. "Let's face the facts. We haven't known each other that long anyway. It's not like we've been a couple for three years or anything."

"I can't believe that just because I'm busy you're breaking up with me," Apple said. "And right before I have to work!"

"It's not just that you're busy," Lyon said. "And there's no good time for me to have this conversation with you. Everyone is busy, but they still find time for their boy-friends. Maybe you really are too busy right now for me. When I met you, you were different. You didn't like going to clubs. You were just . . . you were just different."

Apple didn't know how to respond. She knew she hadn't been spending time with Lyon, and she felt bad about it. But she'd always just thought that he'd be there for her no matter what. Or at least wait it out a little longer. Who gave up on relationships so quickly? She thought of her mother, who said that your partner should be loyal like a best friend—always there for you and supporting you. Lyon was throwing in the towel so easily. It angered her.

"Fine," Apple said, getting out of the car. "Have a nice life!" She slammed the car door. She usually didn't do mad. When she was mad, she fumed silently.

Apple continued to fume as she walked into *Angst*. How dare he break up with her? How long had he been waiting to do this? Didn't he know what he was missing out on? Didn't he understand that she was working hard at *Angst*, and that part of her job was to be social?

When Apple walked in, Morgan threw her the latest issue of *Angst* magazine.

"You're going to die when you see this," said Morgan excitedly. "You look beautiful."

Apple had completely forgotten about the photo shoot. It had been a few weeks since it happened.

Apple flipped the magazine open.

She couldn't believe what she saw. In the three-page spread, two of the pages were dedicated to photos of Apple. On the third page, there was a small photo of her mother, her aunt, and her father.

"I can't believe this," Apple said. "We spent two hours taking photos and they just used the ones of me? What about my mother? I thought they wanted a behind-the-scenes look at the life of Dr. Bee Bee Berg."

"Well, you are more the demographic of *Angst*," Morgan explained. "I thought you'd be thrilled! It even mentions that you hang out with celebrities. It's so cool.

You should be honored. They have a quote from Sloan Starr saying that you're a 'cool chick.' This is amazing! Who would think that a few weeks ago, you were just another intimidated-looking intern? I remember you walking in here, so unconfident, and now you've done a complete turnaround. You're a celebrity now. So, how does it feel?"

Apple wasn't so sure. She had hung out only that once with Sloan and a few of his friends, some of whom she had just learned were in bands. It's not like she was best friends with them or anything.

Apple also wondered if her mother was going to be mad. She had been led to believe that the story was going to be about her. No, Apple shouldn't worry. Apple was her daughter, after all. Her mother should be proud, if anything.

Wait until Lyon sees this, thought Apple, feeling both revengeful and hurt. Then he'll know for sure what he's missing out on.

"Is something wrong, Apple?" Morgan asked.

"No, it's just weird being in the spotlight," said Apple.

Morgan gave her a look that said, "Come on! Who are you kidding? You like it!"

"Okay, fine. It's pretty fun. I just didn't think it would change my entire life," Apple said.

"What do you mean?" Morgan asked.

"Some other time," said Apple. She couldn't talk about Lyon right now. She knew that if she started to, she would burst out in tears. She already missed him and felt awful about how she had slammed the car door. Her mother always said people should break up with class and dignity.

Apple had just acted like a two-year-old who didn't get the toy she wanted. Morgan told her to have a good day and be proud of herself and then Apple walked down to the dungeon, where Emme was already hard at work.

"What's wrong?" Emme asked immediately.

Like Apple's mother, Emme was good at reading people's facial expressions.

"Lyon just broke up with me," Apple said, feeling such a rush of dizziness that she suddenly had to sit down.

"Oh, no! Are you okay?" Emme asked, sounding concerned.

"I think I'm in shock. I don't have time to be in shock or go through heartbreak right now. I have to do my advice column today, and then I have to meet my aunt and my mother for a late dinner and I can't get out of it. I just don't know how I'm going to get the advice column in today! But I need too. Michael already gave me an extension on it, and he wasn't pleased about it either."

When Emme looked at her with pity, Apple started to sob. She usually didn't cry in front of anyone, but she couldn't help it. Her first real boyfriend had just broken up with her.

Emme ran over to Apple and handed her a tissue.

"Apple, please don't cry. Please. Don't worry about Lyon. I know if you really want him you can get him back. But remember, he wasn't exactly supportive of your life right now. He was clingy and jealous. He didn't let you just be. This may be a good thing," Emme said.

Apple sniffed. Maybe Emme had a point.

"Listen, I'll do your column for you," Emme said, now holding Apple's limp hand.

"What?" Apple asked, shocked.

"Just give me the questions. Don't worry. No one will ever know," Emme whispered.

Apple must have given her a strange look, because Emme leaned in as if she were sharing a secret.

"Come on, Apple! Seriously, how hard is it to answer those questions? Anyone who has half a brain could answer those questions. Am I right?"

Apple didn't want to admit it, but Emme wasn't exactly wrong. Still, she hesitated.

"What? Don't you think I can answer them? Do I not give you good advice?" Emme pressed.

"No, you do. It's just that . . . well, I just don't want to get in trouble," Apple started.

"No one will know! Where are the questions?" Emme asked, standing up.

Apple sat behind her computer and opened the five questions Michael had sent her earlier in the week. Emme skimmed them, reading over Apple's shoulder.

"Easy to answer," she said after reading the first question.

"Easy to answer," she said, continuing to read. "I already have an answer for that," Emme said, as she continued to scan the questions.

Apple wasn't sure about it, but she was sure that in her state, after just being dumped, she couldn't be objective. Right now, she hated all men and relationships. And she shouldn't doubt Emme's ability. Emme was smart and such a hard worker. She could probably whip out the answers quicker than Apple could, especially since Apple could barely stop crying.

"Are you sure, Emme?" she asked.

"I'm sure. Why don't you just sneak out of here and go home and relax? You can't concentrate right now. I remember the last time my boyfriend broke up with me. I was shattered. I couldn't get out of bed for, like, three weeks! But it's what you have to go through. So go home, get into bed. The sooner you start the heartbreak phase, the sooner it will be over. If Michael comes looking for you, I'll just tell him you're in the restroom or helping Charlotte."

"I can't start the heartbreak phase. I have to go out for dinner with my mother and aunt," moaned Apple. She started to sob harder, while Emme stroked her hair like she was a new pet.

"Poor you," Emme said. "Don't worry, Apple. This is just a bad day. You'll feel better. And don't worry. I've got things covered here. I'll get to work on your computer right now to answer those questions and send them to Michael. He'll never know!"

Apple just nodded. "Thanks, Emme."

"Don't worry about it. There's no one I would rather help out," said Emme.

Apple managed to sneak out of the building by a side door. Thank God for Emme. She really was saving her ass. She felt grateful to her new friend, who was right. All Apple wanted to do was go home, get into bed, and cry.

twenty-six

There was no way Apple could get out of going to dinner with her aunt and her mother.

When she had called her aunt a couple of hours earlier, her aunt had picked up and said, "Whatever it is you have to say, I don't want to hear it. I'll see you at dinner tonight," and had hung up before Apple could say one word.

The dinner had been set up weeks ago, to celebrate Aunt Hazel's upcoming wedding, just for the bride and the bridesmaids, which meant it was a dinner for Hazel, Apple, and Dr. Berg. They were going to Toaster, a recently opened restaurant that had become a hotspot for celebrities, local politicians, and socialites.

"How did you get a table here?" Apple asked her aunt as the three of them drove to the restaurant. "Emme told me they had a waiting list of about three weeks."

"It was easy! I just told them it was for Dr. Bee Bee

Berg of the *Queen of Hearts* and Apple Berg of *Angst* magazine, and they said of course they had room!"

"You're kidding?" said Dr. Berg, though Apple knew it wasn't the first time her aunt had used her mother's name for perks. Aunt Hazel often said she was "Dr. Berg's personal assistant" to get ahead on wait lists for designer purses before they arrived in stores.

"That's really quite sad," said Apple.

"Well, how else was I going to get to eat here?" her aunt moaned. "It's my celebratory dinner, and I should be able to have it wherever I want."

As Apple got out of the car at the valet, flashbulbs suddenly went off.

"I think they're taking photos of you, Apple!" her aunt exclaimed.

"Me?" Apple asked. "No, they're definitely taking them of Mom."

"Can we just get one of the mother and daughter?" one of the paparazzi screamed out, waving at Apple's aunt to move out of the way.

"Thanks a lot! We're here celebrating because of me!" her Aunt Hazel huffed. "And I'm just pushed to the side. It's my bridal dinner!"

"I don't think they care," Apple told her aunt, laughing. Suddenly, Apple didn't feel so gloomy. There was something about posing and seeing flashbulbs that got her mind off the fact she had been dumped today.

"Now just one of Apple!" the photographer screamed out.

Apple posed as she heard her aunt say, "How does it feel now, Bee Bee?"

Apple felt momentarily bad for her mother, who looked shocked that suddenly there were people who wanted Apple's picture and not hers. She looked a bit dismayed.

"That's enough, Apple," her mother said. "Let's go."

She didn't want to start a fight in public with her mother. So she smiled one more time for the cameras and followed her mother and her aunt inside the restaurant.

"You're turning out to be quite the attention whore," her aunt said.

"Hazel! Don't talk that way to Apple," her mother said.

"It's true!" her aunt huffed.

"So what?" Apple asked. "I'm having fun."

"Just not too much fun, I hope," said her mother. "I don't want you getting caught up in all that."

"All what?" Apple asked.

"Listen, Apple. You're a good person. You always have been. And being in the public eye can change people. Just read *Angst* magazine and you'll see. Fame can be addictive."

Was her mother actually jealous of her success?

Apple had time to ponder that thought while she glanced over the menu.

"You're so skinny now! Can you please eat more than a salad?" her mother asked while a waiter stood before them awaiting their order.

"Are you crazy? You know better than anyone that the camera adds ten pounds," Apple said.

"I also know that you don't have to worry about

that. You look great just the way you are. In fact, you really are looking too skinny," said her mother.

"Oh, how very motherly of you," Apple responded.

"Wow. You really have a sarcastic side to you tonight," her aunt said, shooting her a look. Apple was stunned. It was usually Apple and her aunt who ganged up on her mother, but now her aunt was sticking up for her mother, and they were ganging up on Apple. "And you have to fit into the bridesmaid's dress. And since you never showed up for the fitting, I had to give them one of your dresses from your closet. You have to stay the same size, or you're going to ruin my wedding! It's in two weeks!"

"Calm down, Hazel. Apple isn't going to ruin your wedding. Let's just all take a breath. We're here to toast you!" her mother said.

"Okay, you're right. I just don't want anything to go wrong," her aunt said, taking a big sip of her champagne.

"Don't worry, Hazel. Nothing is going to ruin your wedding. You are going to be a beautiful bride," her mother said.

"I know I shouldn't, because I have to fit into the wedding gown, but I'm going to get the fries. Are you joining me, Apple? I mean, this is my dinner, and I don't want to be the only one eating calories," her aunt muttered.

"It's called willpower. I'll just stick with the lettuce," Apple said.

Apple somehow managed to get through dinner, although her heart wasn't in it. She nodded and laughed at the right times. Her mother looked at her strangely once or twice, but Apple figured she would just think her daughter was overly tired.

She hadn't told anyone, aside from Emme, about her breakup with Lyon. She also hadn't told her aunt or her mother about the upcoming issue of *Angst*, which featured mostly Apple. Aunt Hazel will be disappointed too, thought Apple. She also couldn't shake the feeling that she was a bad employee for allowing Emme to do her column, even if she hadn't been in the right state of mind herself. For the first time that she could remember, she didn't want to call Happy or Brooklyn. She felt scared to call them, just in case they treated her like they had at the Spiral Staircase this morning, dismissively. She had no one she wanted to talk to, and for a moment she felt a great sadness. She felt lonely, and yet she hadn't ever been so popular or so well known.

At home, Apple checked her e-mail one last time and was surprised to see there was a message from Sloan.

"Come out with me sometime? XO Sloan," he had sent.

She couldn't believe it. Sloan was asking her out? On a real date?

At least the night ended on a high note. Lyon may have dumped her, her mother may be annoying her, her aunt may be mad at her, and her friends may not want to talk to her, but there was someone who was interested in hanging out with Apple. And Sloan Starr wasn't just *anyone*.

♡

Apple needn't have worried. The next issue of *Angst* came out and no one seemed to think anything other than that Apple's advice was great. Emme winked at her. Apple had gotten away with it. She thanked Emme again.

"Any time!" Emme said, refusing to listen to any more of Apple's profuse thank-you's.

Apple didn't feel down now. Even Emme was amazed at how well she was taking the breakup and told her that it was a good sign, that the breakup was meant to be. Zen had, over the weeks, stopped trying to get in touch with her at all. Apple felt only relief over that. Yes, she once had been in love with him, and their kisses had been phenomenal, but there was no way it was going to work out with them. It was too complicated, what with him being Happy's ex, and she was busy with work. Apple hadn't bothered getting in touch with Zen either, which Emme also told Apple said a lot.

Apple had an exciting night ahead of her. She had to tell someone. News like this was too good to keep to herself. Though she was well aware that things had fallen off the rails a bit with Happy and Brooklyn, she wanted to share it with them. She didn't exactly miss Lyon, but she realized that she really did miss Happy and Brooklyn.

"Happy! Oh, my God. I feel like we haven't spoken forever! You're not going to believe what I'm about to do," Apple screeched into the phone when Happy picked up.

"Well, if it isn't the famous Apple," responded Happy.

Was it just Apple? Happy didn't seem so happy to hear from her, even though they hadn't really talked in days.

"You're not going to believe who I'm about to meet up with," Apple said excitedly, trying to ignore the awkwardness and Happy's tone. "On a date!"

"I bet I can't," said Happy flatly.

"Come on, just try!" Apple begged.

"I don't know. I really have no idea," Happy responded, despondently. She obviously wasn't in the mood for any guessing games.

"Fine. I'll just tell you, then. Sloan. Sloan Starr! Can you believe it?"

"Really?" said Happy, sounding a little more interested. "He asked you out on a date?"

"Yes!" screeched Apple. "A real date!"

She knew Happy had to be interested now.

"Aren't you going to ask how it happened?" Apple said.

"Tell me," said Happy, sounding more eager. Apple was relieved that Happy seemed to want to hear the story. That meant Happy was still interested in Apple's life and was acting like a friend.

Apple launched into the story of how Sloan had showed up at *Angst* earlier that day for his television taping, and said that if Apple didn't interview him, he'd refuse to do it.

Nancy and Michael had been as shocked as Apple to hear Sloan's demand. Apple wasn't even sure she *could* interview him. She didn't know how to interview people. But Sloan had held firm to his request.

"Just read the cards," Michael had advised her as Celia retouched her makeup, "and you'll be fine. Just talk to him like you're talking to a friend."

Apple did as Michael suggested and the interview went amazingly. She even forgot they were on camera, she was so into their conversation. She threw out questions as if she were talking to a friend, ignoring most of the questions that Michael had given her. Michael was impressed. After the interview, Sloan casually asked Apple to meet up with him later that night, to "really get to know each other."

"Can you believe it?" Apple asked Happy, after telling her the story.

"No," said Happy. "I really can't."

"Okay, you have to meet up with us after," Apple said.

"I wish!" Happy said. "But I really can't."

Had her best friend gone crazy? Happy, at least the Happy Apple thought she knew, would NEVER turn down a chance to hang out with a real celebrity.

"But you're obsessed with him. Don't worry! I'll get you on the list! You have to be on a list, but it's not a problem, Happy. Come! Everyone will be so jealous, and you've always wanted to meet him in person!"

"I really can't," Happy said again, sounding disappointed.

"Yes, you can," Apple said.

What was Happy's problem? She was usually all about the fun. She couldn't believe her celebrity-obsessed best friend was turning down a chance to meet Sloan Starr. And Apple was going out of her way to include her.

"No, Apple. I can't. Don't you remember we have our math exam tomorrow?" Happy asked.

"Oh, God. I totally forgot. Why didn't you remind me?" Apple moaned.

"Oh, I'm sorry," said Happy, not sounding sorry at all. "But this is the first time you've called in days. And you've skipped more classes in the past couple months than Brooklyn has all year. And that's really saying something."

"You're right," Apple said, feeling worried. "There's no way I can pass the exam."

"No, it's not good. You should really stay home tonight and study," Happy suggested.

"Well, there's no way I'm canceling on Sloan. I mean, that would be so rude," said Apple, glancing at her textbook on her desk, feeling guilty about not studying at all.

"Right. You're just not canceling because it's Sloan. You know, you used to have your priorities straight," Happy told Apple. "I'm not sure who you are anymore."

"What's that supposed to mean?" Apple asked. She didn't have time to get into an argument with Happy, especially about math class. She was meeting Sloan and she needed to get ready and pick out something really fabulous to wear. She didn't understand why Happy was being such a party pooper. Happy would get a great mark even if she didn't stay home tonight.

"Well, I mean, you shouldn't worry that much. It's not like the math teacher isn't marrying your aunt. There's no way he'd fail you, I don't think. Oh, by the way, we picked out her centerpieces," Happy said to Apple. "We still need to find her a dress, though."

"What do you mean you picked out her center-pieces?" Apple said.

"Hazel didn't tell you?" Happy asked.

"No, I haven't had time to talk to her," Apple responded

Apple knew that her aunt loved Happy, but was it possible that they had gone out, without Apple, to get her aunt ready for her wedding?

"Well, I don't have time to talk now either. I have to study for the exam, like everyone else," Happy said.

"Oh, come on, Happy!" Apple said. She couldn't believe Happy was being so harsh to her. "Why are you being this way?"

"Okay, fine. Sorry. I'm just freaking out a little. I have four more chapters to get through. What are you going to do? Study or Sloan?" Happy asked.

"What do you mean? I'm going out with Sloan. I'm going to fail the test whether I stay in and study or not. So I may as well go out and have some fun," said Apple.

"Well, have a good time," Happy said. "I can't wait to hear all about it. Or I'm sure I'll at least *read* about it somewhere."

She hung up on Apple.

Apple didn't even have the chance to ask Happy her opinion on what she should wear.

Happy picked up instantly when Apple redialed.

"So did you come to your senses?" Happy said, before saying hello.

"What?" Apple asked.

"About studying?" Happy asked. "Have you decided to stay in?"

"No. I was calling to ask you your thoughts on that pink dress I bought," Apple said. "Do you think Sloan will like it?"

"Are you serious, Apple?" Happy muttered.

"Yes, why?"

"You're really unbelievable," Happy said, adding, "You're not the same!"

No, thought Apple. Happy was the one behaving unbelievably. She couldn't believe that Happy was helping her aunt with her wedding. Sure, Apple hadn't been around, but it was her family, not Happy's. And Apple had always been supportive of Happy when it came to new men, so why wasn't Happy reciprocating? And if Apple had to hear, from one more person, that she had changed . . . Maybe she had changed. So what? Why was change such a bad thing? Wasn't that what everyone had always told her? Why did Apple feel like everyone was just trying to hold her back?

twenty-seven

a pple didn't know exactly how it happened. It seemed just like minutes ago that she and Sloan had breezed into the club after dinner at a small restaurant, and now they were kissing. Apple was kissing Sloan Starr!

"Oh, peachy Apple," Sloan murmured into Apple's hair. "Applesauce. Apple pie."

Apple giggled. She usually hated it when people made up nicknames. People always thought they were being so clever. As if Sloan was the first to call her Applesauce. He had no idea. She had been called that nickname probably a billion times throughout her life.

Still, Apple let him believe that she had never heard that before and that he was, indeed, being clever and charming.

"Stop saying that!" she said flirtatiously.

Apple kissed him back vigorously and thought, If only Lyon could see me now. Though she couldn't help but think that Lyon was a better kisser than Sloan. Maybe it was because Sloan was new, and she was used to Lyon's lips.

She also thought, If only Happy could see me now!

Apple hadn't spoken to Lyon—he hadn't called and he hadn't responded to the couple of text messages she'd sent him just to say hi—and it bothered Apple. It bothered her that she still thought about Lyon, and that it had gone from so good to so bad so quickly. But she also couldn't believe that some guy at her school wouldn't want her when clearly people more famous, actual celebrities like Sloan Starr, did. Yes, there was definitely something wrong with Lyon, Apple concluded.

"That's a pretty sexy outfit you have on," Sloan whispered in her ear.

"Thank you," said Apple, batting her eyelashes like she had seen Happy do many times. "I try."

"Obviously, you don't have a boyfriend anymore," Sloan said.

"Nope. I'm single," Apple said, hoping she sounded breezy, as if losing Lyon was no big deal.

Apple noticed there were dozens of girls trying to get Sloan's attention.

"Don't you notice all the girls flirting with you?" Apple asked Sloan. It was so painfully obvious. One girl, right in front of Apple, had slid a napkin toward Sloan and told him, "Read it later." Apple couldn't read the words, but she did see a phone number. She couldn't help but gloat inside a little as she noticed Sloan just nod dismissively. Still, he hadn't thrown out the napkin.

He had put it in his pocket. Whatever, thought Apple. He probably didn't want to hurt her feelings.

"Well, you're the apple of my eye, sweetie," Sloan said.

Apple knew in her heart it was a pickup line, but she also couldn't help from falling a bit for Sloan. Looks-wise, he did remind her of Lyon. But Sloan was better-looking or at least had the attitude. Apple wasn't sure if it was his attitude that made him more attractive than Lyon.

Apple and Sloan talked all night. Rather, Sloan talked all night about all the celebrities he had interviewed and which ones he liked the best. Apple listened with rapt attention. They kissed often. Happy would want to know all about these inside scoops of gossip. Boy, would Happy regret not coming out tonight. Apple couldn't wait to tell her what she had missed.

♡

Apple woke up. She knew immediately that she had slept through something big. She looked at her alarm clock. It was almost two o'clock in the afternoon. How had she slept in so late? She smiled, recollecting the events of last night as she stretched her arms and let out a loud yawn.

She had kissed Sloan Starr! He wanted to be with her! Apple couldn't believe it.

She looked around for her BlackBerry, which she found on the floor next to her bed. Her heart pounded as she looked through her messages. There was a message from Sloan, telling her what a great time he had had. Apple texted him immediately. He texted her back instantly. They made plans to meet up later that night.

Apple lay back in bed. She couldn't believe how tired she was. Her phone rang. Apple picked it up excitedly. Maybe it was Sloan?

"Apple, where were you?" Happy said.

"I was out with Sloan," Apple responded. "You know that."

"No, this morning! You completely missed the exam!" said Happy.

"Oh, my God," said Apple. "I totally forgot."

"Yeah, you did. So how was last night?" Happy asked. Apple knew that Happy couldn't help herself. Yes, they weren't getting along so well these days, but Happy would still want to know all the juicy details. And if juicy gossip about hanging out with Sloan Starr was all it took to reel Happy back in, then Apple would certainly divulge.

"It was unbelievable," Apple gushed, after she told Happy about her night with Sloan. "We're going out again tonight. Come out with us tonight! You have to this time."

"You're going out with him again?" Happy asked.

"Yes," Apple said.

"What are you going to do about the exam?" Happy asked.

"Oh, that. Maybe I'll try to work something out with Hazel. She'll have my back," Apple said.

"You sure about that?" Happy wondered, and Apple wasn't exactly sure what she was getting at.

"Oh, who knows? She's so caught up with her wedding. So you are coming out tonight, right? I'm not going to take no for an answer."

"Fine, I guess so. Can I bring the gang?" Happy asked.

"Like who?" Apple pressed.

"What do you mean? The gang! Brooklyn, Zen, Hopper, whoever else. Or is it exclusive?" Happy asked sarcastically.

"It's not that it's exclusive. I just . . ."

Apple wasn't sure exactly what she felt. She was looking forward to hanging out with Happy, and even Brooklyn, but wasn't sure about inviting the whole gang, especially Zen, whom she had managed to forget about.

But they were her friends. And she had this fabulous new group of friends, and they should all get to know each other.

"So what's going on with you and Zen?" Apple asked, trying to keep Happy on the phone. "You guys are cool to hang out together still?"

Happy didn't respond immediately. When she did, her voice was curt. "Um, we broke up for good, like, three weeks ago," she answered. "But, yes, we're still friends."

Apple was shocked. How did she not know this news, especially from her best friend?

"Why didn't you tell me? Are you okay?" Apple asked.

"Yes, I'm fine. I would have told you, but you seemed so busy. And I figured somehow you'd hear from someone else."

"Happy, you know I'm never too busy for you," Apple said.

"Well, it hasn't seemed that way," Happy said. "I've been kind of lonely, actually."

Happy explained how she had realized that Hot and Disturbed Guy was really too disturbed for her liking.

"Well, tonight we're going to have a blast," Apple said, trying to sound enthusiastic. "Sloan hangs out with all these people who are actors and actresses, and you can meet them and maybe they'll give you tips on breaking into the business. You could even ask Sloan!"

"You think?" Happy said, her voice sounding lighter.

"I'll make it happen!" Apple said.

"Thanks, Apple," said Happy. "We'll talk later."

Apple felt good. It was going to be a great night.

♡

Apple went to Happy's house first. Apple always loved hanging out at Happy's place, and it was months since she had been there.

"So how is Zen?" Apple asked. Now that Happy and Zen were through, Apple felt she had gotten away with something and was grateful. Happy would never find out about that. She had gotten away with a lot lately, thought Apple. First she had gotten away with not writing Apple's Angst, and now she was getting away with kissing Zen.

"He seems fine. We still talk. We're still friends. In fact, I think he has started to date someone else," Happy said. She didn't sound jealous at all.

"Really?" Apple asked curiously. "How do you know?"

"I can just tell," Happy said. Apple knew she couldn't press the issue, because she would sound overly interested.

"And what really happened with Therapy Guy?" Apple asked, though her mind was on what girl Zen was interested in. Maybe that's why he had stopped trying to get in touch with her and not, as she had assumed, because Apple just didn't respond.

"Well, it turns out the thrill wore off pretty quickly," Happy laughed. "Once Zen and I ended it, that spark was gone too."

Apple felt relieved. Even if Happy ever found out that she and Zen had kissed, surely she couldn't be a hypocrite, since she had cheated on Zen.

"And you and Sloan?" Happy asked. "What's up with that?"

"I guess you could say we're a couple," Apple said. "Or at least we're on our way to being one."

Apple wasn't sure how true this was. But Sloan was texting her all the time, and really seemed into her. Of course they were going to end up together. Apple could feel it.

"Well, I can't wait to meet him. He's got to pass my test!" Happy said, just like the old Happy.

Apple and Happy met Emme and three of her friends at the restaurant. Sloan showed up shortly after, and Apple proudly introduced Happy as her best friend. Happy was in a good mood, and Apple couldn't help but notice that Sloan was being super-attentive to her. Apple was pleased. She wanted her best friend to like her new love interest, and her new love interest had to like her best friend.

"I can't believe how well we're getting treated here," Happy whispered to Apple at one point. "I mean, they just keep serving you and you don't have to wait. And they keep asking if we need anything."

"I know, right? I think it's because of Sloan and his friends," Apple whispered back.

"Or because of you," Happy said, raising her eyebrows.

"Right."

"Seriously, Apple. I know you don't pay attention to these things, but you're everywhere. People now know your name just as much as they know your mother's! You're all over the Web!"

Happy, clearly, had had a little too much to drink. On their way out, a photographer asked Sloan for a photograph. Sloan grabbed Happy and Apple on each of his arms, and all three smiled giddily for the camera. They parted ways there. Sloan was moving to another club, but Happy wanted to go home, and Apple knew it was only right to go with her best friend.

Apple called the car service and they waited to be picked up. When they arrived at Happy's house, Happy gave Apple a big hug.

"Thanks for the night. You're right. It was fun. And Sloan said he'd help me! And I got some really good contacts from some of his friends."

Apple was pleased. She knew Happy would love Sloan. She felt like everything was different now, but different in a good way. Change can be good, thought Apple.

♡

"You're in the paper again," her aunt said, standing over Apple, who was still in bed.

"What time is it?" Apple asked, rubbing her eyes.

"It's time for you to get out of bed," Hazel responded.

"What's in the paper?" Apple asked. She was used to this kind of wakeup call from her aunt now. She couldn't seem to remember a time when her face wasn't in the entertainment section of a paper or her name wasn't being mentioned on a blog.

"Oh, just a great photograph of you, Happy, and that Sloan guy smiling for the camera," her aunt said breezily.

"Happy will be thrilled," Apple said.

"Well, maybe," her aunt said, uncertainly. "I mean, she certainly looks beautiful."

"What do you mean, *maybe*?" Apple asked.

"Well, the headline is, um . . . well, I think it's pretty hilarious!" her aunt said, laughing. When Hazel thought things were hilarious, they usually weren't. Like her personality, her humor was unique.

"What does it say?" Apple asked, though she wasn't sure she wanted to hear the answer.

"The headline is 'Former boyfriend stealer and *Angst* employee Apple, back on track with best friend. Will they be fighting over Sloan next? Who will win this round?'" her aunt read, adding drum sounds at the end.

Apple felt sick to her stomach. She had thought that the whole appearance on her mother's talk show had blown over, that people had short memories and wouldn't remember. And now it was being blown up even bigger. People were being reminded again of what Apple had done.

"That's not funny!" Apple said. "Happy and I aren't fighting over Sloan. He's with me. We were all just hanging out. There was nothing at all interesting about that."

"That's why it's so funny!" her aunt said, laughing. She continued to laugh at her all the way to school.

Apple worried about what Happy would think of her photograph and that headline. But Happy, surprisingly, didn't want to talk about it at all.

"I don't trust Emme," Happy told Apple, after Apple rushed into school and, along with Brooklyn, they headed to the washroom to fix their hair and makeup. Happy, in fact, had laughed off the headline in the paper, which made Apple feel relieved. Apple thought Happy actually enjoyed the extra attention.

"Why not?" Apple asked, blotting her lips on a piece of toilet paper.

"I just don't," Happy said.

"I don't either," said Brooklyn, who was standing with them. Brooklyn never wore makeup. She didn't believe in it.

"You don't trust her because Happy doesn't," laughed Apple.

"That's not true," Brooklyn said, looking hurt. "I have my own opinions. There's something about her vibe that is off."

"I have to agree with Brooklyn," Happy said. "There's just something off about her. I can't describe it."

"Well, did she say something to you?" Apple asked.

"No, she was very nice," said Happy.

"So, then, what's the problem?" Apple pressed.

"Hey, if you like her, we like her," Brooklyn said, eyeing Happy.

"Good. Because I do like her. She really looks out for me at work," said Apple. She didn't tell them what Emme had done for her. In fact, Emme had done her answers last week again because Sloan had told Apple about an event at the last minute. Emme completely understood that Apple shouldn't miss it.

"Good," said Happy. "But I have to tell you there was something off about her. Just something not genuine. Then again, what is it they say? You can't trust anyone in this business."

Apple thought that maybe Happy was jealous. This was the first time in their lives that Apple had new friends outside Cactus High.

"You know," she said, "sometimes I think that we just live in our own little bubble. We've all been friends for so long and we never hang out with new people. I'm not saying that's bad, but for argument's sake, would you say that maybe we just don't know what it's like to meet new friends, or how to meet new friends?"

"Maybe," responded Happy.

Later that day, Apple headed to the *Angst* offices, which now felt like a second home.

"I think you should get paid," Emme told Apple, out of the blue.

They were sitting outside catching some rays on a five-minute break. Emme sipped her diet soda.

"What do you mean?" Apple asked.

"Well, you're just giving *Angst* magazine *so* much press," Emme said. "You're getting your picture taken. Sloan Starr only wanted you to interview him. You're doing a lot for the magazine, and what are they giving you in return?"

"An opportunity," Apple answered, but it came out sounding more like a question.

"Sure, but you grasped that opportunity and now you're a celebrity yourself," Emme said.

"Oh, I don't think so," Apple said.

"Please! You're on buses! Your photo is on websites. And it was in the paper again today. Seriously, you're giving *Angst* so much more than they're giving you." Emme sighed, as if it was all so unfair.

Apple liked that Emme looked out for her. She should be more like Emme, have more of a business sense. She never would have even thought to ask to be paid.

"Maybe you're right," Apple said, taking in what Emme had told her.

"I *know* I'm right. If I were in your shoes and all this stuff was happening to me, I wouldn't be used like that. I'd demand payment," Emme said.

"Maybe you are right," Apple said again, this time more confidently.

"Again, I *am* right. But Fancy Nancy isn't going to reach out to you and make the offer to pay you. Why would she? But if you get paid, maybe I'll get paid," Emme said, winking.

"Thanks, Emme. I should do this for both of us," Apple said.

"You're welcome," said Emme, finishing off her soda.

twenty-eight

$a$pple asked Morgan how she could go about
getting some face time with Fancy Nancy.

"Is something wrong?" Morgan asked, looking concerned. "You're not thinking of quitting, are you?"

"No, I just need to talk to her about something,"
Apple said.

Surprisingly, Apple got a call from Morgan less than
an hour later.

"She'll meet you today at three. She has to be at an
event by four, so you'll have fifteen minutes with her."

Apple thanked Morgan.

"Oh, and Apple, there's a ton of mail for you here.
I'll get someone to send it down."

Apple couldn't believe the stack of mail that shortly
appeared before her. They were all invitations: for
charity events, television awards, even birthday parties
for people she didn't know.

But Apple didn't have time to look through the stack

of mail addressed to her. She had to write her advice column, which was due in the next ten minutes. She whipped it off half-heartedly. Emme, thankfully, was there to help her again, and she seemed to like helping Apple think through the questions. In fact, Apple hated to admit it, but Emme was really good at giving advice. She was quicker at it than Apple was and came up with some really pithy lines.

At three o'clock, after a quick pep talk from Emme, Apple walked meekly into Fancy Nancy's office. Fancy Nancy was on the phone and motioned for Apple to take a seat.

"I'm glad you wanted to meet today," Fancy Nancy said. "There's something I want to talk to you about. In fact, I was going to ask you to come meet me today."

Apple was surprised. What was it that Fancy Nancy wanted to talk to her about? Maybe she was going to compliment her on all the attention Apple was bringing to *Angst* magazine.

"Why don't you begin, Apple?" Fancy Nancy said.

Apple immediately felt nervous and wondered if asking for money was a mistake. But Fancy Nancy was looking at her expectantly and with a hint of impatience.

"So?" Fancy Nancy pressed.

"Well," started Apple, "I was just thinking that . . . well, I think I should be getting paid. Not a lot or anything, it's just that I am doing a lot of work here and it doesn't seem fair, exactly, that I'm not getting something in return."

Fancy Nancy looked at Apple with an amused smile on her face. Apple hadn't been expecting that. Fancy

Nancy didn't speak immediately, which made Apple feel even more uncomfortable. Finally, Fancy Nancy spoke, in a tone that was clear as crystal.

"So, Apple, you think you should be paid. Tell me why, dear," she asked, as if she was trying not to laugh. Apple felt like it was a trick question and wasn't sure how to answer.

Apple definitely wasn't expecting this. She tried to remember what Emme had told her, that she was bringing a lot of press to *Angst* magazine, and that they were using her, and that she should be getting something in return.

"It's just that . . . well, I'm bringing a lot of press to *Angst* and, well, people should get paid," Apple said, sounding childish.

"Okay, Apple, I'll consider your argument. You *are* bringing a lot of press to *Angst* magazine," Fancy Nancy said, drumming her manicured nails on her desk.

Maybe she had gotten through to her, Apple thought, loosening up.

"But not all of it, you see, is good press," Fancy Nancy said, looking at Apple intently.

"Sorry?" Apple responded. Everyone had told her—Happy, Sloan, Guy, her aunt—that all press was good press.

"You are out at clubs. Yes, I do read gossip websites. You aren't exactly sending out a good message or being a good role model," said Fancy Nancy. "You're out there partying with your friends in the middle of the week when you should be either doing your homework or working here, at *Angst*."

Apple definitely wasn't expecting this. She had thought Fancy Nancy would be happy that she was out with celebrities.

"And, yes, I will admit that you are great on television and there is a ton of buzz about you right now. However, this could go one of two ways. I know you've been lazy about your column, which is fine. I've seen it time and time again. You're not the first, nor will you be the last, to get caught up in your fifteen minutes of fame. But consider this a warning," Fancy Nancy said. "You get only one."

"A warning?" Apple asked meekly.

"Yes, a warning. We here at *Angst* don't care whom you date. We don't care how many celebrity friends you have. You're here to do a job. You can't let your personal life get in the way of that. So you are on probation as of now. I warned you at the beginning that at *Angst*, we are role models. And I wasn't kidding around. In fact, if you weren't Bee Bee Berg's daughter, you wouldn't have even gotten this warning," Fancy Nancy said.

Apple was shocked. She wasn't going to be getting paid, obviously. Fancy Nancy didn't seem to care that Apple was bringing press to the magazine. In fact, she seemed disappointed with her.

"Are we done?" Fancy Nancy asked.

Apple just nodded. She couldn't form a sentence, not even to say, "Thank you for your time."

"Oh, Apple? One more thing?" Fancy Nancy said, just as Apple was about to walk out. Apple felt her heart beat. Maybe Fancy Nancy realized that she had been a little too harsh and wanted to apologize.

"You can't use the car service anymore. That was to get you home from the offices, not to use as your own personal chauffeur to take you home from clubs."

♡

Apple had to catch her breath. She felt like she'd had the wind knocked out of her. She needed a few minutes alone and couldn't bear just yet to see Emme. She walked into the kitchen area. Luckily, she was alone. She felt faint and had to sit down. She grabbed a chair at the communal lunch table (where no one actually ate, because they were all chained to their desks) and took a seat.

"Late night or bad day?" a voice asked suddenly.

"Oh, Michael, you scared me," said Apple. She inhaled and exhaled deeply, trying to control the tears she knew were about to fall.

And then they did.

Michael put his coffee cup on the counter and raced over to her. Over the past few weeks, they had had many short chitchats in this area, with Michael always making Apple laugh about something, or Apple making Michael laugh over her outings or her aunt's wedding-related antics.

"Oh, dear. Oh, dear, it can't be that bad," he said soothingly, grabbing her hand. "Tell me what's wrong. Is it, you know, that time of the month?"

Apple couldn't help but laugh, which came out more as a snort.

"No, it's not. It's just . . ." Apple said, and started

to sob again. "It's just . . . well, sometimes it seems like everything is too much, you know?"

She couldn't stand to tell Michael what Fancy Nancy had just told her. She felt like she was letting everyone down. And she certainly didn't want to let Michael down. He had been nothing but supportive to her since her first day. She should have asked Michael if he thought it was a good idea to ask Fancy Nancy for a raise before she had done it. Why hadn't she thought of that?

"I think you're just having a bad day," Michael said, reaching behind him, grabbing a Kleenex and handing it to Apple. "You have a great life. Fabulous friends, a new hot boyfriend, apparently, a family who love you, not to mention all your *Angst* fans who read you and watch you on television."

Apple started to sob louder. If Michael only knew that Emme was doing more work on Apple's Angst than she was, that Fancy Nancy was one step away from firing her, that Sloan hadn't returned either her phone messages or her texts today, that her friendship with Brooklyn and Happy was rocky, that her aunt was furious that she hadn't helped out on her wedding at all.

"Think about my life," Michael said. "I work for *Angst* 24/7. I go to parties but don't have that many close friends. Everyone likes me just because they want press in *Angst*. Or at least that's how I feel. I can't really trust anyone, which is probably why I'm single. I don't know if a guy wants to be with me for me, or because he thinks I can do something for him."

Apple smiled at Michael warmly.

"I can't believe a guy like you is single! You're so sweet and nice," Apple said.

"Me neither! I'm such a catch!" Michael said, and they laughed.

"You need to put things in perspective," he continued. "You're young! You have your whole life in front of you. This is just a bad day. Come on, I can't have my star employee in tears. You need to have some fun. Do you have any big parties to go to?"

"Well, I have my aunt's wedding," Apple said. "It's not exactly a party. It's more like a function."

"Oh, weddings. Everyone always says you meet people at weddings. Not me! I'm usually stuck at the senior citizens' table or the kids' table. People don't know what to do with me," Michael said.

"Actually, my parents met at a wedding," Apple told Michael, her tears drying up. "And now they've been married for twenty years!"

"Dr. Bee Bee Berg met her husband at a wedding?" Michael asked. "Interesting."

"You know, you should come," Apple announced, as if she had just come up with the most brilliant of ideas.

"To your aunt's wedding? Won't she wonder who I am and what I'm doing there?" Michael asked, laughing.

"No. She invited her garbage collector this morning. Trust me, she won't notice and she won't care," Apple said.

Apple could tell Michael needed prodding.

"Come on! You can meet my mother," Apple teased. "And who knows, you might even meet someone special. If it happened to my mother, it could happen to you. Plus I don't think anyone there is going to be looking for press in *Angst* magazine! My aunt is going to make sure she's the only topic of conversation that day. Trust me."

Michael nodded slowly.

"Please, Michael. It will cheer me up if you come," Apple begged. "For me, please? You'll come?"

"For you," he said. "But it's kind of strange."

"So what?" Apple said, and told him she'd e-mail him the details. "Just fawn over my aunt and it will all be good. And like I said, you might meet someone!"

"Well, I guess you never know," Michael said, though he didn't sound very convinced.

Apple smiled and made a mental note to tell her aunt there was one more guest. She knew her aunt wouldn't mind.

When she got back to the dungeon, Emme was eagerly waiting to hear the news about the meeting with Fancy Nancy. Apple was to mortified to tell her what Fancy Nancy had said.

"She said she'd take it into consideration," Apple told her, lying through her teeth.

"Well, that's not bad! In fact, that's good! We should go celebrate tonight!"

Though that was the last thing Apple felt like doing—she felt like going home and crying—she had to put on a brave face.

"You go home," said Emme, practically shooing Apple out. "And I'll finish up here. And then we'll all meet up later."

Thank God for Emme, thought Apple. Apple didn't want to be at *Angst*. She didn't want to worry about running into Fancy Nancy, that was for certain.

twenty-nine

When Apple came downstairs from her nap, her mother, aunt, father, and Guy were all sitting around, looking serious. Apple wondered if something bad had happened.

"What's up?" Apple asked glassy-eyed.

"You tell us," her mother said.

"Oh, is this because I'm home right now? I wasn't feeling well, so I came home from work early," said Apple. "I think I may be coming down with something."

They all glanced at each other.

"What?" Apple asked. Why was everyone looking at her like she had grown a third head?

"I said, 'What?'" Apple asked impatiently.

"Come down, honey," her father said, looking at her mother for backup.

"Don't 'honey' her," her mother jumped in. "She missed a math exam!"

"And she hasn't been going to classes," her aunt added.

"Who are you? The police?" Apple asked, looking at her aunt. "How do you know what I've been doing?"

"Um, remember my fiancé?" her aunt said. "He's in the know, you know! He said a lot of the teachers are worried about you, not just him."

"Right. So just because you're marrying my math teacher you get to find out what I've been doing? It's so not fair," Apple huffed.

"Well, life isn't fair," her mother said.

Apple rolled her eyes.

"It's an invasion of privacy," Apple continued. "No one else is being spied on by her teacher!"

"Tonight you are staying in. Hazel spoke to Jim and he said you could make up the test. So tonight you are in and studying," her mother said. "You're lucky you're getting this second chance."

"Yeah!" threw in Hazel. "I had to beg him to let you do this."

"I have plans," Apple said, looking her mother directly in the eyes.

"Cancel them," her mother said, looking Apple straight in the eyes.

"I'm not canceling them," Apple said.

"Apple, you're grounded," her mother said.

"Does that mean I don't have to go to Aunt Hazel's wedding next week?" Apple asked.

"I don't know who you think you are, but you had better get your life in order, Apple. I don't like what you're becoming. Do you?" her mother asked.

"This is what people do. If you actually tuned in to modern society, you'd know that it's not about work all the time," Apple said.

"Yes, it is," said her mother. "But school comes first. If your grades don't pick up, or you miss one more exam, I'm going to have to put my foot down and you won't be allowed to go to *Angst* even for work."

"You can't do that!" Apple said. "Part of the job is going out! Don't you know that?"

"I don't think it's part of the job," said her mother. "I'm going to call Nancy."

Apple looked at her mother with horror. Who did her mother think she was?

"Mother!" Apple screamed. "You'd better not call her! You don't know anything! You don't even know that your wardrobe is out of style! There are more colors out there than white!"

Apple stormed out of the kitchen. She could see that her mother was going to come after her, and she saw her father pull her mother's arm to hold her back.

Apple jumped into the shower. She didn't want to hear her parents and her aunt "discussing" her, though she knew that was exactly what they were doing.

After her parents went to sleep, Apple snuck out of the house. She was happy that they always went to bed early. Sloan had, finally, sent a short note saying he may be going to the club they had gone to a couple nights earlier but wasn't exactly sure when he was getting out of work. Apple felt like Sloan was pulling back from her, but she plastered on a smile for her friends. Emme had come, and so had Happy and Brooklyn. She could barely muster up the energy to admit her worries to Happy and Emme when they asked Apple where her "boyfriend" was. She just shrugged and said, "He'll come."

♡

When Apple saw Sloan come into the club, she felt a huge sense of relief. She may have almost lost her job, but losing her new boyfriend on the same day would be too much. So what if Sloan was hanging out with a bunch of girls? Happy noticed the distressed look on Apple's face when she saw him surrounded and told her that it was part of his job to be nice to fans.

When Apple finally got Sloan alone, she asked him, bluntly, if he'd like to be her date for her aunt's wedding. She pretended not to be bothered that it had taken him almost thirty minutes to come up to her. And even when she found herself talking to him alone, it felt like she was being rushed.

"Like, a date, date?" Sloan asked.

"Well, yes, my date," Apple said.

"I'm not sure about weddings. That's quite a serious commitment," said Sloan. Apple knew Sloan was acting far from eager. He was acting, in fact, as if he would rather stay at home and do nothing than to be her date at Hazel's wedding.

"Please," Apple heard herself beg. "Please come with me."

Sloan refused to commit.

She couldn't believe this day. Everything was off, from the warning from Fancy Nancy to her parents' lecturing her, to everything! And now Sloan wouldn't commit to being her date at her aunt's wedding.

"Well, I guess I should go," Apple said, trying to catch Sloan's eye. She tried not to let it bother her when he barely acknowledged she was leaving, especially right in front of her friends. Apple wanted to give him the benefit of the doubt. Maybe he had had a bad day too, she thought.

She told Sloan that she would call him tomorrow, but he didn't seem to hear her. He was too busy laughing over something Happy, or someone else, had just said.

♡

"He hit on me," Happy told Apple at the Spiral Staircase the next morning.

"What are you talking about?" Apple asked, trying not to sound as grumpy as she felt.

"Sloan. Right after you left," Happy said.

"Sloan hit on you?" Apple asked. "Sloan Starr hit on you?"

"Yes, Sloan Starr. Who else named Sloan do we know? Of course Sloan Starr," Happy said.

"I'm so sick of hearing his name," Brooklyn said. "He's like the opposite of Britney and Madonna. He's known by two names."

Happy laughed. Apple didn't.

"Come on! It's funny," Happy said to Apple. "Brooklyn is right. I so can't picture him just as a Sloan. He's such a Sloan Starr!"

"I don't think it's so funny that my boyfriend was hitting on you," Apple said. "And don't make fun of his name!"

Happy snorted loudly.

"He's so not your boyfriend," she told Apple.

"What do you mean?" Apple asked. "We've been out a lot. Our picture was taken together a lot of times. Everyone *thinks* he's my boyfriend. He's going to be my date for Hazel's wedding."

Apple knew the last part wasn't exactly true. In fact, it was a downright lie. But Apple still had a few days to work on him. She knew that there was time to convince Sloan Starr that going to the wedding with her wouldn't be that big a deal. She would even tell him that he'd get to meet her mother, if that's what it would take. Apple pictured them walking into the reception arm in arm. She also made a mental note to ask Celia to restraighten her hair. It was starting to get wavy, another thing to add to Apple's plate of worries. She just couldn't, or didn't want to, believe that Sloan Starr had hit on Happy.

"He was hitting on me! Right in front of everyone. You left, so you didn't see. But he asked for my digits. He said he could get me a meeting with some casting directors," Happy said. She didn't seem to notice that these words pained Apple.

"Maybe he was just being nice. Maybe he really was trying to help you," Apple suggested.

"Trust me, I know when someone is just being nice and when they're trying to get with me," said Happy knowingly, picking a piece of fluff from her dress.

"Well, you don't know everything," muttered Apple.

"What did you just say?" Happy demanded.

"Come on, guys," Brooklyn said. "Let's not turn this into something it's not."

"It's called *reality*, and Apple needs a reality check—and fast," said Happy.

Zen, Hopper, and everyone else sitting on the Spiral Staircase around them, including Lyon, suddenly became silent. They couldn't believe what they were witnessing.

"*You* need a reality check," retorted Apple.

"No, you do!" Happy said, grabbing her bag and standing up taller.

"Guys, stop!" pleaded Brooklyn in a meek voice.

"I'm not stating anything that's not entirely obvious to everyone except precious Apple. Oh, we wouldn't want to hurt Apple's feelings," mimicked Happy. "Oh, Apple, the celebrity. Oh, we can't tell her THE TRUTH! *She* doesn't tell the TRUTH! I know you kissed Zen. You think I don't know? Emme called me and told me! Yeah, your good friend Emme!" Happy said, her voice rising. "I told you she was shady and you wouldn't listen. I've been keeping it in because I didn't really care and I thought you'd eventually tell me. But you were never going to, were you?"

Apple's mind immediately went to Lyon and his reaction. She thought he'd be so hurt by hearing this, especially this way, that it didn't register that Happy had said Emme had told her. She looked quickly at Lyon, who didn't look hurt or jealous. He looked like he felt sorry for Apple, which made Apple even angrier. Why did a nobody like Lyon feel sorry for her? She was the one whose face was plastered everywhere. She was the one hanging out with fashionable new friends. She was the one having all the fun.

Why did she care so much about what Lyon thought?

"Okay, that's enough, Happy," Apple responded, her voice rising as well. "You're the one who can't see the truth. You're the one who can't accept the fact that I have a great job and new friends, and that for the first time I'm the one in the spotlight. And you cheated on Zen with that guy at your therapist's office! So you can't be a hypocrite. Who are you to talk!"

Zen looked shocked, as did Happy, as did Brooklyn. Not only was Apple yelling, she had divulged a big secret.

"Well, Zen doesn't care. He has a foolie friend in Emme!" Happy finally sputtered out.

"What?" screeched Apple. She looked at Zen, who looked to the ground slyly while Hopper pounded him on the back and said, "Way to go, man!"

"Emme told me that last night. Didn't you know?" Happy said, egging Apple on. "Apparently, they've been foolie friends for weeks!"

Could that be true? Was that the reason Zen hadn't been in touch with her? Had it had nothing to do with the fact that he didn't know what to say to Apple and everything to do with the fact that he was fooling around with Emme? Or was Happy just trying to ruin Apple's friendship with Emme? Happy hadn't liked Emme from the start. There was no way that this was true.

"You're such a liar, Happy," Apple screamed. She could feel her face bursting red. "You'll do anything to be the center of attention."

Happy was so mad, she raised a finger, as if to shake it at Apple. Instead, she just stormed off. Apple looked at Zen for confirmation of what Happy had just said. But he refused to look at her. Apple stormed off too, leaving Brooklyn meditating on her mat, Lyon looking stunned, Hopper shaking his head, Zen looking sly, and the rest of the school whispering.

thirty

"Hey, babe. I see you got into a fight today with your best friend," said Sloan. Apple was sitting behind her desk at *Angst*. Every time she thought of her fight with Happy—which was every second—she shook so hard she was still furious. Every time she thought of Happy, her heart raced and she broke out in a sweat. She needed to talk to Emme, who, for the first time, wasn't at the office before Apple. She hadn't returned any of Apple's desperate messages either.

"Hey! I thought you'd never call me back. I've left you, like, four messages today," said Apple. She knew she sounded like a nag, but she couldn't help it. "What are you talking about, a fight with my best friend?"

"Are you in front of your computer?" Sloan asked.

"Yes. I'm at work," Apple responded.

Sloan told her to type in a Web address.

Apple typed in the address and couldn't believe her eyes. There was a photograph of her and Happy.

Happy was pointing in her face, looking furious. Only Happy could pull off looking so beautiful while being mad. Before Apple remembered that she was furious at her, she felt a moment of pride for her friend.

"Where did they get that?" Apple wondered. The photograph was obviously taken during the scene at school that day.

"Someone must have taken it with their cell phone," Sloan said.

She read the caption: "Teen advice columnist needs help!"

"This is awful," said Apple. "I think I'm going to cry."

"Don't cry. All press is good press," said Sloan. "You know you've made it when you're on this website."

"Well, do I look okay?" Apple said.

"You look gorgeous," Sloan said. "But, babe, I got to go."

"So you want to take me out tonight and make me forget this awful day?" Apple asked.

"I wish, but I don't think I should be seen with you right now," Sloan said.

Apple couldn't believe it. Sloan didn't even pretend that he was sad about this. She couldn't believe that not only had he become so hard to get in touch with, but he didn't even want to be seen with her.

"What do you mean? You just told me that all press is good press."

"Well, maybe not *all* press," said Sloan. "I'll catch up with you sometime. Maybe I'll see you around."

"What about the—" But Apple didn't get the chance to ask Sloan if he would be her date for her aunt's wedding, even as a favor. He had already hung up.

When the e-mail popped up in her inbox from Fancy Nancy, Apple really wasn't even all that shocked.

♡

"Oh, Apple, I'm so sorry!" cried Michael. Apple was walking home. She had seen that it was an *Angst* number on her phone and thought it might be Fancy Nancy, telling her that she had changed her mind, that she had made a mistake. It wasn't.

"I had no idea what was going on. Nancy just told me that Emme came to see her, and then she told me that she had fired you! Over e-mail! Anyway, tell me Emme is lying! Please tell me," Michael begged. Obviously, it had gotten back to Michael that Emme had ratted Apple out, had gone to Fancy Nancy and told her that she had been doing the Apple's Angst column for weeks.

"She's not. I deserved to be fired," Apple said. She was walking at a snail's pace. She couldn't believe that Emme was so evil. She knew, in her gut, that it was also true she had been fooling around with Zen all this time.

"Oh, Apple! I feel awful," Michael moaned.

"Why do you feel awful? I'm the one who did it," Apple said quietly. She wasn't sure what she felt worse about—that Emme had done all of that to her, or that she had let Emme do Apple's Angst in the first place. Apple may have been naive when it came to Emme, but she had agreed to let Emme do her work. She had only herself to blame for that.

"I feel awful because interns are like my babies, and this reflects badly on me too! Why didn't you come to me if you felt overwhelmed?" Michael moaned.

"I'm sorry," cried Apple. "I thought I could handle it. Everyone else seems to handle everything on their own."

"I wish you had said something," Michael said. "I can't believe that Emme went behind my back as well, directly to Fancy Nancy!"

"You call her that too?" Apple said, shocked to hear the words "Fancy Nancy" come from Michael's mouth.

"Of course! Everyone does," Michael said.

Apple laughed. She couldn't believe she had managed a laugh when her whole world had fallen apart. Apple had no idea how she was going to break the news that she had been fired from her intern job. She would be the laughing stock of the entire school. She couldn't bear to imagine her mother's reaction. Her mother, Apple knew, would be not only furious but disappointed, which was somehow worse. But why shouldn't her mother be disappointed? Apple *was* a disappointment.

Apple wondered how long she could go before telling anyone. Could she pretend to still be going to the office? Could she apologize profusely to Fancy Nancy and try to get her job back?

"Is there anything I can do for you?" Michael said. "Anything?"

"Actually," said Apple, after a pause. "There is one thing . . ."

thirty-one

"This totally makes up for everything!" screeched Aunt Hazel. "You are now officially the best bridesmaid ever."

"Shh! Don't move," said Celia. "You must calm down."

As a wedding present, and an "I'm sorry for being the worst bridesmaid in history" present, Apple had presented Celia, the celebrity makeup and hair artist, to her aunt on her wedding day, which was today. Michael had pulled through with Apple's favor. She was sure he had had to work to convince Celia to do this, but she was here. Her aunt was in the makeup chair, dressed in a beautiful gown Michael had also managed to grab from the magazine's wardrobe closet. The magazine was going to do a spread on celebrity weddings, and her aunt had fit beautifully into a gown worn by Julia Roberts in a recent movie. Because her aunt had always been more like her sister, Apple knew her size exactly. Hazel was stunned when Apple had presented the gift.

"Where's Mom?" Apple wondered.

Aunt Hazel directed her eyes toward the restroom.

"Can you believe this day is here?" her aunt said, grabbing Apple's hand.

"I tell you not to move, and you move!" scolded Celia.

Apple couldn't believe that her aunt's wedding day had arrived. Everything in the past few weeks, from her great rise at *Angst* to her great fall, had seemed to happen so fast. Apple felt like she had been through a tornado.

She looked at herself in the mirror. The light green bridesmaid's dress wasn't actually that bad. It was actually pretty sophisticated for her aunt's taste. Apple was pleasantly surprised. Though she felt horrible inside, at least she didn't look it. Her aunt could see this.

"Happy helped pick out the style and color," said her aunt. "So now you don't have to be embarrassed in front of your friends."

Apple couldn't believe that she would have to face her friends at her aunt's wedding either.

"Great. So you invited all my friends?" muttered Apple.

Apple had sworn Aunt Hazel to secrecy after telling her that she had lost her unpaid job at *Angst*. Her aunt had been surprisingly understanding, probably because she had lost many jobs in her life. Apple hadn't mentioned her fight with her friends, though, because she didn't want to ruin the day for her aunt.

"Of course I did," Aunt Hazel said. "Your friends are like family. And you're my family, which makes them my family."

"Are they all coming?" muttered Apple.

"Of course they are! They love me. What is up with you?" her aunt asked, looking perplexed.

"Nothing," Apple muttered. "Nothing at all."

"Do I look all right?" her aunt asked, standing up from the makeup chair. Celia looked like she was about to cry, taking in the sight of the blushing bride.

"You look beautiful," Apple told her aunt.

It was true. She hadn't seen her aunt look so stunning in her entire life. She had a glow. Apple felt her tears well up.

"This is the happiest day of my life," her aunt moaned.

Apple didn't want to ruin the day for her aunt. It was just one more day Apple had to get through. Just one day, Apple thought to herself. And it was a once-in-a-lifetime moment for her aunt. Apple was trying to be *in the present*, as Brooklyn always told her to be. She could get through this. And she would try her best to enjoy herself as well.

Luckily, her mother had been so caught up with Crazy Aunt Hazel's wedding, she hadn't seemed to notice that Apple wasn't going out, or barely even leaving her room.

Apple cried with her mother as, from the front row, they watched her aunt walk down the aisle and marry Apple's math teacher.

For a brief moment, Apple felt joy. At least things were looking good for her aunt. If things could turn out for Crazy Aunt Hazel, surely they could turn around for Apple. They had to.

$$\heartsuit$$

Apple was seated with her friends for the post-wedding dinner. She couldn't believe how uncomfortable it was. Luckily, there were speeches, and Apple made sure to sit down at the table right before they began. Her aunt couldn't have made a worse seating plan if she had tried. Not that her aunt knew what was going on.

Happy refused to look at Apple. Zen refused to look at Happy. Lyon was looking at his date, a girl Apple vaguely recognized from school. Her aunt really had invited everyone. Brooklyn was ignoring Hopper. And everyone was ignoring Apple.

It was a mess. Apple sat down. "Hey," Lyon said. "This is Sara," he said.

"Hey."

Lyon rubbed Sara's back. Apple missed that.

"What? No date?" Happy whispered to Apple as they watched her aunt get up to make her speech.

"Shut up, Happy!" Apple said. "Do *you* have a date?"

"She'll have a date when she decides she can be with one person," said Zen.

"You should talk," said Lyon. "Aren't you the one with all the foolie friends?"

"Yeah, you should talk," Happy repeated to Zen.

"Who are *you* to talk?" Hopper asked Happy. "Don't you have a therapy guy as a foolie friend?"

"Don't talk to her like that," Brooklyn told Hopper.

And then it all blew up. Everyone was suddenly yelling at everyone. Hopper and Brooklyn were going at it. Zen and Happy were going at it. Lyon was shooting Apple dirty looks, and Apple was yelling at Zen for fooling around with Evil Emme.

"SHUT UP, ALL OF YOU," screamed Hazel into the microphone. "This is my special day! This is not about you! I repeat, this is not about you! It's about me! It's about ME!"

They all turned, along with the three hundred other guests, to where her aunt was standing, on a stage, at the front of the room. Her aunt looked crazy, her eyes wild, and she was bashing her bouquet around. Apple hadn't realized how loud they were. The guests, along with her parents and Mr. Kelly, all looked toward Apple's table.

It may have been Guy, it may have been Happy, but someone in the room started to laugh. The laugh was contagious. Someone else started to laugh along, then someone else. Soon enough Apple felt herself doubling over in laughter.

"I'm glad you find this all so funny. What's so funny?" her aunt demanded into the microphone, which made everyone just laugh harder. Mr. Kelly walked to her, whispered something in her ear. Her aunt looked appeased and told the crowd that she'd come back to speak soon.

"I was such a bitch," said Happy, wrapping her arm around Apple, laughing hard.

"No, I was!" Apple said, laughing so hard she felt tears come to her eyes. "I was fired!" Apple screamed out.

"You were WHAT?" screeched her mother from the other side of the room. She should have known that her mother had ears, along with eyes, at the back of her head.

"I was fired," Apple repeated. "I was fired."

Apple watched as Mr. Kelly, her new uncle, whisked her aunt onto the dance floor. He was the only one, it seemed, who could make her aunt look so dreamy, even if Apple and her friends had ruined her perfect day. Maybe they *were* meant to be, thought Apple. Other guests started to dance alongside them, and Apple felt the pang of having no one to dance with. Well, there was Guy, who was hovering around.

"I can talk to Fancy Nancy for you," said Michael, coming up behind Apple. "She listens to me. I can convince her to give you another chance."

"That's so sweet of you. Guy says thanks, that's so nice," said Guy, looking at Michael, then sticking out his hand. "I'm Guy."

"Oh, I'm sorry. Guy, this is Michael. My boss . . . well, former boss at *Angst*," said Apple. Guy had run up to Apple, wanting to know what happened, and had remained at their table.

"Apple!" her mother said, coming toward Apple's table. "I need to speak to you right now!" Apple grabbed Happy's hand, and Happy squeezed back.

"Would you like to come to my table for a drink?" Guy asked Michael.

"Good idea. I think we should leave them alone," Michael said, nodding toward Apple and her mother. Apple watched as Guy and Michael took off together, laughing their way to the bar.

"And you thought our relationship was confusing," whispered Hopper to Brooklyn. "You know, all of this makes me appreciate you all that much more."

"Ah, that's so sweet," said Brooklyn. "I appreciate you too."

"Happy," said Apple. "You know I appreciate you, right?"

"Yes, I appreciate you too," laughed Happy.

thirty-two

" L et me just get dressed," Apple said. "I have a day
before summer school starts, and what better way
to spend it than with my friends?"

Happy and Brooklyn were in her bedroom, waiting
for Apple.

Happy threw the copy of *Angst* magazine that she
had been reading on Apple's bedroom floor with
disgust. On the cover was a photograph of Emme. "Ask
Emme!" read the headline. Happy then picked up the
magazine and tossed it into the trash. "Where it
belongs!" she announced.

"Hear, hear!" said Brooklyn. "I've never wished evil
on anyone before, but I wish evil on Emme."

"Oh, don't worry, Brooklyn," said Happy. "She'll
get hers. What goes around comes around. And no one
messes with my best friend."

Michael had filled in Guy—they were a couple immediately after Hazel's wedding and now barely left each

other's sides—who had filled in her mother, who had told her aunt, who had told Apple what happened.

Emme told Nancy that she had been doing Apple's job. And Fancy Nancy just gave it to her. She apparently liked Emme's "work ethic."

Michael said Fancy Nancy would have Apple back, but Apple couldn't bear to face Emme or Fancy Nancy, nor did she want to walk into those offices ever again.

Apple knew her mother would, eventually, start talking to her again. She had to. Apple had apologized profusely to her, after listening to her rant about getting caught up in fame, not doing her job, and almost failing school. Plus, her aunt was on her honeymoon, so her mother would need someone to talk to. Apple had sent a handwritten letter of apology to Fancy Nancy, as she did Lyon. Lyon had called and actually apologized to Apple.

"I really was overbearing," he had said. "I just wasn't mature enough to handle a girlfriend so in the spotlight, you know. I really did get all clingy and jealous. I'm sorry too."

They had said they would remain friends, though Apple thought this was doubtful.

Apple didn't imagine she'd ever hear from Sloan Starr again. The last time Apple checked the celebrity website, he was hanging out with a friend of Emme's.

Apple was never going to look at the gossip websites again. Or at least she was going to try not to. At least not until they featured Happy, which could happen sooner than later.

Happy had gotten a call to audition for a television

show. An agent had seen her photos in the paper and on websites, and had asked to represent her.

"If I get this role, you have to come with me," Happy said to her friends.

"Right! If my mother lets me," said Apple. "If she ever speaks to me again."

"Oh, she will. Come on! So many more people watch her show now because of you," Brooklyn said.

"That's true!" Happy agreed. "I read somewhere that she's never been more popular. Did you notice that she's even changed her wardrobe? Yesterday she was wearing pink! Didn't you see?" Happy asked.

"No," said Apple. "I was studying all day, remember?"

"Oh, it was brilliant. It was all about backstabbing co-workers," said a gleeful Happy. "Don't worry. She didn't mention you, Emme, or *Angst* by name, but if they're watching, they'll know."

"Yeah, that's their karma coming back," said Brooklyn.

Wow, thought Apple. Her mother may not be talking to her, but she was loyal. She was sticking up for Apple in the only way she knew how: on her talk show.

"Can you believe that *both* of you guys AND Emme kissed Zen," Brooklyn said.

"Don't remind us!" screeched Apple and Happy in unison. The thought of Zen kissing Emme made Apple's stomach turn. Emme had ditched Zen the same day she had ruined Apple's career at *Angst*. Zen, apparently, didn't really care. He had enjoyed her only as a foolie friend.

"What did I ever see in him?" asked Happy.

"I was just thinking that, about me!" said Apple. "But he was a better kisser than Sloan."

"Really?" gushed Happy.

"Really," said Apple.

"Do you mind if I post that somewhere online?" laughed Happy. "That's juicy stuff!"

"Go ahead!" said Apple.

Apple knew that Happy would get the job. She knew, as Brooklyn said, that it was Happy's fate to be on a television show.

"I think I've had enough with celebrities," moaned Apple. "I want you to be a star, but I don't think I can deal with everything else that comes with it," Apple said. It was true. Unlike her mother, she wasn't cut out for more than fifteen minutes of fame. She didn't want to be in the spotlight. She felt as if she had been holding her breath for the past couple of months and now could finally breathe again. It was nice.

"Well, at least no one's taking your photograph anymore," said Brooklyn.

"Yeah, I'm old news," Apple laughed. "Now I can eat without worrying about looking bad on television!"

Apple had spent the past week pigging out on pizza and hamburgers and fries. Why had she ever given that up?

"And they wouldn't be able to recognize you anyway, because your hair is different," said Brooklyn.

"It's not different," said Apple. "It's back to normal."

Apple's boings were finally back. It was as if her hair knew she had been fired.

"The way it should be," said Happy, pulling on one of Apple's boings.

"Yes," agreed Apple. "Everything is the way it should be."

"I should get that printed on a shirt!" said Brooklyn.

Apple smiled at Happy, who smiled back at her. "You should," said Happy.

Brooklyn stood up taller and cleared her throat loudly, as if she were a teacher at the beginning of a class, trying to get the students to settle down. Happy and Apple glanced toward their friend with interest. Clearly, she wanted to tell them something important.

"Because of you guys and your boy nightmares, Hopper realized that I was sane and now wants to be exclusive!" Brooklyn announced.

"That's great!" Apple said.

"You know, you two should start a matchmaking business," Brooklyn said. "You got me and Hopper together. And Hazel and Mr. Kelly together. And Guy and Michael together."

Happy and Apple looked at each other.

"That's not a bad idea," said Happy slowly. "How fun would that be, Apple? We could totally do it."

"You think?" Apple asked. It wasn't a bad idea. It could be fun.

"Let's go discuss it over manicures. We may destroy our own relationships, but we also bring people together!" Happy said excitedly.

"Maybe we should! Okay, I'm ready to go," Apple said. She thought about matchmaking and how nice it would be to worry about someone *else's* love life. It WASN'T a bad idea.

She took one last glance at herself in the mirror. Apple took in her curly hair, her white tank top, and her ripped jean shorts. Yes, she was finally looking back at herself.